Farrel's LAST CASE

GERALD R. WRIGHT

Order this book online at www.trafford.com
or email orders@trafford.com

Most Trafford titles are also available at major online book retailers.

Printed in the United States of America.

ISBN: 978-1-4907-0853-9 (sc)
ISBN: 978-1-4907-0855-3 (hc)
ISBN: 978-1-4907-0854-6 (e)

Library of Congress Control Number: 2013912812

Trafford rev. 07/10/2013

www.trafford.com

North America & international
toll-free: 1 888 232 4444 (USA & Canada)
fax: 812 355 4082

For Barbara

'. . . the evil that men do lives after them . . .'

-Julius Caesar, Shakespeare

1

Detective Chief Inspector Ian Farrel was not naturally the superstitious type. However, today was the thirteenth and it was a Friday. In actual fact, as coincidence would have it, he was having a bad day. He had had bad days before—a lot of them. Many of them Fridays and many the thirteenth, but then again Saturday to Thursdays, odd dates, even dates and days off work also figured in his bad or not-so-good days.

Four years ago his wife left him. Coincidentally, that day happened to be a Friday the thirteenth. She'd had enough of his excessive work schedule, the long hours and the number of days he worked on his job without taking a break. It was too much. She needed him to be around to take her out and spend money on her, but she came to realise his job came first—it always came first. So, she wanted out.

Farrel was a good cop. He had always been a good cop ever since he started out as a beat officer. He hated to think that criminals were getting away with murder. Well, not necessarily murder but thieving from the old folks and beating people up, to name but two. Parking offences had never been his cup of tea when he was on the beat. He managed to develop a method of saying 'get the hell out of here with that car' in a way that offenders could not really complain about.

He was promoted and then worked his way up to become a member of the Criminal Investigation Department. During this latter part of his career he gained respect as well as a fearful reputation, not only in the Underworld but also with his colleagues. He had thrown himself into the job wholeheartedly, almost as if he were the only crime fighter in the entire country.

So, his wife left him and rather quickly took up with a slick, smart aleck import-export operator, who seemed to be able to take time off at the drop of a hat and spend a great deal of money on her.

Farrel despised the man for taking her from him as well as his home comforts, but he was unable to do anything about it. It was not surprising then that he was extremely satisfied, to say nothing of amused, when the son-of-a-bitch was arrested by a neighbouring force for business irregularities: running drugs into the country, embezzlement, fraud, money laundering, unpaid taxes, and, of course, not paying the fines for his motoring offences. The book that they threw at him was rather large and heavy with the judge sentencing him to seven years. Later Farrel rang the officer in charge of the case to congratulate him on a job well done. The other policeman never knew the real reason behind the congratulatory call.

Almost immediately after, his ex wanted to return to him, but, with as much good will as he could muster, Farell turned her down. She had, after all, betrayed him once and played fast and loose with a member of the criminal fraternity. He explained that he wouldn't be able to trust her again and argued that it was possible she could do something similar again and cause him still more embarrassment.

The problem was that he was still a young man and he missed the comforts of a home life. He had moved into a two-bedroom apartment and catered for himself, even though that meant eating out in cafés, in the police canteen or grabbing a takeaway from the local fast-food joints. Yes, it was a bad diet, but at least he didn't have to waste time preparing meals or doing the washing up. He worked all the hours he could, and the apartment, in reality, only served as a dormitory.

As time passed, he became a rather tetchy individual, running on a short fuse and unable to suffer fools gladly. The squad recognised his bad days as well as the better ones. The good days usually consisted of an arrest or when some criminal was sent down for a long time. Those were days for a small celebration.

Gradually, his men came to the conclusion that perhaps it was a good thing Farrel was a detective and not a judge, for if he were, not only would the nation's prisons be full to overflowing, but the country would be building prisons at an unprecedented rate to keep up with his sentencing.

Things had not been going well lately and everyone knew that today was not a good day for Farrel. It was definitely a bad day. They all recognised the signs, except that is for the young man who had recently joined the squad. Now the men were gathered for the normal morning briefing.

"That's not what I heard," Farrel shouted in irritation, as he glared disdainfully, his steel blue eyes fixated on the young Detective Constable who had just volunteered a piece of information. At six foot three, Farrel looked down upon most people including the young DC at five feet ten inches.

Outside it was a beautiful day. The morning sun streamed through the large windows of the squad office which faced southeast. Farrel though, was not a man to notice or be influenced by such weather or anything else that Mother Nature bestowed on or withheld from him. He was well known for his cynicism and pessimism, and today was certainly not the time for being unable to deliver a positive piece of information.

"In fact, that story is absurd," he continued. "I don't know where you got it from, but if that cheap little crook Tommy Acton were on holiday, it would be one the judge had given him, or a job that Big Mick Jeanes had sent him on. Anyway, if that *were* the case, lovely little Jill Franks would be with him, but she's not, she's still around here somewhere, and, from what I understand, she's keeping her pretty little head down because someone has scared her witless."

The young, clean-cut, immaculately dressed DC Richard Copley flushed with embarrassment and shuffled his feet nervously, his eyes downcast glued to the floor. Some of the men in the room grimaced, some winced and others grinned a little self-consciously. After all, each had at some point during their service with him experienced the rough edge of their superior's tongue. Been there, done that, got the T-shirt was a thought that probably crossed each man's mind. They knew that the young man had recently joined the police service straight from university. His college tie bore witness to that and he was quite likely to be promoted very soon due to his qualifications and connections.

Farrel knew that this did not sit well with some of the older, hard-bitten men in the squad. They had survived through sheer hard work and putting their reputations and sometimes even their lives on the line in what on occasions was a very murky business. The young man's superior manner and educated accent did not help either, but everyone admitted that he never knowingly used them to his own advantage. He was just a very fast learner.

Farrel himself had joined the police service as a young twenty year old and in the intervening years—he was coming up to complete twenty-two years' service—he had worked his way up to his present rank. His reputation was highly respected by his seniors and almost revered, if grudgingly, by other police officers. He was, of course, not without his critics, who would point to his very unorthodox methods to gain the necessary results, yet they could never deny they were effective and always within the law—if a little dubious, according to the purists.

Farrel cast his eye upon each member of the squad one by one for some sign of progress. DS George Preston, his 'loyal sidekick', as he thought of him, perhaps two or three years his senior and some five inches shorter but more heavily built, was a highly confident officer who commanded respect from the rest of the group. If Farrel needed to delegate an important job to anyone, or share a confidence, he would turn to George. Now though, as his boss turned to him, Preston briefly shook his head. "Nothing guv," he murmured quietly.

Farrel switched his gaze to DC Alan Perkins, a reliable man if ever there was one, who always looked on the brighter side of things but never missed a trick in a serious situation.

He too shook his head. "No, guv," he answered disappointedly.

DC Dick Johnson had heard nothing reliable and neither had sour-faced DC Peter Rowles.

This lack of information irked Farrel and it showed on his face.

"Shut that bloody window," he snapped abruptly, his voice rising angrily as a road drill unexpectedly started its loud, clanging chatter in the car park three floors below, right under the open squad office window. "How the hell can anyone think properly with that racket going on outside?"

Someone rushed to close it, but it made little difference inside the office. Farrel rolled his eyes towards the ceiling and mouthed a silent obscenity. "Has *anyone* heard *anything*?" he impatiently asked again with a growing tone of annoyance.

There was a negative sound in the murmuring within the squad members. Of course they had all heard rumours, but nothing substantial. And they knew that the DCI only wanted something real to go on and not 'silly bloody fairy stories' as he so often put it.

"I've heard," he announced in a somewhat bitter, superior tone, "from pretty good authority that little Tommy won't be wasting any more of our time. Sadly, he seems to have found out something he shouldn't have, and the story goes that he's been dropped off somewhere between Dover and Calais and told to swim home, so to speak."

"Didn't know he could swim, guv," the bright cockney voice of DC Perkins piped up. At five foot nine, he was the shortest man in the squad, but he overcame this disadvantage by being a bit of a clown at times.

"He couldn't," Farrel confirmed. "At least not when tied to something heavy. Mind you, that's only what I heard. It seems a bit far-fetched to me. At present, it's only hearsay, and I hope it's not correct, but, all the same, someone has heard something along those lines. So, gentlemen," he concluded as he looked around the office at the others, "it's up to us to find out whether he is alive or not, and, very importantly, what he knew that would make someone desperate enough to give him impromptu swimming lessons, if they did in fact do that." With this he glanced at his notebook then slammed it shut. "Let's get to it then. Look in all those dirty, slimy places that you know so well, turn over a few stones and find out what the maggots living under them know. I have no doubt that something big is going down or is about to go down in this neck of the woods. So, let's find out what it is and do it to them before they do it to us, as someone, somewhere, once said."

The officers all shuffled from the room except DC Copley. Farrel turned and marched into his office—a small area in the corner of the main detective room. The temporary walls were some six feet high and Farrel could see over the top of them when he stood up. The lower half was made from painted white plasterboard and the upper portion, frosted glass. The door was similarly constructed and now stood open. He sat down in the chair behind his cluttered desk, sighed and put his hands, palms down, onto the scattered papers covering it. A sudden movement caused him to look up to where Copley hovered in the open doorway.

"Yes?" he asked curtly.

"I'm sorry if I wasted your time, sir," the young DC adopted an apologetic approach, "but that was the story I heard from a guy in the pub last night." Farrel sighed and rolled his eyes skywards—it was a habit of his and manifested itself when he was in a bad mood. "What did he look like?" He asked the question almost as if expecting a stupid reply.

"Thin-faced, about five foot seven, very slim build, balding, had a smallish moustache and wore a dark suit. He said he knew you."

Farrel thought for a moment and grimaced. "Scar, left eyebrow?"

"Yes, a big one."

"He knows me alright. I've felt his collar on numerous occasions. I gave him that scar and ever since he's been looking to put one over on me. He tells a bloody good story, but don't ever trust a word he says. If he tells you it's five o'clock on Friday 23, check your watch and calendar before you believe him. Did you give him any money?"

"Good grief, sir. No, sir."

"Well, perhaps you're not as stupid as I was beginning to think you were," Farrel responded in his abrupt and unkindly manner.

"Thank you, sir. I'm sorry, sir."

Farrel sighed and looked at the young officer.

"Look, son," he softened his tone, perhaps remembering his earlier less-confident days in the service, "this job's not easy. In fact, it's bloody soul-destroying. Not, I may add," he continued with a hint of bitterness creeping in, "for those sitting in plush offices pushing paper and men around and making pronouncements to the press. Down here, you have to use your initiative and intuition and work your butt off."

"Yes, sir. I realise that."

"You've a lot to learn, son," Farrel lectured. "At the moment, you're thinking I'm a bit of a bastard, I know, but, let me reassure you, I'm really the embodiment of sweetness and light. Mind you, I wouldn't expect my ex-wife to confirm that. I have tremendous respect for all the men in the squad. They won't admit it but they love me like a brother, and after a while, you'll find that I'm even nicer than your favourite uncle."

He paused and looked down with another sigh at the piles of paperwork cluttering up his desk, most of it needing urgent attention—and he with so little time to do it—and sighed yet again. After a moment or two, he looked up and raised his eyebrows as if surprised to see Copley still standing there. "Well then, don't just stand there, son. Sod off and get some work done. We're looking to catch some villains today and maybe even a killer."

Copley left the office, somewhat crestfallen.

Farrel breathed inwards. Perhaps he had been a bit harsh on the young officer and had used language that the young man's uncle, the Assistant Chief Constable, was not likely to approve of. But, there it was. The naïve officer had to learn and the Chief Constable himself had assigned him to Farrel so that he could be trained up for 'great things', as he had put it.

He cleared an area of his desk with the intention of getting through some of the more urgent pieces of work, swore quietly under his breath as he looked at the ever-increasing pile of paperwork and picked up the phone.

He dialled a number and was about to hang up when the phone was suddenly answered. "Liz, it's Farrel. I need to see you." There was a short pause. "Is tonight convenient?" There was another moment of silence as the reply came back. "Fine," he said, "your place at eight o'clock, okay? . . . See you then." He hung up.

Hell. He stared at the phone. *What I'd give for just one straightforward case every now and then.*

2

Farell pulled up near Elizabeth's place just after 8.30 p.m. It was dark by then. He parked his car under a streetlight and walked the 300 yards or so to the main gate of the apartment block where she lived. That way, he thought, his arrival was less noticeable.

The apartment block was situated in a leafy part of Larchester. The imposing façade, perimeter wall and electronically controlled gates reflected its classy surroundings. He punched in the security number Elizabeth had given him so that he could enter the building relatively unobtrusively. It was probably better that no one saw him.

Elizabeth's expensive apartment was on the fourth floor and at the end of a bright and beautifully kept hallway complete with various potted green plants. Through the small security observation hole of her door a clear view of the whole approach from the lift was possible. There was also a CCTV camera on the wall above the lift door. Farell rang the doorbell and noticed a light shine briefly through the security viewer as the inside cover was drawn back. Seconds later the heavy door swung open.

The first time that Farell had seen Elizabeth Coulter again was six months or so earlier, although they had a friendship many years before. They met by chance in a café in a nearby village and had drunk coffee together and talked about old times. After that, they had met on a number of occasions for a coffee or a meal.

Elizabeth had a past and it was that, that interested Farrel. At first, Farrel thought her past might have even proved useful to him. Odd little snippets came out during their conversations that related to those people who operated very close to the edge of the law, and Elizabeth hadn't attempted to hide anything from him, even though she knew he was an 'important' cop.

"Hello, handsome." It was Elizabeth's way of greeting him when they met. "*More* problems? More bad news? Come on in."

Farrel stepped inside and Elizabeth closed the door behind him. He noticed that she turned the dead latch. He gave her a kiss on the cheek. He had known Elizabeth, or Liz, as he usually referred to her, ever since their schooldays. She was a very attractive woman, around his own age, with an engaging smile that showed a perfect set of teeth. The fact that she wore glasses in no way detracted from her good looks, and Farrel thought they probably even enhanced her beautiful brown eyes.

Whoever said 'men don't make passes at girls who wear glasses' was an absolute idiot, he thought. He did not return her light greeting or her smile.

"Huh," was all he said.

"*Still* feeling bitter about women?" she asked him.

"Only some, but it's always good to see you, Liz," he replied at last, thinking back to the time they had been much closer. He slipped off his coat and hung it on the hallstand before following her into the lounge.

"You're looking really good, girl," he said, as he slowly ran his eyes over her. She had a rather fuller figure than when she was younger, but, at fortyish and five foot six inches tall, she still turned heads.

Farrel's thoughts began to wander. Her features were those that most men admired: high cheekbones with an aquiline nose and full lips. Her dark brown hair, he knew, was her own. She was no dumb blonde and never had been. "But then, you always have looked good," he complemented her.

She laughed lightly and her eyes shone.

He looked around approvingly at the room. It was his first visit here. Other meetings had been in cafés and restaurants.

The furniture was expensive: a black leather three-seater sofa, a two-seater and an easy chair that looked towards a large fireplace that contained an ornate flame-effect fire and beside which sat a large flat screen television. The clock on the sideboard showed 8.25 p.m.

"Come and sit down," she invited him. "Make yourself comfortable and tell me about all those troubles."

"Thanks," he mumbled and crossed to the large armchair, slumping into the plumped up cushions.

"Scotch, isn't it?" she asked, half turning towards him from her well stocked drinks cabinet.

"You remember," he approved, showing that he was pleasantly surprised.

"There's a lot I remember about you, Ian."

It was a long time since anyone had called him by his first name. Normally it was 'sir', 'guv' or just straightforward 'Farrel'. It was a good feeling.

"You haven't been to my place before, have you? Just seen you outside, that's all," she complained.

He said nothing in reply.

Liz sat on the sofa facing him, hitched her skirt up a little further than necessary and crossed her legs. *Damn good legs*, he thought, as his eyes dwelt upon them.

She giggled when she saw him do it. "What are you thinking about now?" she asked provocatively.

Again, he did not reply.

"That summer's day in the park in the little woodland?" she suggested, her left eyebrow rose to accentuate the question.

He smiled; something he did very little of these days. He thought back to the time to which she was referring, and he remembered it well.

"So, you're a mind reader now?" he said, lightening up and chuckling at the memory. "Long time ago that was."

She flashed him a wicked grin. "Good though, wasn't it?"

"Bloody good," he confirmed.

She laughed again.

"I may have said it before, but you really did fall on your feet, girl," he continued, as he looked around again at the large room with its luxurious curtains, carpet and decoration. "Whoever said 'crime doesn't pay' was talking a load of crap and through the back of his head at the same time!"

"Yeah, it paid well enough. I've got nearly everything I need." She looked up at him, her face now pensive and serious. "My biggest regret is that I chose Harry instead of you. Thought he was an honest bloke, but he was crooked as hell."

"Had a high old time though while it lasted, didn't you?"

"For a while, but then things changed. Look at that security door, the big gates and all the other things. Those days were scary. I'm still nervous about going out alone after dark, even now. There are still people out there who might like to have a go at me just for old time's sake, and for what Harry did."

"He got in too deep," Farrel noted and shook his head, "and couldn't handle the big boys."

"He *did* want out though," Elizabeth told him sadly. "He was scared because he knew everything about everything that was going on."

"And that's why they killed him," Farrel stated flatly. "They couldn't afford to let him go *and* let him live. Something like it is starting up again, if I'm not very much mistaken."

"Yes, that's possible. I've heard a whisper or two," she nodded. "They're only whispers though, mind you. That's all they ever are or ever were. I still see some of the wives and girlfriends of Harry's old mates, and I hear things, you know. I listen but keep my mouth shut."

"Really?" he raised his eyebrows but was not surprised. She had mentioned little things like this before over a cup of coffee or a dinner somewhere, but then he said quickly, "I hope you haven't taken any risks and found out something you shouldn't have."

"Not a chance," she assured him. "After we met and talked these last few months, I had an idea you'd be around when you thought something really big might happen, so I just listened; thought what I heard may be of use sometime. You'd always been good to me when we were kids, so why shouldn't I help you out if I could?"

Farrel thought back to those teenage and twenty-something years, when he and Elizabeth were reckoned to be an item. That was before he had joined the police force, and she had chosen to marry one of his old school friends. Harry had subsequently turned to crime and paid the ultimate price for crossing a particularly nasty hoodlum.

"So, what's the news on the street?" he asked.

She stood up, sauntered over to him and took his hand. He stood too, unsure of quite what to do. He inhaled her perfume. It had been so long since he had last shopped for perfume for his ex that he could not place it, but he knew instinctively that it was expensive. She stood so close to him that he could feel the warmth of her body. *She's still a cracker.* His pulse quickened.

"Not so fast, Mr Ian 'important policeman' Farrel," she warned, "I'll trade you something."

"And what's that?" It was a rhetorical question and he knew it, but he was now very pleasantly intrigued.

"I've got something you want and you've got something I want," she said, looking him straight in the eye and grasping his hand firmly. Then she led him from the lounge, across the hall and through the door of the master bedroom.

His mind strayed back to that summer's day in the park.

The bed covers were turned back neatly.

"Well?" she asked, turning to him. "Deal, or no deal?"

"You drive a hard bargain, ma'am," he replied with fake sigh.

"Don't lie," she laughed, as she pulled him towards to the bed. "And it's been a decent time since Harry's been gone, don't you think?"

Farrel nodded—yes, he definitely thought, it had been a decent time since Harry had been gone!

3

F arrel dragged his eyes open and rubbed them as he tried to focus on the digital clock positioned in the corner of the bedside table. The alarm had not been set.

"God, it's seven thirty," he muttered, as he sprung up quickly almost tripping over himself in the process.

"What's the time?" a sleepy voice from the other side of the bed enquired.

"Half seven and I'm late."

"Can't you be a bit late, just for once?" Elizabeth turned over languidly to look at him. She smiled and pouted her lips. "Stay just a little longer?"

Farrel wanted to stay. That was for damn sure. He knew that under that sheet all she was wearing was that enticing smile. "Sorry, kiddo," he forced himself to say. "I really must be on time today. I have a very important meeting first thing."

"Was our 'trade' worth it?" she asked in a husky voice.

He looked down at her; the dreamy look on her face, the half smile, her half-closed eyes with their long lashes and her dark brown hair tumbling across the pillow.

"Absolutely," he said sincerely. *More than worth it,* he had to admit to himself. The meeting was the last place on earth he wanted to be this morning. "In fact, I seemed to get everything I needed, or didn't you notice?"

She giggled and stretched sensuously again, taking a deep breath inwards. "So did I," she murmured. "It was a good trade."

The sheet slipped. Farrel inhaled deeply.

"A bit like the old days, yes?" she wanted to know as she propped herself on her elbow. The sheet fell away completely.

"Absolutely," he repeated. "You haven't changed at all in your old age."

"You cheeky bugger," she giggled, as she heaved a pillow across the bed at him.

"Except," he added very quickly and with great sincerity, "you're much better."

He showered quickly and found something that looked similar to a razor he used at home, only it was a lady's shaver and did not achieve the standard he preferred. It would have to do. He dressed and returned to the bedroom. He crossed to the bed where Elizabeth was still giving him a very strong 'come-on'. He bent down and kissed her. She was warm, still sleepy and very desirable.

"When will you come back?" she wanted to know. He did not tell her he would much prefer not to go in the first place.

"When I can," he replied. "It won't be too long, I promise." Another kiss and he let himself out of the flat and quickly returned to his car.

As he drove to the office he reflected upon the previous night. Had it been a wise thing to do? Had his motives been the right ones? It had been great, but Elizabeth was, after all, the widow of a criminal. In addition, she had left Farrel for that criminal all those years before and benefited from ill-gotten gains until Harry, her husband had been eliminated by the mob.

It would perhaps cloud his reputation.

He wondered if it had really been in pursuit of information that had led him to Elizabeth's bedroom last night. Maybe it was, or maybe it was Elizabeth using him for her own reasons.

The more he thought about it, his confusion grew.

Better let things settle down and see what develops. There's no need to rush things. No need to get too serious. Look what happened all that time ago. She left me for a crook.

She was a widow with no man around. He was a divorced man with no woman around and as celibate as most priests for four years. What was he supposed to do?

4

The briefing was scheduled for eight thirty, but Farrel called in on his mobile to say he would be a few minutes late. At nine o'clock he strode into the room. There were a few sharp intakes of breath and smothered smiles from those assembled as they looked at his poorly-shaven face and the dark patches under his eyes. He was always clean-shaven and smart each morning, but today things were different.

"Are you okay, guv?" DS Preston enquired with concern in his voice, but at the same time just able to mask a smile.

"Yeah, I'm fine," the DCI replied curtly. "Didn't sleep too well last night, that's all." He thought briefly back to the real reason.

The members of the squad stood quietly waiting to be informed of any updates since their last meeting. They always stood during these briefings. That way, in Farrel's philosophy, everyone would stay focused on matters in hand and time would not be wasted with 'small talk'.

No one had heard anything of any real value and so kept most of what they had heard to a minimum.

At last Farrel took over. "I think we may now be in possession of just a few more bits of info," he began. "Mind you, I wouldn't say it's gospel at this point, but the whisper is that Big Mick doesn't rule the roost any more—he thinks he still does, but it seems that some big boys from the Continent have moved into the area and muscled in on his action. At the moment it appears that they are operating somewhere on the London Road Industrial Estate, allegedly Unit 5 and possibly Unit 6."

"What's their angle?" Detective Sergeant Preston asked.

"Rumour has it that they're men from the East and possibly into drugs, maybe people smuggling and even running guns. At least that's what it looks like, so we have to check it out."

"Men from the East, eh," Perkins piped up in his usual cheery cockney voice. "But they ain't the Magi. Oh dear, what a pity!"

Farrel smiled briefly. "You could say that," he said. "Anyway, it looks as if the big cheese and problem in this neck of the woods is in fact small fry from now on. However, there's always the possibility they may join forces and we don't need that. So, keep your ears to the ground. We need as much info as we can get. It doesn't matter how little or insignificant it seems." He shot a glance at DC Copley. "We all need to know about it and log it. I want that board," he indicated to the large white board they always used to collate information when investigating a complex matter, "full of information. We can discard anything unnecessary later. Copley, you're the whizz kid on computers. I want you to log everything, cross-reference everything and search and research every item that you are asked, okay?"

"Yes, guv," Copley replied, looking as if he felt he had at last received some sort of recognition from the DCI. Farrel, in turn, felt he had atoned in a small way for his outburst at the young man the day before. Relationships were perhaps about to improve.

"What's the source of the info, guv?" Rowles chipped in. "Is it really reliable?"

"It's as reliable a source as we have as yet," Farrel replied impatiently. *That was a strange question from one officer to another.* "Why? Do you have a problem with that?"

"No, guv," Rowles replied quickly, and with a shrug of his shoulders added, "just wondered."

Every group seemed to have its own 'black sheep' and this group's was Rowles. He was bitter about being passed over for promotion and his demeanour, often petulant, showed it.

The squad left the office to carry out their respective enquiries. Copley took his seat in front of his computer and logged on.

Farrel stood behind him. "Right then, son," Farrel said, "I'll give you what I know now. No names at present, of course." He shot a glance at the backs of the departing squad members. "I'll leave the rest up to your initiative and intuition."

"Yes, guv," Copley said, now feeling almost completely rehabilitated. "I've got a list of vehicle numbers, names of firms on the industrial estate and any *foreign* persons in the area." He stressed this term, Farrel thought, in order to remain politically correct, *just like his bloody uncle*, he thought.

Copley continued, "And, I'll run checks on anything else that shows up or seems relevant. It seemed to be a good idea to check out everything in and around the industrial estate."

"Well done," Farrel said impressed. "I'll leave you to it then, and, don't forget, I want to be the first to know of anything new."

"Of course, guv."

The rest of the day passed off quietly. No bodies had come to light, but Tommy Acton was still unaccounted for and Jill Franks had still not been spotted in her usual haunts.

Surveillance was organised for the industrial park in question from dusk until half past midnight. The local patrols had been quite adamant that nothing moved around there after midnight, not even the girls.

5

Farrel looked around the area disapprovingly as he left his car and walked towards the vehicle in which DS Preston and DC Jackson sat watching. The sergeant opened the window of the car as he approached.

"I remember when all this was open fields," Farrel observed looking about him. "Now look at it. What a dump!"

"Well, the good news is that nothing's happened so far, guv," Preston reported.

"Okay," Farrel commanded, "go and have your break. I'll take over. Maybe *tovarich* Igor or whatever his name is and wherever he comes from, will do something tonight."

The other two officers drove off and Farrel took over the watch. He had set up the surveillance on what he thought was reliable information, but so far it had not produced anything approaching a result.

The newcomers were, at present, an unknown quantity. He knew everyone in the squad was used to being patient; that was the way they caught the 'big fish', and this 'Igor' fellow and his associates were being considered as 'big fish' and very careful not to lay themselves open to detection and arrest.

He sat alone in his unmarked car. It was about eight o'clock on a Friday evening late in October. The evenings were drawing in but the weather was still quite mild. The light industry park, which included several small storage and warehouse units dotted around, had been developed on the edge of the town on what had been at one time the municipal waste dump. The remaining part of the area had been left untouched. A chain-link fence had originally surrounded that remaining undeveloped area, but after years of neglect the fence had deteriorated and had been damaged by vandals and fly-tippers. The inside had grown into a mixture of young trees, bushes and scrub around which piles of builders' rubble had been deposited. Other fly-tipped materials had been thrown over the surrounding chain-link fence that remained and even more had been dumped outside it by locals not wanting to make a trip to the local official tip. *What a mess*, he thought. As the lengths of broken fence had increased, so too had the amount of rubbish deposited there. *Rat heaven!*

The industrial units opposite were a variety of types and mainly constructed out of concrete and steel. Some had high double doors whilst others had the up-and-over garage type, and yet others still had single doors and windows at ground level. Some of the units had windows on the first floor and lights still shone from some of them, but dirt and graffiti covered most. *Probably to obscure anything that was going on inside,* Farrel thought.

The subject of the surveillance was Unit 5, which had an up-and-over door. It was closed, but he could see light coming from both the ground level windows and those higher up.

He had parked his car off the road on the rough ground just off the pavement and under the heavy shadow of the trees where he knew his presence was less likely to be noticed. The weak streetlights illuminated only the roads around the units on the other side of the road.

Many of the businesses employed night watchmen if their goods were deemed to be of high value and others used security companies that visited at intervals during the hours of darkness, checking the premises and logging the times of their inspections.

Cars drifted slowly around the dimly lit streets in search of the girls who plied their trade there. Police patrols also drove around it from time to time, but any problem that the girls presented seemed to merit a very low priority. He watched as they flitted around in the shadows of the buildings and approached the occasional kerb crawler. None of them appeared to relish the idea of working in the deeper shadows close to the wooded area where he had positioned his car. Everything was quiet. He liked a quiet life wherever possible, but it was not the way to get a result. He looked around in an attempt to pick up even the slightest hint of criminal activity.

"What are you up to tonight *tovarich*?" he murmured softly towards the grey concrete building with its dirty grey door scrawled with graffiti; the type of building you could easily associate with dubious goings-on.

Suddenly, there was a sharp rap on the car's front passenger window which made him start. A pretty face atop a shapely female torso appeared to his left, silhouetted in the window. The front of a low-cut, tightly fitting red top was open halfway and looked to Farrel as if it were struggling to restrain a very full bosom that was attempting an escape.

He pressed the button to open the window. The face that came into a much clearer view had large hazel eyes and was framed by dark brown hair that shone even in the weak lamplight from across the street. The lips were full and accentuated the pleasant smile. The mouth was perhaps a little wide, but that was no bad thing, he considered. There was little sign of make-up; so very different from many of these girls he had dealt with before. *What did someone once say . . . a smile is the best make-up?* It was a face he recognised as its owner stooped down closer to talk to him. As he sat in the darkness of the car the girl could not see his features clearly.

"Looking for a nice time, darling?" she purred.

"Hop in," he invited.

Quickly she opened the door and slid onto the seat, her mini skirt sliding higher until it became nothing more than a short pelmet, and her ample bosom straining even harder to escape its confinement. She slammed the door shut and Farrel closed the window. He leaned towards her so that she could see his face more clearly in the small amount of light that entered through the windscreen. "Hello Julie," he said brightly. "How are you these days?"

She shot him a glance of horror. "Oh my God," she groaned, "Farrel."

"Right first time," he said smiling.

Quickly, she turned to grab the handle of the door to escape, but with his left hand he gently grabbed her right forearm.

"Hang on a minute," he said, "I'm not in vice. Relax."

She stopped and turned back towards him with a hesitant smile, but there was still a look of suspicion on those attractive features.

"So, you *would* like a nice time?" she enquired somewhat dubiously.

"Maybe," he teased, "and I promise I won't nick you."

"I can't make you out," she said sounding confused. "You're a copper, aren't you? Coppers nick girls like me, so why are you being nice?"

"Don't you know why?"

"No."

"Ask your mum."

"She died last year. It was cancer. Didn't you hear?"

Farrel was shocked. No, he hadn't heard. In the dimness of the car's interior, his face fell.

"Oh, I'm so sorry, Julie," he genuinely sympathised.

"You knew her then?" she asked almost in disbelief.

"We were at school together, that's all. She was in the year above. I always liked her and I always spoke to her when I saw her. I even remember you in a buggy."

"She had a good idea of what I was doing the odd times I did it," Julie confessed, sounding guilty.

"But you've never been a real pro—not at all regular."

"Not very successful either," she laughed dolefully. "Can't put my heart into it, you see." She fell silent for a few moments. "You ain't such a bad old bastard after all," she mused at last. Then, as if realising something for the first time, "And you ain't all that old neither. Mum was forty-two when she died a year ago, so that puts you about . . ."

"Okay, okay," he cut in.

"Prime of life," she chuckled and leaned towards him.

The tight-fitting top was appearing to lose the battle.

"You know, where I come from everybody refers to you as 'old' Farrel," she teased, "but you *ain't* old. I like that."

"Careful, I'm still old enough to nick you though," he chided.

"What for?" she challenged.

"For being rude to a policeman who's a lot older than you are."

They both grinned.

"If you've let me off, I guess I owe you one," she added pouting her lips, "and it'd have to be for free."

He looked into her eyes. *I'd like that*, he admitted to himself, *I'd like that very much, but not just now*. As far as he was aware, all she ever did this for was to put food on the table and pay the rent.

He sucked in a breath in preparation to change the mood then put his hand into the inside pocket of his jacket and took out his wallet. He removed two twenty-pound notes, folded them and carefully and slowly tucked them down into her cleavage, noting how warm it felt.

"Payment for your time," he stated. "Please note, *time.*"

He wanted information and he was prepared to pay for it, especially if the 'nark' was as attractive as Julie was.

"Just sit a while and talk to me about what goes on around here," he said.

They sat and small-talked for a time about why she was occasionally on the game, what had started it and why she didn't quit. Her story was a sad one from the beginning. Her mother had been a single teenage mum with no support from an absent teenage father. With a daughter to keep, she had needed support and had turned to a number of boyfriends who turned out to be irresponsible and whom Julie grew up calling 'uncle'. Many of them unfortunately liked schoolgirls as well as the older women.

"It just seemed to evolve even though I hated it," she said angrily but with resignation. Farrel felt genuine sympathy growing for her. He had never really thought too much about the diverse reasons why the girls did what they did. *Did she really have any choice?* He felt as though maybe he wanted to help her somehow. Then the copper in him reasserted itself. *I'll have to work harder at being a bastard.* However, when he looked into her eyes again, he saw what he thought was helplessness.

As the time passed, he changed the course of the conversation.

"So, what goes on around here?" he asked looking around at the outside.

"What do you mean? I work."

"Not that. I mean in those units over there where the lights are on."

"I don't know. I'm not here *all* the time, you know. It's all part of the job description."

"But when you are?"

"I've no idea, but some nights there's a lot of coming and going over there at number five and the next one, six."

"Like what?"

"Who knows? Strange things sometimes," she said, and attempted to change the subject. "Look, are you sure you wouldn't like me to give you a nice time? You've paid for it, you know."

"What strange things?" he persisted.

"Well, big vans come. They open those big doors in number six. The van drives in. The doors close and in a couple of minutes or so the doors open again and it drives out. Never seems to stay long at all."

"Same van every time?"

"Yes. I think so."

"What happens then?"

"Er . . . they close the doors, but then there seems to be a babble of noise going on inside."

"A babble?"

"Like lots of voices."

"Saying what?"

"I can't really hear from out here, but I get the feeling they're foreigners in there."

Farrel thought for a moment. "That figures," he said, thinking out loud.

"When the white van goes, another van arrives," Julie continued. "I think it's either dark blue or black, and the same thing happens again. It drives in and after a few minutes, it drives out again. Once a punter dropped me off here," she went on, "and after he left, a big guy, foreign he was, came over and told me to 'fuck off'. I told him this is my pitch and that I have a job to do, but he told me again to 'fuck off' if I knew what was good for me. If I didn't, he said he would rearrange my face and a few other things."

"Bastard," muttered Farrel. "Anything else?"

"Yes. Although I was rather scared at the time, I noticed a scar across his left cheek; a big one it was, from the bottom of his ear to his nose. It was horrible."

"Pity it wasn't four inches lower," Farrel thought aloud.

"Why?"

"Because, my dear, that's where his carotid artery is, and if whoever cut him had hit that, you wouldn't have had any trouble with him now."

"Just before I left," she said, "someone from inside number six called out to him."

"Saying what?"

"Don't know. It sounded foreign and something about *Igor* or something like that." She looked at him quizzically.

Farrel leaned forward with a quiet chuckle and kissed her lightly on the cheek. Then he sat back. "Fantastic!" he chortled.

She gave him a very strange look. "What was?" she asked, "Do you feel alright? Looks like you *do* need a few lessons. I could give you some though. Maybe you really would *like* a nice time?"

"Not right now," he said, "but you have made me happier than you know."

She gave him another puzzled look. "But I . . ." she started.

"It's what you have *told* me. I'll explain it all later, but I don't think you should hang around here anymore."

"It's my pitch," she protested.

"It could be dangerous for you. You may have seen things that you shouldn't have, and I'm worried for your safety."

She started to complain, but something outside the car must have caught her attention because she suddenly threw her arms around him and pulled him close to her.

"Somebody's coming from number six," she whispered hurriedly. "Make it look good," and he felt her full lips on his, her tongue toying with his. At first, he was taken aback but very pleasantly surprised and responded to the situation in what he considered was the appropriate fashion, easing the top of her neckline down to liberate her bosom. It was warm, smooth, and pliant and he savoured the feeling. At the same time, he noticed her hand sliding up his thigh from his knee. *Is she play-acting or what?*

Suddenly, there was a rap on the front passenger window of the car. Farrel opened the electrically operated window from his side and leaned across towards the voice.

"What you do here?" demanded a foreign voice. *East European, Russian or Ukrainian* Farrel thought, *certainly Slavic.* Julie hurriedly covered herself and Farrel felt her body stiffen.

"Why? What do you mean?" Farrel asked in innocent annoyance and adopting a very superior tone of voice. "Bloody well obvious, isn't it, old boy?" It was his time to play-act.

The man ignored Farrel's remark and addressed Julie. "I know you," he said, "I tell you before 'fuck off'. Keep away from here."

"This is my pitch," Julie stated forcefully.

"When I say 'fuck off', I mean it . . . and you stay away," the Slav added, his voice full of menace.

"Okay, old boy," Farrel cut in, now appearing to want to placate the man, "We're going, aren't we, my dear?" He shot a quick glance towards Julie.

"But—" she started.

"Sh," Farrel hissed and gunned the engine into life. He selected first gear and started to drive away.

"He's a nasty bastard," he said as he drove.

About a quarter of a mile along the road he pulled over and stopped. "You could be in danger Julie," he reiterated.

"Why? What's gonna happen?"

"Who knows, but I'm sure that son-of-a-bitch had a gun under his left arm. That could mean he's right handed and that little piece of information might be useful sometime in the future," he added, as if speaking to himself. "Where do you live now?" he asked her.

"14, Queen's Park Road, Flat 25. Just off Queen's Park Avenue."

"Nice area," he noted and she nodded.

"That was a bit scary," she admitted, her voice slightly shaky.

Farrel touched her arm to try to reassure her. "Keep away from there in future," he advised her, "they're nasty people."

"Please don't frighten me anymore," she pleaded. "I feel bad enough already, but after all, it's my pitch."

They approached Julie's apartment block, but before exiting the car she removed a smart black coat from a tote bag she had been carrying and slipped it on over her working clothes. It certainly looked more in keeping with this neighbourhood and so different from her beat. As the car stopped, she leaned across and gently kissed Farrel.

Perhaps someone looking on might think I'm her boyfriend dropping her off. Indeed it would seem reasonable enough for anyone to think it.

"Would you like to come in for a drink?" she invited.

He looked closely at her and saw her in a brighter light. *She really is a peach. Why does she have to do that for a living?* He would dearly have loved to take up her offer. *Stay for breakfast too!*

"Better not," he said kindly, "I've got a lot of work to do before I finish tonight."

"Pity," she said, "but thanks for everything this evening, and I do mean *everything*."

"My pleasure."

"Mine too," she replied, giving him a knowing smile.

"Keep away from the estate," he advised again.

"I have to work."

"Stay away," he insisted as she opened the door and climbed out. She turned round and looked at him through the open door, her eyes gentle as they met his.

"I have to work, but thanks for your concern and care." She threw him a kiss. "Good night," she whispered and closed the door.

Farrel watched her go into the main door of the block. *Nice rear end too*, he mused. He sat for a few moments pondering the last hour. Right now his thoughts were in a jumble. He had felt greatly attracted to her those last twenty or so minutes and his concern for her seemed to be very real. The added thought that he could be so close to the 'Slavs', as he now referred to them, did not faze him even though they were likely to be ready to use firearms. It was Julie's face that kept crowding into his thoughts. She could be in much more danger than anyone had thought and she certainly did not deserve that.

6

Farrel worked through to eleven thirty that evening, planning and re-planning strategies as he saw weaknesses in each one. Nothing could be left to the vagaries of Lady Luck. You had to be absolutely certain of your next move and then four or five more moves beyond that if you were to trap the 'Slavs'. It was a bit like playing chess and he guessed that *Igor* and his henchmen knew how to do that too.

He left the office and drove home to his flat on the first floor of a smart block on the edge of town. It was where he could normally switch off and relax, watch TV or listen to his collection of CDs. It depended on his mood as to what genre of music he would play; classical if he felt relaxed, or jazz, or even perhaps part of his collection of country and western songs. He had always considered himself as a bit of a country boy or even maybe a cowboy, but not the sort of 'cowboys' who operated these days. He liked simple, down-to-earth lyrics and easy-to-listen-to tunes.

He poured himself a large Scotch, put on a CD without really looking at it and selected the random mode. Then he sat in his favourite brown leather armchair to relax. Chris de Burgh sang *Lady in Red. Damn it,* he thought as Julie's face appeared and he recalled the sight of that cleavage within the half-open red blouse. He remembered too that kiss and the brief fondling that had taken place in the car. *I need to relax,* he thought, but she remained there and his thoughts returned to his earlier fears for her safety.

Why was he so damned concerned about that? She would most probably be known to him if he were in vice, but he was not and all she was to him was just another very attractive young woman whom he was worried about, perhaps unreasonably so.

This is stupid, Farrel, she's just a young whore. But young whore or not she still merits protection, his other self argued. *And anyway, who is there to protect her?*

These thoughts bothered him until around 2.00 a.m. when finally he drained his third double whisky and went to bed. Sleep did not come easily. In fact, it did not come at all until around 4.00 a.m. His worry for Julie seemed to consume him almost to the point of being an obsession. Why, he kept asking himself, why this feeling that suddenly this woman, who was very streetwise, needed looking after? The more he thought, the more he became aware of being strongly attracted to her. *But she is only a whore,* he kept reminding himself.

Then he thought about those people he'd dealt with in the past, whose deeds were far worse than those of this young, attractive woman, renting out her body just to make a living. Those people who harmed others. Julie was not doing any harm. Had it been the kisses and fondling that had triggered this almost forgotten part of his life? Again, confused thoughts plagued him until he finally drifted off into a fitful sleep with dreams of Julie in the front seat of the car.

7

At nine o'clock the next morning the briefing took place in the office. All the members of the squad were present. Farrel related the events of the night before and what he had heard had happened on previous evenings. He purposely omitted using Julie's name at this point, or their very brief intimate encounter.

"How did you come by this info, guv?" Detective Constable Rowles inquired.

"Just someone I met."

"During that time you relieved us?" DC Jackson asked.

Farrel nodded.

"Do we need to know who it was?" Rowles asked again. Farrel turned and looked him straight in the eyes. Rowles knew that impatient look. He had seen it many times before.

"Why?"

Rowles looked uncomfortable and averted his eyes. "I just thought perhaps you might want us to know . . . for protection . . . or whatever," he shrugged.

"I'll handle that bit," Farrel replied curtly.

The briefing broke up after it had been decided to reimpose the surveillance later in the day.

*

At ten thirty that evening Farrel called off the watch. Julie had told him that all the activity seemed to take place mid to late evening when Units 5 and 6 closed up. He thought that if things were too quiet, any dubious activity would draw attention to itself.

At 10.45 p.m. he drove into the road for a brief visit to satisfy himself that all was well. He stopped at the same spot he had parked the previous night, cut the engine and switched off the lights.

He thought back to twenty-four hours ago and hoped that Julie had heeded his advice and stayed away from the area just to be on the safe side. He still could not explain, even to himself, the reason for his concern.

All was quiet. No lights shone from the windows of Units 5 or 6 and he breathed a sigh of relief. At that moment there was a rap on the passenger window. He turned and saw Julie's face above the cleavage he had so admired the evening before, but this time she was not smiling and offering him a nice time. This time her face was pale, even in the weak streetlights, and she looked scared. He unlocked the door and she slid in beside him quickly.

"What the—" he began, but she was shaking so badly that he postponed the tirade he was about to direct at her. He reached across and took her hand; it was ice cold and trembling. "It's okay, Julie," he said quickly, yet quietly to reassure her, "it's okay. What the hell's happened?"

She looked at him, her eyes wide open and showing even more fear than he had recognised at first. "Oh Farrel, thank God it's you," she stammered. "But what made you come around here?"

"Copper's intuition, perhaps," he lied, not wanting to let on that it was her safety that really bothered him. *What the hell am I thinking about? I'm not paid to look after stupid young whores who don't take good advice.* However, just as quickly that other part of him, the voice deep inside asked: *Has she become special?* He stopped musing when her voice cut across his thoughts.

"I'm frightened, Farrel."

"Why? What's happened?"

"I know you told me not to come, but it's my pitch and all that . . ."

"Yeah, yeah," he said impatiently.

"Well, about fifteen minutes ago a large van went into number six . . ."

"Damn," he interjected, "I pulled them off too early."

It was clear by her frown that Julie did not understand the outburst. "Anyway," she continued, "the doors closed and all the lights came on in both units . . ."

"Carry on."

"Well, then I heard shouting, a lot of shouting. I think some of the voices came from women."

"And?"

"Suddenly, that side door opened," she gestured to the side door of number six, "and a woman ran out quickly followed by a man who grabbed her and slapped and punched her around the head. She collapsed in a heap and the man just dragged her back inside. As he did so, he looked around to see if anyone had witnessed what had gone on." She hesitated again.

"And?"

"I think he may have caught sight of me, but I can't be sure."

Farrel swore. "That's all we need, you being a good witness and then being seen, putting yourself right in harm's way. Why the hell didn't you keep well clear like I told you?"

"I ran and hid," she said hurriedly in her own defence, "and then I heard a loud bang."

"What was it? Metal on metal, a door slamming or a shot?" he asked.

"Don't know. Anyway, the door of number five opened after a moment or two and a small van reversed out and drove off fast. That's all I know. Then I saw your car. You came about five minutes after it left."

"Did you see a number or a name on the side?"

"No."

"Colour?"

"White or a very light colour."

Farrel paused and thought. *It's always a bloody white van.*

"What's going on? What's going to happen?" she asked nervously.

He looked across at her. In the dimness of the weak streetlights he saw her not as a self-assured, streetwise woman on her beat, but much more a frightened, white-faced little girl.

"If he did see you," he warned, "you could be in a lot of danger."

"Oh, thank you very much," she retorted, the fear in her voice was all too obvious. "I don't know if he *did* see me, but he came back out and started to cross the street heading in my direction. I think he must have seen some car headlights coming, most probably yours, because he turned and went back into the building. Within seconds, the van backed out and the lights in the building went out. Then the van drove off a few minutes before you arrived."

"That's it then," Farrel stated, "I'm not taking any more chances. Right now, in my opinion, you are, or may be, an important material witness to something or other. I'm not sure what at the moment, but we sure as hell have to take care of you." He did not add that he did not want a possible murder on his patch—hers. She was frightened enough already.

"Who's we?" she asked.

"The police," he replied. He looked at his watch. "Good grief, is that the time? It looks as if it has to be me, not we. There's nowhere at this time of night to take you and I want to keep you well away from the office. Somewhere where I can be sure you're safe. I have a strange feeling about this case."

She settled back into the seat appearing a little less fearful. "I don't mind that," she said. They drove to her flat and Farrel parked as close to the entrance as he could.

"Go and get some clothes, enough for a few days, and come back as quickly as you can," he instructed. "Don't say anything to anyone. If they did see you, they'll soon trace you to here. I'm going to take you to a safe house after."

"Where's that?"

"You'll find out soon enough." He did not want her to know. Even at this time of night she might see someone in the building and without realising it let something slip. If she had been seen and recognised, Farrel knew full well it would be a very simple matter for them to trace her home address. She was very vulnerable right now.

Within fifteen minutes she was back, having bundled some clothes into a rather large holdall. She threw it onto the back seat and climbed into the front beside him. "Where are we going?" she asked at last. "Where's this safe house?"

"My place," Farrel replied.

8

Farrel parked the car in the usual spot outside his apartment. He checked that no one was around to see Julie and led her up the back stairway. No one ever used the stairs unless the lift was not in service. Despite the absence of other people he did completely relax until they were both inside.

"This is nice," Julie commented as she quickly scanned the living area. There were still a few bits and pieces dotted around the place indicating that at one time a woman had lived there, although generally the place took on the appearance of a male's domain—functional.

"It does the job," Farrel replied without enthusiasm. "For me anyway."

"Wife?" Julie queried.

"Left four years ago. She couldn't put up with my job and what goes with it—the hours and that sort of thing—you know. She found someone who worked less hours and so had more energy." A note of bitterness crept into his voice.

"Pity," she said, still looking around. Farrel led her out of the living room, into the hall and thence into the second bedroom. It was quite small but adequate.

"It's not a suite," he said apologetically, "but it will have to do for the time being."

"It'll be absolutely fine," she confirmed with a smile.

They had a snack which Farrel rustled up with what there was in the fridge. Usually he would eat his meals in the police canteen or pick up take-away food on his way home. From time to time, he replenished his fridge with pre-packed foods. He could not even guess how many times he had eaten food after its sell-by date or even its use-by date either. He always considered, after his ex's cooking, he could eat anything and stay healthy.

Julie drank an orange juice whilst he imbibed his usual double Scotch. It had been a disturbing few hours; worrying for Farrel and very frightening for Julie and they each retired to their beds around eleven thirty.

Farrel lay awake for a long time mulling over what had happened that night. Every time he seemed to get comfortable his conflicting thoughts prevented sleep coming. All was quiet in the next room and he assumed that Julie was asleep, but suddenly he heard her cry out. Then it was quiet again. *A bad dream*, he thought.

The silence continued, but after another sleepless twenty minutes or so it happened again. *Poor kid. Who knows what sort of life she's had, then this.*

Eventually, he drifted into sleep but was awakened as before by the fearful cries from the next room. He lay awake for a long time as those disturbing thoughts kept returning to his mind. Why was he so concerned about this young woman so close by in the next bedroom? Was it his policeman's mind that nagged him regarding her safety, or was it something more personal?

He finally nodded off again. How long he slept he did not know but he came back to wakefulness at the sound of his bedroom door being opened very quietly. He lifted his head cautiously off the pillow and listened. A small shaft of light entered from the streetlights outside to illuminate the room slightly.

"Farrel, are you awake?" whispered a quiet, frightened little voice.

"Why? What's wrong?" he asked as he roused.

"I'm scared. I can't sleep and when I do, I dream about 'scar face' and he's after me. It's so scary."

"You'll be fine," he assured her. "I'm close by."

"Not close enough, though," she said as she stood beside his bed. Then she lifted the bedclothes and slipped under them.

Is this wise his conscience queried. *You could be making a big mistake.*

"I need to be with someone right now," she said with a trembling voice.

"I'll sleep in the chair in the lounge," he said, somehow remembering to consider his career and reputation at this point.

"No, no, you don't understand. You'd still be in a different room," she said, sliding further into the bed. "When I was a kid and got scared at night, I used to get in bed with my mum and then I felt safe," she explained.

"But I'm not your mum," Farrel stated the obvious.

"I had noticed," she retorted, "but I'll feel better anyway."

God, what am I getting myself into?

They talked and as they did so, she seemed to become more relaxed and told him much more of her young life.

"But," she emphasised, "I've never done drugs."

"I'm glad to hear that, Julie," Farrel said, sounding more like a father than a stranger. Although, did he consider himself a stranger right now?

He turned over, his back to her, and eventually drifted off to sleep again thinking about what a dilemma he was in as he did so. Should he move, or stay where he was and take the consequences? However, sleep came first and gave him the answer.

When he awoke next he found Julie's head propped up against his shoulder and her warm body much closer to his than it had been before. He could smell the lingering perfume she had been wearing—it was pleasant, not the most expensive, but pleasant. Julie was still sleeping. He stayed still for as long as he could, not daring to move and disturb her. When he realised that he couldn't remain in this position all morning, he moved, and as he did so, Julie awoke with a start and a little cry.

"Sh . . . it's okay," he murmured softly. "You're safe."

"Mm . . . I know," she mumbled sleepily and moved even closer.

After his divorce, Farrel had thrown himself into his work with what some people thought of as unreasonable fervour and to the exclusion of all other things, but now the warmth of her body so close to his seemed to awaken feelings that for so long he had missed and that had lain dormant.

"Mm . . ." she murmured softly, "Farrel is human after all."

Farrel felt sure that had there been enough light in the bedroom he would have seen a smile on those lovely lips.

"Go to sleep," he ordered but with not half as much authority to show that he really meant it.

"Not now," she murmured again as she put her arm over him and snuggled closer still. "Feeling warm and safe is a marvellous feeling."

Farrel, the strong-willed hard headed cop, knew he was losing the battle.

"Don't be a 'cold fish' cop," she cooed in his ear, "Forget about being a gentleman. I owe you, you know."

Farrel surrendered.

They made love, taking their time, *not like the usual 'quickie' she obviously dispenses*, he thought, *more as if she really means it.*

Afterwards they lay quietly together.

"You okay?" she asked a few minutes later. She must have sensed Farrel's discomfort.

"I'm sorry," he said.

"Sorry for what? You didn't take advantage of me, you know that," she whispered.

"But . . ." he began.

"But nothing," she insisted. "You said you would look after me, and it seems to me you're keeping your promise and making a damn good job of it too."

"Yes, but . . ." he began again.

She stroked his face.

"Didn't you like it?" she asked, a hint of hurt and disappointment tinged her voice. He felt her warm lips brush against his shoulder.

"It's not that . . ."

"Mm . . . ?"

"Yes, of course I did." He now felt her lips on his cheek.

"You're a good man, Farrel," she said as she ran her hand over his chest, "and I feel very safe here."

The warmth, the touch and her breath on his neck once more triggered his natural male instincts, and desire took over.

"Well, well," she groaned appreciatively, "you really are a good man."

"Sorry," he apologised, but with not a great deal of credibility, "I can't help it."

"Hmm . . ." she murmured, as she drew him close.

They made love again and afterwards both fell asleep, not waking until daybreak.

9

Farrel left Julie after a 6.30 a.m. breakfast with orders to stay there until he returned. She was still too frightened to argue and agreed.

As he drove to the office his mind began to fill with conflicting thoughts. *What the hell am I doing? I spend a night with a criminal's widow and two nights later with a young woman who is, to all intents and purposes, an apprentice whore.*

Both women could ruin his reputation and possibly his career, but four years of celibacy had weighted heavily upon him and what else could a red-blooded man do?

Both nights had been like two birthdays rolled into one. It was like being a starving man, close to death, having a sumptuous meal set before him. Would the man choose to starve?

Elizabeth was roughly Farrel's age; Julie was half of it. How would he feel if either of them found out about it? Could he keep it from them? Should he keep it from them? How would he feel when he next saw Elizabeth? If she offered a 'trade', as she had put it, what would he do when he returned to his apartment and Julie?

Things were becoming complicated. Was he beginning to feel guilty? Should he feel that way? They were, the three of them, free agents, but all the same there was an element of guilt plus a fear for his reputation, which he surely had to consider.

As he had done the previous time, he shrugged and decided to let things take their course. *I never did like that divorce-diet anyway*, he admitted, and then immediately, he felt guilty.

*

The squad gathered at nine o'clock that morning. The other members noted that Farrel was in a very amenable mood, very different from his usual morning behaviour. He recounted the events of the previous evening, but did not divulge the name of his source nor her whereabouts. He certainly did not mention what had gone on in the privacy of his own bedroom. Each officer wanted to know where the information came from; it was certainly intriguing, but no one asked. They all realised after working with him that he would let everyone know when he considered the time to be right. Preston recognised that Farrel was preoccupied and worried as well.

Before he had left Julie that morning he had given her instructions to sit down quietly whilst he was away and write down everything she could remember about what had taken place at the industrial estate that evening and anything else she could remember about previous evenings. Being alone she could perhaps spend time on quiet recollection. She was eager to help and said she would make notes and then write as full a statement as she possibly could.

"So, it seems to me," he said to the squad, "that we need to spend a little more time around the industrial estate."

The others nodded and murmured their agreement.

"I'll draw up a rota," he said, "and arrange for cameras etc. etc., and, if possible, we'll use an empty unit as close by as we can get; if there is one, of course. There's no point sitting outside in the cars; we'll soon stand out like a sore thumb."

"Will that be twenty-four seven, then?" Rowles asked

"Why?" Farrel asked quickly. "Spoil your beauty sleep, will it?"

Rowles smiled and gave a short, nervous laugh; he did not have a very good sense of humour and this reply put him in the spotlight, which he did not relish.

"No reason, guv," he said. "Just like to know what arrangements to make, that's all."

Farrel returned his attention to the rest of the group.

"I don't want this to get about," he said. "No leaks, no idle chat. Is that clear? I'll let the Chief Constable know what we're doing. He's the only other one who needs to know any information."

"Sounds like this could be quite a big deal, guv," Perkins observed in his usual bright if somewhat flippant manner."

"That could be the understatement of the year, my boy," Farrel said.

As the briefing session ended and the officers went about their other duties, Farrel called Rowles back to him.

"I'd like to find out just what Jill Franks knows," he said.

"Okay, guv," Rowles replied. "I'll go and find her and have a chat with her."

"Thanks, but I'd like to have a chat with her myself and in the quietness of the office. No need to frighten her any more than I think she may be already. Just bring her in to start off with."

"Right. Any particular time?" Rowles asked.

Farrel thought for a moment. "Around four o'clock this afternoon," he said eventually. "That'll give me time to see the Chief Constable."

As Rowles left, Farrel noticed that Copley was busy on his beloved computer.

"Excuse me, guv," he said.

Farrel walked over to the workstation.

"I've been working on the machine here," he said, "and found out that there are a number of units on the London Road estate that are unoccupied."

"Really?" said Farrel. "That's interesting."

"Yes, there's one just to the rear of numbers five and six."

"Yes?" Farrel smiled. "So, what are you saying?"

"Better than that, there's one just round that bend in the street that could give us a clear view of the front of those units, providing, of course, that there are no tall bushes in the way."

"How did you find all this out?"

"Just looked up a few local letting agents' websites. And then there's the map, naturally."

"Naturally . . ." Farrel echoed. "Where'd you get the map from?"

"It's the local area map on the screen here."

Farrel stooped and looked over Copley's shoulder and smiled. There was the map showing clearly the vacant unit that the young DC had mentioned.

"Good work, Copley," he said. He felt that not using the usual term, son, was likely to give the young man a greater feeling of belonging now. "We'll use both sites. I'll organise it with the Chief Constable. I'm sure it won't be any trouble." He turned on his heel and marched towards the door. As he did so, he half-turned back and called over his shoulder, "Keep doing that and we'll soon have all the villains inside."

Copley returned to pounding his keyboard.

*

Arranging a meeting with the Chief Constable took far longer than he had anticipated. *I suppose he's pontificating about something to some dignitary*, he thought as he waited impatiently in the smart headquarters office with its oak panelling, brass fittings and windows, some of which contained stained glass. The longer he waited the more impatient he became, but he had to control himself. After all, he needed something from the top brass. He saw his requirements as essential to doing his job efficiently, whereas they would, in all probability, consider it a favour and possibly object to it on cost considerations.

Eventually, he was shown into the Chief Constable's office, but the man he was hoping to see was not there. He knew the Chief Constable, who, in turn, knew him well, and although not always approving of Farrel's methods, knew that he was a good police officer, even if something of a maverick. Facing him across the desk sat the Assistant Chief Constable, Michael Copley, OBE. The two had never, for some reason Farrel could not fathom out, got on. Perhaps it was because they came from different ends of the spectrum, the other side of the tracks. But there it was; there was this gulf. Farrel's heart fell. *Not much chance of any help here.*

"Ah, Chief Inspector," the Assistant Chief Constable said in his inimitable superior, university-type voice, "what brings you here?"

Farrel did his level best to stand to attention in accordance with difference in their ranks, but not out of respect for the man.

He cleared his throat. "Good morning, sir," he said as politely as he could.

The Assistant Chief Constable, however, was long acquainted with Farell, and both men knew the situation was going to be rather frosty. Very formally, Farrel outlined the present lines of enquiry and his ideas for furthering them.

ACC Copley appeared reasonably interested, but it was he, Farrel, who wanted the help, and he would have to work hard to convince his senior officer to agree to the extra expenses involved. Cameras for the officers to gather evidence was not a problem, but using the vacant units on the estate, now that was different. That could be costly.

"I'm not sure we can go to that," the ACC pondered. "I'll have to look into it. I can see your point, but . . ."

"It seemed like a good idea to me," Farrel now saw an opportunity open up. "We have a young DC in the squad, a bit of a whizz on computers, who brought it up in the briefing . . ." He paused for effect and it worked; the Assistant Chief Constable was all ears, and then Farrel, as if the realisation had just struck him as he looked searchingly at the other man added, "A relation, I believe, sir?" he asked, "I had heard . . ."

"Yes, Chief Inspector. He's my nephew."

"Ah . . ." Farrel said.

"His idea, you say?"

Farrel nodded.

"Hmm . . . leave it with me; I'm sure we can sort something out. Go and get yourself a coffee, and I'll have my secretary call you."

"Thank you, sir," Farrell said and turned towards the office door. He was about to turn the shiny brass knob when ACC Copley called.

"How's the young man doing, Chief Inspector?"

Got you, Farrel thought gleefully. He had played his cards well.

"He's doing very well, sir," he said turning back to the Assistant Chief Constable. "He's very keen, still a bit green as you would expect, but he's a quick learner. I think he'll go far . . . and soon, if you ask me." *That's just what you wanted to hear isn't it*, he thought as he turned back to the door, opened it and left as the ACC picked up his phone. It appeared that DC Copley was likely to be more use to the squad than anyone had first thought.

Thirty minutes later Farrel had finished his second coffee when a phone call took him back to Copley's office. This time he was invited to sit on a chair, which he did.

"Everything's fine," Copley said. "Out of respect, I contacted the Chief Constable, told him of DC Copley's idea and he straightaway agreed with me. The more I thought about it, the more the idea made good sense. So now, as they say, Chief Inspector, go for it."

"Yes, sir. Thank you, sir," Farrel said as he stood up and moved towards the door.

"And tell young . . . Copley from me . . . well done," the ACC called to him.

"I certainly will, sir," replied Farrel as he closed the door behind him. He smiled outwardly but chuckled inwardly. *I'm still a conniving old bastard.*

10

Before he left headquarters Farrel called in on the resources people. Everything had been made available to him: a collection of video cameras with a variety of zoom lenses, night-vision glasses, scopes and several dedicated radios, which could be used only by those on observations without the fear of anyone else listening in. Farrel was satisfied with the cooperation he had received from the 'top brass', as he referred to them, usually with a hint of distaste in his voice. The surveillance could now take place without being parked in the vicinity and drawing anyone's attention to them.

At 4.15 p.m. that afternoon, Rowles brought Jill Franks into the office. She was a pretty, dark-haired woman of about twenty, five foot two and of slim build. She was very nervous and Farrel thought that perhaps it had not been such a good idea to send Rowles to fetch her; maybe Perkins would have been a better man. He would at least have brought a little humour into the proceedings and made the girl feel more relaxed.

Farrel took her into one of the interview rooms and George Preston sat the other side of the one-way glass window. The tape machine was not switched on and Farrel and the girl sat easily, side-by-side, each with a cup of tea.

"I just want to ask you a few questions, Jill," Farrel said quietly; he could be kind and reassuring when the need arose. "You're not in any trouble. Let me tell you that before we go any further."

"I don't know why you want to talk to me, Mr Farrel," she said, still slightly nervous and on her guard. After all, Farrel considered, she was the girlfriend of one of the local villains and may feel threatened by being at the police station.

"I don't know anything about anything . . . honest," she added.

"Don't worry about that, Jill," he soothed, "but we are concerned about Tommy: no one seems to have seen him around . . . and . . . well . . . you know . . . stories start. Mind you, we don't want him, but, after the rumours, we would like to know that he's still okay. Has Big Mick sent him somewhere on . . . say . . . an errand . . . or something?"

Jill sat with her hands folded in her lap, and Farrel could see that she was clenching and unclenching her fingers, obviously upset.

"I don't know, Mr Farrel," she said. "I haven't seen or heard from Tommy for four days now and I'm getting really worried. I'm sure he hasn't gone anywhere for Mick, or he would have said."

"Has he said anything about someone else moving into the area?"

"What do you mean?"

"Another group . . . like Big Mick's?"

"I don't think so, but he did say he'd heard some foreigners had moved into the London Road Estate, but he didn't say anything else."

Farrel questioned her about her relationship with Tommy Acton; was it good? Had Tommy been seeing anyone else?

Had he been going out at odd times and not said where he was going? He learned that Jill and Tommy were as close as anyone could be, and there were no problems as far as she was concerned.

"He's been out later than usual sometimes," she said. "I didn't think anything of it, but now I'm very worried. Where do you think he is?"

Farrel took one of his business cards out of his pocket and handed it to her. "Look, Jill, if you need me or any sort of help, get in touch. The phone number is on the card but keep it well out of the way. I wouldn't like Mick Jeanes to find you had my number; he might jump to conclusions, and I'm sure that wouldn't do you, Tommy or me any good now, would it?"

"No, I don't think it would," she said, as she slipped the card into a small inside pocket in her handbag. "I promise I'll let you know when he comes back, but that's all I'll tell you. After all, he's all I've got."

"Okay, Jill," Farrel said as he patted the back of her hand, "thanks for your help." He escorted her from the police station by way of a back door, so as not to make it obvious she had been inside talking to him.

11

The rotas were ready for activating when Farrel considered it best to start. The surveillance equipment was ready and waiting in a cupboard to which Farrel had the only key, and at six thirty that evening, he left the office.

He drove the fifteen minutes it took for him to reach his flat and parked his car in the underground car park. He used the lift and at the front door inserted the key into the lock and tried to turn it, but it refused to budge. Julie had done exactly as he had instructed her that morning and had secured the door from inside. He rang the bell and after a few moments the door opened a little way. Julie peered nervously through the small gap with the security chain still claiming the entrance to the flat.

"Oh, it's you," she said sounding relieved, quickly closing the door. She released the chain and then reopened it. As he stepped inside, she offered her face up to him for a kiss, and he duly obliged. She stepped back and he drew in a quick breath in surprise. This evening Julie was wearing a dark blue dress with large white spots—not the sort of attire that he had seen her wearing just recently. True, it had a slightly plunging V-shaped neckline, which together with its broad white belt enhanced her figure, but it reached just below her knees and gave her the appearance of a beautiful, sophisticated young woman. He stood motionless for a moment, stunned at her appearance and for once lost for words.

"Well," she said, "What do you think?" giving him a twirl and smiling broadly

"You look fantastic and what have you done to your hair?" he said, noticing that she now had it shoulder length rather than in a ponytail.

"Like it?"

He took his time taking in the sight. "Very much." He nodded his approval then he screwed his face up a little. "What's that smell?" he asked, sniffing.

"It's something called polish," she giggled. "The flat's okay, but you really should spend more time cleaning it."

He had to admit the smell was indeed a fresh one, and wherever he looked all the solid surfaces gleamed.

"I thought I should earn my keep, not having anything else to do all day," she said. She then gave him a wicked smile. "Or did I do that last night?"

Farrel grinned rather sheepishly, took off his coat, hung it on the coat stand there in the hall and walked into the living room. On the coffee table, close to his chair, his whisky glass contained a very generous double measure of his favourite spirit. Julie stood beside him as he looked round and down into her eyes. There was no need for him to thank her; the look on his face already showed that clearly.

"I thought you might like a little snifter after work," she said.

Farrel smiled and shook his head.

"You're brilliant," he said, and before he realised it, he had put his arm around her shoulder, pulled her close to him and given her a kiss on the cheek.

"By the way," he said, sniffing the air again, "what's that other smell?"

"Home cooking, or don't you like that?"

"Like that?" he echoed, his mind drifting back years to the time when he used to return home after a day's work to home cooking. But then as that relationship had cooled, his wife had either wanted to eat out or bought in fast food or plated meals to be reheated. "It's been a long time since I had a decent home-cooked meal, and this smells real good."

"Good, it'll be ready in about . . ." she glanced at the clock positioned above the fireplace, "twenty minutes."

As she sashayed into the kitchen, Farrel sat down, picked up his drink and sipped it. *This feels good,* he thought, as he gazed into his glass. What a girl! The trouble was he was about twenty years older than her, but that did not stop the feeling that was undeniably developing inside him. He had felt it the previous night and now seeing her as she was now, it hit him even harder; he wanted to be with her, not as a police officer guarding an important material witness, but as a friend, a lover or perhaps even more. But no, this could not be. There would not be a future for them. The ages and his position; there was so much difference between them. Then a realisation cut through his thoughts.

"Julie," he called, "what's for dinner?"

"Come and see, it's ready now."

He went into the kitchen.

"The starter is smoked mackerel with horseradish sauce, followed by grilled steak with potatoes, peas, and broccoli, with tiramisu for dessert. Is that okay?"

"Fantastic, but where did the food come from? There was none of that in the fridge or larder this morning."

Julie pulled a face. She had not thought too much about explaining this. "I . . . er . . . er . . . sort of . . . um . . . popped out for it this morning," she said, dreading what might come. And come it did.

"You did what!" Farrel exploded in disbelief. "You did what?"

"I was very careful," she said, trying to placate him. "I wore something completely different from normal."

"I don't care about that. You went out alone. You could have been seen by some of those men, and they could have followed you here. *Then* what do you think could have happened?"

"I had to get us some food," she said in an attempt to excuse herself. "Just a minute . . ." She disappeared into her bedroom and reappeared after a few minutes.

Farrel's jaw dropped. She stood before him dressed in a scruffy, dirty, light brown raincoat, a headscarf over her dark brown hair and unpolished and well-worn shoes. To complete her appearance, she wore a pair of heavy, dark horn-rimmed glasses, and, for effect, an unlit half cigarette hung from her pale lips. Farrel stood and stared. That was all he could reasonably do. Then he saw the funny side. At first, he smiled; the smile became a broad grin and culminated in a peal of laughter.

"My God, you look awful," he said, still chuckling.

"Well, do you think anyone would have recognised me?" she asked, taking the cigarette from between her lips.

"No one would have recognised you, at least not from a distance," he said still trying to stifle his laughter. "In fact, *I* wouldn't have known you from a distance, but I'm not so sure close up," he admitted.

Julie's face relaxed, a smile replaced her grimace.

However, close up, she'd never be taken for an old woman. Not in a million years. She's too damned attractive and vivacious.

"But, please, don't you dare go out alone again," he ordered.

"It worked though, didn't it?"

"Yes, but let's not push our luck. Tell me what food to get, and I'll pick it up during the day, and if you get fed up being in here, we'll go out somewhere a fair distance away for a meal on Friday evening, but I really can't promise anything right now."

Julie pouted in disappointment, but then after a brief thought smiled. "It's only Tuesday," she said, "does that mean I'll still be here then?"

"Ah . . . well . . . I haven't had a chance to get a place sorted out for you just yet. I've been too busy."

"Oh, that's okay. I don't mind. I feel safe here with you. I like it, really."

Not half as much as I enjoy your being here.

"I guess dinner's ready now," she said, and disappeared into the bedroom. She reappeared dressed as before and Farrel smiled in appreciation.

"That's better," he said, "now I'll really enjoy the meal."

After the last morsel of dessert had been cleaned from the dish, Julie presented him with her statement of everything she could remember. It was not the most clear and concise statement he had ever read; the grammar and spelling amused him, but he did not show it, and at least it was a start.

"That's good, Julie," he said, "and when you get to thinking a bit more about things, you'll remember even more. We need as much info as we can get. We know very little at the moment, but what you've given us here is an excellent start."

12

Farrel awoke at six thirty the next morning. He thought back to the meal the evening before, the brandy which followed it and the time they had spent curled up together on the sofa before retiring—if retiring could in some way be construed as the correct word. He had slept very well indeed afterwards.

There was a sound from the kitchen. The other side of the bed was empty and Julie was carrying out her housekeeping role again. He showered and then entered the living room. A morning feast was ready and waiting for him: orange juice, cereal, eggs, bacon, sausage, toast and coffee. He could not remember the last time he had enjoyed such luxuries as in the last two days. It was too good to be true and too good to last.

They spent breakfast sharing pleasantries across the table. She looked radiant even though she was only wearing a dressing gown. She had changed so much in just 48 hours and Farrel thoroughly approved of that change.

Breakfast over, he rose, grabbed his jacket off the coat stand in the hall and putting it on, he headed for the door. Before he left Julie gave him the once-over. She straightened his tie, which did not need straightening, ran her hands under the reveres of his jacket and brushed an imaginary piece of cotton off his shoulder.

"You'll do, Mr Detective Chief Inspector," she said as she stroked his cheek with the back of her hand. The only response he could give was to bend lower and kiss her. A kiss that lasted some considerable time longer than was necessary for a man just leaving home and going to work.

"Keep the door locked and on the chain. Don't open it to anyone and don't go out, not even looking like a bag lady."

"I promise but please don't be late home."

"Okay. Is there anything I can get today?"

She thought for a moment. "I'll need some clothes from my place," she remembered. "Could you call in and get some for me?"

She dashed back into the bedroom, brought out her holdall and handed him a set of keys. "I'm sure you'll make the right choices," she said with a wink.

Farrel smiled in return. He felt embarrassed yet thought he had not let on, but he had, of course. "Okay, I'll get them," he promised.

*

Within thirty minutes of arriving at the office, the various items of surveillance equipment had been inspected, and to Farrel's surprise, or maybe relief, Copley had volunteered to set them up when and where required.

*

At four o'clock the next morning, they met on the waste ground opposite the front of the two units and set each piece of equipment up so that any vehicle within the vicinity would be recorded. Having completed this to Farrel's satisfaction, Copley produced one other item: a remote battery-powered video camera with an aerial. Anything it picked up would be sent to the control centre located in the building overlooking the units and recorded for future use. As the camera was so small, it was secured to the trunk of a small tree in order to observe the front doors straight on. All that was needed was a clear view of the doors and an unobstructed line to the receiving aerial in the control centre.

"Nice work, young man," Farrel said approvingly when everything was ready. Copley appeared satisfied too, noting that the guv'nor no longer referred to him as 'son'. They re-entered the control room, as it was now called, and Copley powered up the equipment. They checked and rechecked the systems to ensure that each part was operating as it should and recording everything onto a hard disc. At an appropriate time each day, an officer would remove the disc and take it back to the squad office where it would be viewed by Copley and analysed for vehicle types and numbers, and also people seen arriving or leaving.

*

Back at the office Farrel explained that nothing useful could be done at this stage as there was no hard and fast evidence of a pattern of how the 'villains' worked. He wanted to know as much as possible about who used the units and when. He wanted photographs, clear photographs, of each individual there, and he wanted to know whether they were known to other British police forces. Maybe Interpol or another International law-enforcement agency would be interested. He required details on every car, van or truck that visited, the full description, colour and, of course, registration numbers. He also wanted to find out if the hours they operated were fixed or flexible and on which days they were different.

"I need everything about this lot before we do anything," he instructed at the next briefing. "Copley, here, will be monitoring all the information that comes from the control, and that will be manned, in the first instance, twenty-four seven. I'll lay on some help from the uniform boys so that we can work it in shifts and still keep up with some of the other work we have to do."

Shift work was not entirely popular with any of the officers, but they all considered that at least they would be getting some rest time and share the observation time with colleagues.

Later, Farrel rang Julie to make sure she was doing what he had instructed and had not gone shopping looking like a female tramp.

"Have you been out?" he asked.

"No, you told me to stay in."

"Good girl," he said feeling relieved. She was quite likely to go out knowing that her disguise had worked once, however, anyone standing nearby would soon see through it. He was still worried for her safety.

"I'm not a little girl," she huffed, "but I'll do as you say. By the way, have you picked up my things yet?"

"No, not yet. I haven't had a chance."

"There's not a great deal left there so bring what you think best. What you would like me to wear if we go out for a meal?"

"A meal?" he answered incredulously. "My God, woman, we have no idea what's out there." Immediately he regretted his outburst. "Maybe we can do that soon," he conceded more kindly.

"I'm glad I'm a woman now," she said with a little laugh.

Some woman too ran though his mind.

"Bring what you think, though," she said.

"Okay, but please, Julie, stay in. Don't go out."

"I promise," she agreed, "but please don't be too late."

He rang off, making a mental note to make much more of an effort to find her a safe place to stay, yet he liked having her around. It did not take him long to realise that he was reluctantly becoming emotionally involved. *I'll get a place for her tomorrow . . . or maybe the next day . . . or the next*, he silently promised himself.

On his way home he passed by her flat. He managed to push the key into the mortise lock with some difficulty, yet it finally opened after a few hefty twists. As he entered the hall he had a strange feeling that all was not well. Things lay around in a haphazard way—not at all like Julie, at his place anyway. She was so neat and tidy. He took a quick look through each room. Nothing was broken and nothing appeared to have been taken as there were items of some value on her dressing table. He opened the drawers and scooped up as many pieces of clothing he thought she might need and placed them neatly in a pile on the bed before moving to the wardrobe. He selected three dresses and a coat that he was happy for Julie to wear if they went out together and placed them on the top of the other clothes. He could not possibly pass any opinion on the clothes he had scooped up and stuffed them into the bottom of the bag. They sure as hell looked interesting though.

As he left the flat, he bumped into Julie's neighbour who happened to be in the hallway. She looked at Farrel closely.

"Is everything all right?" she asked with a frown on her face.

"I think so," Farrel replied. "Why do you ask?"

"There was a man here this morning," the woman said. "He seemed to be having difficulty getting in, but he managed somehow. He said he lived there, but I've never seen him before."

Farrel frowned and thought for a moment. "What did he look like?" he asked.

"I think he was foreign, but that's very unusual for this place. He said his girlfriend lives there. Now you come along too. What's going on? Shall I call the police?"

"There's no need for that," Farrel said. "Julie is a friend of mine and has asked me to call in and pick up a few things."

"Oh, you know Julie then?" the woman said. "So I guess it's alright. The other man seemed a bit vague when I asked him who he was looking for."

"What did he look like?" Farrel asked again.

"Definitely European . . . North or maybe East European . . . I suppose he could have been Russian or something like that . . . fair skinned. About your height and size."

"Thank you," Farrel said.

"Oh, and I noticed that he had a nasty scar on his left cheek. I told you that though, didn't I?"

"No, you didn't mention that, but thank you anyway."

Farrel picked up the bag and thanked the woman again. He turned and left by way of the lift muttering obscenities under his breath. Things were really beginning to get serious; a witness, a girl, his girl he finally admitted, appeared to be on the hit list of some damned foreign criminals and he did not even know at this stage why.

13

At the briefing the next morning Farrel announced that now was the right time to 'hit' the two units, and that night was likely to be the optimum moment. He felt sure that there was something incriminating in there: anything, even a bloodstain would do.

"I'm making arrangements to obtain a search warrant today, and it shouldn't take long with all the evidence that we have gathered so far," he explained.

True to his word, by lunchtime he had secured the necessary warrant and called the squad together.

"We go tonight. I'll head up the front with Perkins and Copley, whilst you, George, watch the back with Johnson and Rowles. I want you all back here at eight this evening ready for the 'visit' at nine. Is that clear to everyone?"

They all nodded; a search of a property was something they had done many times before.

"Watch it, Geronimo, the cavalry's coming," Perkins chipped in with his usual light-hearted comments in his inimitable cockney voice. "Who gets to sound the charge?" he asked looking around.

The squad laughed quietly.

"I'll go in first with 'trooper' Perkins here, and as it's Copley first time, he will hang back in case he's needed to stop anyone making a run for it out front and so he can see how we do things around here. We don't want him getting the wrong idea now, do we?"

Again, there were quiet chuckles from everyone. The tension was beginning to build.

"George, you and the other two will only come in from the back if you are needed. I'll keep in touch by radio. I don't want to go in mob-handed and break heads unnecessarily. Our superiors wouldn't like it now, would they?" He shot a sideways glance at Copley and winked at the others.

"No, guv, mustn't upset people, whoever they are," agreed Perkins. Everyone knew that this could be quite a nerve-wracking time and so anything that eased the tension would be quite welcome.

*

At nine that evening, Farrel and the other five parked their cars on the other side of the waste ground from the industrial estate so that their arrival would not be spotted. They moved quietly through the trees and around the bushes to their position.

"Okay, George, off you go with your two. We'll give you ten minutes to get set. That's more than enough time, but I don't want anyone rushing about and announcing our arrival too soon. Perkins, you keep close to me, and, Copley, you stay a little farther back. Be very alert and ready to get back to my car in case we need to give chase, okay?"

"Yes, guv," Copley said. He was obviously very keyed up, even more so than the rest, as this was to be his first 'op'. George

Preston and his group left very quietly and used a circuitous route to get to their positions. Ten minutes elapsed.

"Okay, let's go," Farrel said quietly, and they set off towards the two units. "We'll do number five first. That's the one most likely to have anything going on."

They crossed the road and after trying to look inside number five through a dirty window at the side, they began to approach the door. As if on cue, a white van, the one-ton type, swung round the corner into the street and approached number five. It pulled up in front of the door. The driver sounded a sharp double blast on the horn and it opened immediately.

"Just the job," Farrel said to Perkins, "we'll follow the van in."

The van entered the unit, which was brightly lit. The driver killed the lights and engine, opened the door and climbed out. Farrel and Perkins followed closely. There were three men inside the unit waiting for the van: one, Farrel saw, was Scarface, as he now referred to him, and there were two others. The van driver and the other three men turned to face Farrel and Perkins. *They don't appear to be too surprised*, Farrel thought. *How is that? We've only had the search warrant a few hours.* The thought bothered him but he carried on. He must carry on now, no backing down.

"Good evening, gentlemen," he said politely and very officially, but perhaps with a slight sound of annoyance in his voice. "I am Detective Chief Inspector Farrel of the local Criminal Investigation Department and I have a warrant to search these premises. My colleague is Detective Constable Perkins."

"What you mean?" Scarface said in the same foreign accent that Farrel remembered from their previous encounter. Perhaps the other man had not recognised him after all. "Why you come here? We are not criminals. We are foreigners but we are not criminals. Are you racists or something?"

"Not at all," Farrel said politely but somewhat on the defensive. "But we have to check all buildings from time to time to make absolutely sure that everything is in order," and he waved the search warrant towards Scarface. "Now, if you don't mind, we'll have a look around."

"Okay, but don't you damage nothing," Scarface muttered.

The other three stayed in the background and remained silent while Farrel and Perkins carried out a search of the unit.

"Now, next door, please," Farell said.

"Why you want to go there?"

"Because . . ." Farrel stated irritably, and waved the search warrant again. Scarface said something in what Farrel thought to be a foreign language, as he certainly did not understand it but imagined, by the sound of it, to be something obscene. They entered Unit 6 and carried out another search.

Farrel turned to Perkins. "The bastards knew we were coming," he said quietly. Perkins nodded his agreement. "Make it look like a casual look-around but take in as much as you can," he continued.

Neither unit yielded anything illegal and nor did the van, so the two police officers left the premises.

"I hope you are satisfied, Mr Policeman," Scarface said as they left, in a voice which Farrel thought very sarcastic.

"For the moment, *sir*," he replied. "But it may be necessary to visit again later, although I'm sure you wouldn't be doing anything illegal in my country. Good night." With that, he turned on his heel and, followed by Perkins, left the building. The door closed behind them.

Farrel was furious.

"You were right, guv," Perkins said. "They knew we were coming . . . but how?"

"I don't know but I'm bloody well going to find out. Don't mention anything to anyone else at all. I have a strange feeling about this and I don't want anyone to know what happened here, okay?"

"Sure, guv, my lips are sealed."

Farrel knew he could trust Perkins, but now he had a nasty feeling inside that perhaps not everyone was so trustworthy.

14

Back in the squad room, Farrel reported, officially, of course, that they had found nothing out of the ordinary in numbers five or six and that for the moment surveillance was being curtailed. The squad were a little surprised as it appeared that he was giving in too easily. However, as he gave them the news he searched their faces for some kind of reaction, but no one's registered anything except mild surprise. They knew Farrel did things his way.

The meeting broke up and as it did so Farrel called to Copley quietly so that those departing could not hear.

"Copley, you and I need to get together to talk about sorting out the electronic surveillance stuff again."

"Yes, guv."

Farell caught Perkins' eye and indicated for him to hang back too when the rest of the squad left. "It's about time we went and had a little drink," he said. "What about the Royal Oak on the Barnchester road?"

"That sounds like a very good idea," Perkins agreed with a smile.

"You want me along too, guv?" Copley queried with a look of surprise on his face.

"Of course. We have to talk about a lot of things right now. You can drive, Alan," he said turning to Perkins, "okay?"

"Sure thing, guv," Perkins replied. "When?"

"Now . . . let's go."

They quietly left the office and made their way to where Perkins always parked his car and left without anyone spotting them all together.

*

The Royal Oak was very quiet when they arrived. Even so, they sat at a table as far from the bar and possible distractions as they could.

"Right," Farrel instructed, as they made themselves comfortable with their beers. "What I'm about to say is for your ears only, and if anything gets out and I find it came from either of you two, I'll have your guts and a few other things for garters."

"*That* important is it, guv?" Perkins said. "I guess we already started to discuss it earlier, yes?"

Farrel nodded and Copley looked lost. "I can't say anything," Copley said, "as I don't have a clue what you two are talking about, but I imagine you are about to enlighten me in the next few minutes."

"Right," Farrel said again. "This evening's do was not a cock-up as the rest of the squad believe it was from what I said at the debriefing. I still have to make a lot more enquiries before I say any more, but I know I can trust you two. Alan, here, because I've known him for years, and you, Richard, because you are so new to the job and so very keen to get on that blotting your copy book right now will do you a lot of harm."

"Right, guv," Copley replied, still in a state of puzzlement. He was rather surprised that Farrel had used his first name, and rather gratified too.

"The surveillance equipment stays where it is and we monitor it between us," Farrel stated. If everyone thinks that it's all switched off, perhaps they'll let their guard down."

"You're still not telling us everything," Copley said rather nervously, not wanting to upset Farrel.

"No, and I'm not going to at this moment. Someone might think that I don't trust some of my colleagues."

Perkins grimaced and Copley raised his eyebrows, but neither said anything.

15

Life carried on much as normal for the squad, but Farrel, Perkins and Copley were seen less as they continued to monitor the two suspect units on the industrial estate. They met at varying times during the day and then usually in The Royal Oak in the evenings where they compared notes.

Farrel was impressed with Copley's application to the situation and after the third week, he, Perkins and Copley met at eight o'clock one evening in the squad office when everyone else had left for the day.

Copley had collated several pieces of observation over the last three weeks and was eager to show the other two what he had picked up. He played the video showing the times that a white van had arrived at the units.

"What do you see?" he asked them.

"A white van," the other two agreed.

"Only *a* white van?" Copley pressed, stressing the 'a', and he ran the video through again, this time more slowly and using a zoom so that the rear registration number could be read easily.

"Just a minute," Farrel stopped him, "play that through again."

Copley did so. They saw different registration numbers.

"They're different vans," Perkins pointed out. He, like Farrel, was puzzled. "So what does this show? We have a whole number of villains using this place?"

"I thought that at first," Copley said, "but look a little more closely," and he zoomed in a little more. "Look closely at the rear offside of the first van."

They looked intently and agreed there was some damage, perhaps caused by a slight accident or a careless piece of reversing.

"Now, look at the second van," Copley said eagerly.

That van had damage in the same place they noticed. They paused. Farrel looked at Perkins who looked back at Farrel; both with puzzled looks on their faces.

"Now, look at the third van." Copley was warming to the reporting of his findings. Same damage, same place, they agreed.

"And the fourth, and the fifth and the sixth," he said, running through the video with more speed, "and you'll find there are other points of 'similarity' as well," he continued. "Look carefully at the sides of the vans. Can you see when the lighting is right, there's a name that's been over-painted"?

They looked once more as Copley zoomed the video more closely onto the side of the van.

"J. Laxton, Fruiterer," Perkins made out and let out a long breath. "Well, bugger me!"

"Not right now, Alan, this is getting more and more interesting by the minute," Farrel said.

Copley suppressed a grin. He had never realised before that even with the difference in rank, both these men were true colleagues, who possessed not only the desire to catch criminals but a healthy camaraderie.

"Who's this J. Laxton fellow?" Farrel wanted to know. "Do we know yet?"

"He committed suicide three years ago in Bristol after he went bankrupt," Copley enlightened them.

"So what is the real registered number of the van?" Farrel asked.

Copley relayed the original number.

"What about the other numbers?"

"False. They in fact belong to several vans, some of which were written off in accidents, or were stolen and have not been recovered."

"You've been a busy boy," Farrel said to Copley appreciatively.

"Just found it interesting at first, and then as it went on, it became fascinating."

"So, who owns the van right now, as it's obvious that there's only one van with several aliases?"

"It's supposed to be owned by an import-export company calling itself East-West Logistics," Copley replied.

"Okay," Farrel said knowing full well that Copley had a great deal more to tell, "and where's this East-West Logistics located?"

"Its head office is in London, in a street in the East End at the office of a 'Joseph Kos and Sons, Solicitors'."

"I might have known that would be the case. It's quite normal to have a registered office of convenience and it's often a nondescript solicitor, at a nondescript address," Farrel observed, "but do we have an actual address from which the firm operates?"

"That's a bit difficult to say. I've looked on the Internet and as far as I can find out it deals mainly with the Continent, using Dover and Calais as ferry ports."

Farrel said nothing for a few minutes. He looked first at Copley and then Perkins and then back at Copley again.

Copley, too, said nothing at first, but then, "I contacted Europol to see if they had any knowledge of this company."

"And . . ." Farrel was intrigued by the young man's tenacity.

"They say that they too have had suspicions about them, but, like us, they haven't been able to get anything of any substance on them, though they think that it is only a matter of time. I had the impression from Inspector de Large—that's the officer I spoke to in France—that they might have someone inside the organisation, but he wouldn't be drawn on that. He said that since this mob had come to their attention, the police have lost two men. Of course, nothing was certain, because there was no sign of the men for some weeks, and the police there have no idea whether they are either alive or dead. I told him that we were very interested in this company, and he told me he would be in touch if, and when, he discovered anything else. I think he seemed happier to know that there was someone else on the case."

"You've done well, Richard," Farrel said. "When did you find all this out?"

"At odd times over the last few days, either when I wasn't working or when I couldn't sleep."

"Seems to me you don't get a lot of sleep," Perkins said. Farrel muttered his agreement.

"I think we need to think more about this," Farrel said checking his watch. "Let's go and have a drink. I owe you both one, and you, Richard, more than one."

Copley grinned. He felt he'd been accepted at last.

*

The surveillance carried on for the next few days. The three officers continued to watch in person when they could afford the time, or they would analyse the video recordings that had been made during their absences. From these observations it was clear that something was happening at the two units, but everything was taking place inside and behind closed doors.

They had noticed that there was always more activity on Friday evenings. Copley thought that was when the cross-Channel ferry docked on the morning tide. They studied this theory more closely and found that the idea was sound.

"When's the next time the ferry arrives on a Friday morning tide?" Farrel asked.

"This week," Copley informed him. "I checked the times for the next couple of weeks in case you thought there was any mileage in the idea."

"Well done. That's good info," Farrel said, and Perkins smiled and nodded his agreement.

"We'll not say anything until Friday morning at the briefing," Farrel said, still with the thought in mind that somehow the gang knew what the police were doing, "but then we'll pull everyone off what they are working on at the time and go in that night. I won't have any difficulty in getting another search warrant."

16

J ulie was still at his flat when he arrived that evening. He had telephoned earlier leaving a message on the answering machine to let her know what time he would arrive home. He used an agreed pattern of knocks upon arrival so that she would know it was really him. She opened the door and he immediately noted the relief on her face, and also that quite recently she had been crying. He quickly closed the door and she threw her arms around him. She was trembling.

"Hey, hey," he murmured softly, stroking her hair, "what's the matter?"

"I'm scared," she said, the tone of her voice clearly showing it.

"Why, what's happened?"

"I know you'll say it's my imagination, but I feel something weird is happening . . ."

"What's happened?" he persisted.

"Well, the phone's been ringing, several times, in fact, but you told me not to answer it, so I didn't . . ."

"Good . . . and . . . ?"

"I'm sure someone's been outside all day watching the flat. I can't be absolutely certain, but it's very strange and scary."

Farrel nodded and embraced her, patting her back to reassure her. "It's okay," he said. "You did the right thing. Did you go near the window?"

"No, I kept well back in the shadow and to the side, but I'm sure there was somebody out there."

Farrel was worried, but he knew that he could not let Julie know how much; she was scared enough already. She was in danger. Even though she hadn't actually seen a crime being committed, her information went a long way to providing a good deal of circumstantial evidence. He had to find her a safer place to stay.

"I've got us some dinner," she said breaking across his thoughts. "What are you thinking about? You seem deep in thought."

"Just something that happened earlier today," he replied, not letting on that perhaps it was related to what had scared Julie.

"I'm glad you're here now," she said, her voice sounding much more relaxed.

He smiled. "I'm glad I'm here too," he said. "It's the only place I get a really good meal."

She smiled. "Is that all you get here that you like?" she teased him.

"Now, now," he chided, "at my age I have to try to limit the amount of excitement I engage in."

"I hadn't noticed anything of the sort," she said, as if completely disbelieving him.

He knew he was in deep, maybe over his head, but his years of imposed celibacy since his divorce had left a gap that was now being filled in the most pleasant way by this young woman. He knew that in the long term it was not going to work out. The problem was that she needed him for protection and care, and he needed her to help make up for all the years of missed tender loving. Was he in love with her? Probably, yes, very much at this particular moment. Her past did not bother him now, but the age difference did.

They ate the meal and washed up together. Julie, as always, stood very close to him, and when they spoke to each other, they spoke in low tones, which seemed much more intimate. They could feel each other's warmth.

"That was another lovely meal," he said.

"Glad you liked it," she replied. "I like cooking and doing things for you."

Farrel looked around. *Doing things for me*, he thought. *This place is a palace compared to what it was, and bedtime is really something else, but, shit, it has to finish.*

"A penny for them." Her voice once more cut across his thoughts.

He dragged himself out from under them and realised they had suddenly thrust him towards depression at the thought of her going away. "Just thinking about this crap job I have," he lied.

She looked at him puzzled.

"Not this part of it," he said. "The day job." He put his arms around her, drew her close and kissed her long and tenderly. She relaxed against him.

"What's troubling you?" she asked, concerned.

"It's just the job."

They kissed again.

"I'm beginning to hate it. Never thought I'd ever say that, but now I'm not so sure."

"Let's relax and watch a bit of TV," she suggested.

Farrel sat on the sofa and turned on the television. It did not matter what was on, he was far too preoccupied with the case and Julie's safety, but mainly just Julie.

A few minutes later, she appeared from the bedroom and curled up on the sofa close to him. Tonight she had discarded her dressing gown and wore a nightdress that Farrel thought would fall apart if he held her too tightly—it was that delicate. He drew in his breath audibly between his teeth, and she grinned, accepting it as a compliment. He could think of nothing to say.

"I don't like to see you troubled," she said softly, "so I've decided to be your therapist tonight."

His throat and chest tightened. He had to tell her that this would all have to end and that would mean a great many tears, but this was neither the time nor the place. He just didn't have the balls to say something he knew he didn't want to say and that she definitely did not want to hear. It would have a devastating effect upon them both, so he just said, "What's the best treatment then?"

She laid her head on his shoulder and gently kissed his neck below his ear. His pulse rate quickened as it always did and he shuddered, only slightly, but it was the pleasurable feeling it gave him.

"I think we should discuss it in bed," she said, standing up and taking him by the hand. At the same time, she switched off the television. They walked from the lounge and into the hallway. The nightdress slipped lower and lower, until, at the bedroom door, it fell into a soft heap onto the floor.

"Oops," she said, turning to him with a cheeky smile and holding out an inviting hand again to him.

"Is this part of the therapy?" he asked, looking into her eyes.

"A very small part," she said as she opened the bedroom door.

Tonight was not the time to talk about anything to do with the future.

17

The next day, Farrel, Perkins and Copley spent their time planning their next 'visit', as they put it, to Units 5 and 6 on the industrial estate. It was not a difficult thing to do. They would merely replicate the first one.

Farrel lunched alone. It was more of a snack and a pint, but he used the time to get his thoughts into order. First he rang Julie. They had arranged that he would speak into the answering machine, and when Julie was sure it was definitely him, she would answer.

"Are you okay?" he asked.

"Yes, thank you."

"Had a good morning?"

"Yes."

"Does anyone seem to be hanging around today?"

"No, I don't think so."

He ended the call. The voice on the other end was soft and inviting, especially when she said, "I'm missing you. Please don't be late."

Farrel sat quietly for a long time, gazing into his half-drunk pint. Finally, he made a decision. It had to finish. It would be best for them both. The relationship was perfect at this moment, but the age difference was too great. The thing that had finally made him decide was the probability that after everything, Julie would have to move away for her own safety to another town, or even country, and have to assume a completely new identity. The type of criminals he was dealing with at present always seemed to have long arms and particularly long memories, and, therefore, she would have to 'disappear'. Better get it done soon he decided. He already knew his next move. Picking up his mobile phone, he punched in a number. Moments later it was answered.

"Liz?" he said.

"Hello, handsome," came back the cheerful reply. "What can I do for you?"

"I need to see you, Liz."

"Sounds important," she said, her voice serious. "Business rather than pleasure then."

"Afraid so," he said, although seeing Elizabeth had become a pleasure, and right now he needed a friend he could trust. "When can I call round?"

"Give me ten minutes to make myself half decent," she said. "Is that soon enough?"

"Perfect. Thanks, Liz," he answered. "You're a diamond. I'll be there in thirty minutes then."

"Don't be late," she said.

He ended the call.

*

It was three o'clock in the afternoon when he arrived at Elizabeth's place. She had obviously checked through the security viewer. It was something she had become accustomed to ever since her tenuous contact with the local underworld had ended.

She opened the door wide, *nearly as wide as her smile*, Farrel thought. She looked terrific. He considered that perhaps she was more intuitive than he gave her credit for and was already preparing for competition against another woman, but then he put that out of his mind as a completely unworthy thought. She did not need to compete: she was gorgeous and her expensive clothes and make-up showed off her looks beautifully. Under normal circumstances and all things being equal, he would be well down the queue for her attention, but he had found that in his business things were never normal or equal.

The only thing that he thought might swing it his way was that she was around his own age and the fact that they had been very close all those years ago. Confusion was beginning to increase with regard to his love life.

"Have you got new glasses?" was all he could stupidly think to say, so taken by her appearance.

"Is that all you're looking at?" she asked laughing.

"You look fantastic," he said at last, as he bent to kiss her cheek, but she put her arms around his neck and pulled him down towards her.

"Say hello properly," she said, and kissed him firmly on the mouth, her tongue seeking his, and then a little breathlessly, "Coffee's on, would you like some?"

"Please," he too replied a little breathlessly.

She poured the coffee and they sat at the table in her modern, well-appointed kitchen.

"So what's the problem?" she asked after taking a few sips.

"Don't really know where to start," he said, his voice sounded doubtful.

"Pick a spot, any spot," she suggested.

"It's all part of the case I'm on."

"Something to do with Tommy Acton?" she guessed.

"Don't know for sure, but it's likely," he said.

She nodded. "I thought as much. Jill Franks is worried sick."

"I think there may be more to it than just that," Farrel said. "You see, I have a witness. Just one, but one who may well hold the key to prising open a whole can of worms."

"What's your worry then?"

"The witness is in danger, great danger in my opinion. Could be a matter of life and death."

"And you're worried."

"Too right I'm worried. I may already have a murder on my hands and I sure as hell don't want another."

"Do you have the witness in protective custody or care?"

"Sort of."

"What do you mean 'sort of'?"

"Unofficial care," he said.

Elizabeth nodded and thought for a few moments. Then she got up and disappeared into the lounge, returning a few minutes later with two large double whiskies. She put one on the table in front of Farrel then sat and cradled the other in her hands.

"Okay, handsome," she said, "let's hear all of it. Tell it like it really is. I don't want you getting ulcers worrying about it."

"The witness is a young woman," he said simply.

"Ah," she said, sounding as if she knew what was coming. "I did hear that Julie Jackson hasn't been seen around just lately. Story was she'd run off with some Russian bloke," she continued, raising a querying eyebrow, "but she hasn't, has she Ian?"

He shook his head.

"She's your witness. Right?"

"Right," he confirmed. "You should be in the force. I thought I'd kept it under wraps pretty well, but I seem to have been under a misapprehension."

"It's elementary, my dear Farrel," she said. "It's a woman's intuition—a concerned woman's intuition. I think you and I are closer than you really think."

She looked straight into his eyes and he returned the look. Her eyes were tender and said much that he had not even considered until perhaps now. He could not tear his eyes away from hers. He did not want to. They were beautiful eyes but they were also searching eyes. *The eyes are the windows of the soul*, he thought, and now he felt his soul was being laid bare.

"Okay, big, hard copper Farrel, it's you who's taken her in and at the same time put your life and job on the line, yes?"

"Yes," he admitted quietly, and then explained that finding a safe place for her had proved difficult under the circumstances.

She nodded her understanding. "You always were an old softie, a real gentleman," she said, "and not having a woman around for such a long time told on you."

Again, he just nodded.

"I wish you'd come around here more often since Harry died," she went on.

Farrel wished he had too.

"So, now," she said, "you have an attractive, vulnerable young woman who you feel responsible for and who you've become attached to, and I mean attached to."

Farrel did not reply. He merely sipped his whisky and felt guilty.

"How can I help then?" she asked.

Another sip of whisky and then Farrel related how Julie had moved into his flat and the gang appeared to have located her flat.

"I think it's only a matter of time before they trace her to my place. I'm worried, and she's scared," he said.

"Where do I come in?" she asked.

"I wondered if you could put her up for a few days, until, that is, I can get her tucked away safely somewhere," he suggested hesitantly.

"You're a typical man, aren't you?" she said sarcastically.

"What do you mean?"

"Well, you want to put two women together who, by the sounds of it, seriously fancy you and expect them to be buddy buddies."

"Well . . . I . . ." he started.

"Don't worry," she said, "bring her here as soon as you like. I may scratch her eyes out later, but I guess I'll look after her just because it's you who asked."

"Thanks, Liz," he said, relieved. "I was hoping you would." He kissed her.

"I'll do my best," she said. "And you can rest assured that no one will know from me where she is."

"I know," he said. "I know you're loyal."

"It'll cost you though," she stated. "When all this is over and Julie has moved on, it'll cost you plenty."

"It'll be my pleasure to recompense you accordingly, ma'am," he said in mock formality.

"My pleasure too, if I get my way."

They both laughed and it seemed to release the tension a little.

"Do you have to leave just now?" she asked disappointedly as Farrel rose.

"Yes, dammit," he replied with a real note of regret in his voice. "It's a big day tomorrow. I'll tell you all about it later."

"Don't make it too big a night then," she ordered, as she kissed him fondly goodbye at the door. She seemed to anticipate what sort of last night together this could be for Farrel and Julie.

18

The next morning when Farrel left his flat for work, any onlooker would be forgiven for thinking that some old woman, possibly his mother, had left in the car with him. Julie had made an excellent job with her make-up and awful choice of clothes, and Farrel was happy that no one was likely to recognise her.

The previous evening had been traumatic for them both, but particularly for Julie when she realised that Farrel was explaining how important it was she should go to a more secure place.

"I want to stay here with you. I feel safe here," she wept, but as he explained it, she had eventually come to understand that it was a move for the best. Neither had slept much; Farrel, because of his worries about Julie's safety, and Julie because she had to go and leave the only man who had treated her as, she imagined, good men treated good women.

The last few days, she confided to Farrel, had been the best in her life and she did not want to leave them behind. Farrel, for his part, knew it had to end, and as they had talked well into the night, Julie realised too they could not continue this passionate relationship for much longer. She would have to go away and leave him. She had cried a lot, and they had made love a lot as if this would seal their special tie.

*

As they travelled to Elizabeth's flat, Farrel explained that it was far more secure than his place could ever be and she became more relaxed about it.

When they parked the car outside the apartment block, Julie rested her hand on his. "I will be seeing you, wont I?" she asked anxiously.

"Of course," he replied. "You're my star witness and a very important person, and I have to look after you." He looked at her sternly. "And you're special too."

"What's this Elizabeth like?" she asked. "Is she attractive?"

"Liz is a very nice person. She'll look after you. You'll be safe there . . . and yes, she is attractive."

Elizabeth opened the door to them when Farrel rang the bell. The welcome was warm.

"Hello, handsome," her usual greeting to him and she gave him a kiss on the cheek. She looked as lovely as ever, Farrel considered. She then looked past him to Julie and held out a welcoming hand, as she looked her up and down.

"She doesn't always look like this, Liz," Farrel explained hurriedly.

"That's obvious," Elizabeth said, "but close up she'd never pass as an old woman—never in a million years. Come in, coffee's on, as usual." She closed the door and locked it, which made Julie feel a lot more at ease. "So, this is the opposition," Elizabeth stated.

Julie looked embarrassed and glanced nervously at Farrel for assurance.

"Don't worry about Liz, we've been friends for a long time," he said gently.

"I'm only doing this because Ian asked me," Elizabeth explained to Julie. "He can be very persuasive sometimes, you know." She gave a 'you-know-what-I-mean' type of grin. Now it was Farrel's turn to look embarrassed.

Elizabeth showed Julie around the flat, at the same time telling her to call her Liz, and after a leisurely cup of coffee, Farrel took his leave.

"Got a busy day today," he explained. Both women came to the door when he left. Elizabeth kissed him gently on the lips.

"Take care, handsome," she said. "I'll look after Julie."

"Thanks, Liz," he said.

Not to be outdone, Julie too kissed him warmly on the mouth as she said 'goodbye'.

"We'll be okay," Elizabeth, said. "I'm sure us two girls will have plenty to talk about," and she gave him an outrageous wink that Julie did not see. Farrel grinned self-consciously as Liz closed the door. He heard the lock engage.

"Now for those bloody Slavs," he muttered out loud.

19

The briefing did not take up much time and Farrel made no mention of the ongoing electronic surveillance. Neither did he let anyone know that the authorities on the other side of the Channel had been keeping Copley informed of events on their side. Something was definitely on for today. All everyone knew was that the police raid would take the same format as the previous one. It had worked well and there was no reason to think this time should be any different. In addition, until now, no one had been told that the raid would take place today.

The day passed off quietly, and Farrel, like most of his colleagues, ploughed into his backlog of work. Elizabeth had phoned to say that all was going well. Then it was time to go.

*

By nine o'clock in the evening, everyone was in position; all they had to do now was wait.

Farrel knew that the van had to have something of interest on board; drugs or people, it did not matter—it was some sort of contraband.

At nine thirty, the same white van pulled up in front of the closed doors of Unit 5 and sounded the short blast on its horn. The doors opened, the van drove in immediately and the doors closed behind it. Farrel and Perkins, as before, went in, this time, by way of the side door. The other members of the squad, Farell knew, were covering the backs of the buildings in case anyone tried to escape. Copley acted as back up at the front.

On a silent count of three, they burst through the door and found two men, one of whom was 'Scarface', waiting inside, in addition to the two who had arrived moments before in the van. They were about to sit at a small table towards the rear of the unit where four mugs of coffee had been poured. The rear doors of the van stood open and it was evident that it was empty. There had been insufficient time for anything to be off-loaded.

The men turned towards the officers, and to Farrel's mind, they did not seem surprised to see them.

"Oh shit," Farrel heard Perkins mutter quietly, "they've done it again."

"What do you want *now?*" Scarface demanded angrily.

Farrel, although taken aback by what had confronted him as he came through the door, covered it well.

"Just another visit to make sure everything is okay, sir," he said, but his voice was terse.

"You think we are robbers or something?" Scarface demanded.

Farrel shrugged and spread his hands out in front of him. "Well, now," he replied, "why should we think that? Anyway," he continued, holding up the search warrant, "now we are here, perhaps we should check around to make sure that no one has tried to rob *you,* and that your security is up to scratch, so to speak."

As he spoke, he began to wander around, ostensibly in an off-handed manner yet missing nothing. Everything was noted:

windows, doors, equipment and, of course, the inside of the van.

"Everything seems to be in order, sir," Perkins reported.

"You are sure you don't want to arrest us all?" Scarface asked sarcastically. "I see my lawyer," he added. "Just because we are foreign; you think you can . . . what you say . . . 'harass' us? My lawyer will complain to your boss."

"That's your right, Mr . . . terribly sorry, I don't wish to be rude, but I don't know your name and if you're going to make a complaint, I would like to know who's complaining about me." Then his tone changed. "What *is* your name, sir?"

"Minski," Scarface replied, "Ivan Minski. And what is your name?"

Ivan not Igor, Farrel thought. *Not far off.*

"I told you before, sir. Detective Chief Inspector Ian Farrel."

Scarface wrote something down.

During all this time, Perkins had been going quietly from one man to another, making notes of everything he could think of: names, passport details, driver's licence, notes on each man's appearance, details of the van.

Damn good copper, Farrel thought, *he doesn't miss a trick.*

Farrel continued to hold Scarface in conversation until Perkins had completed his work and, when there was nothing more to do, he took his leave with as much politeness and grace as he could muster. Perkins knew he was seething.

Outside, Copley could see by the looks on their faces that not all had gone to plan and so he waited to hear the bad news.

"The bastards knew we were coming again," Farrel spat out. He was livid.

"How could they?" Copley asked.

"God knows," said Farrel, "but they did. At this very moment that place seems squeaky clean, but we know otherwise, don't we?"

"I thought I saw something down the side of a bench just behind the door we went through," Perkins said, "but I couldn't be sure about anything."

"Interesting," Farrel said. "I noticed something too, a stain of some sort, but I thought it could be oil or something similar."

"Blood can be pretty thick too, guv," Perkins noted. "And after what you said about strange loud noises, perhaps we should test a sample—it could be helpful."

Farrel thought for a few moments. "If we go back now, they'll put two and two together and realise that we have serious suspicions about them," he said. "Later perhaps, but I don't want to spook them into anything." Julie's face came to mind as he said it.

By phone, he called the rest of the squad off the surveillance, but he, Perkins and Copley stayed behind together.

"Let's think about it over a pint," he suggested.

*

An hour later, they left The Royal Oak having decided that they needed a sample of whatever had stained the side of the bench. But what was the best way to go about it?

As they stood under a lamp in the car park, Perkins moved his feet and a chinking sound of metal came from the tarmac. They all looked down.

"Oh goodness me," Perkins said in a voice filled with mock surprise and a wide-eyed look of innocence on his face, "look at this." He bent down and picked up what appeared to be a set of keys. "Someone's dropped these," he said. "I wonder who they belong to." He looked more closely at them, turning them this way and that. "They look strange," he continued. "Almost like a skeleton set or bunch of master keys."

There was silence.

"I told you to dispose of those months ago," Farrel said, his voice was quiet and sounded disapproving, not wanting the Assistant Chief Constable's nephew to think that he was complicit in such behaviour.

"Did you, guv," Perkins said. "Oh yes. I must have forgotten. I kept meaning to."

"Anyway," Farrel said, as if deep in thought, "I wonder if they would fit certain locks that we may possibly be interested in?"

Copley said nothing, but in the lamplight a smile flickered across his face.

"Do you mean . . . ?" Perkins said, leaving the question hanging in the air for Copley to think about.

However, Copley was not slow and the smile reappeared.

"Maybe . . ." Farrel replied, "but we'd have to be very careful. What if they've left a guard or watchman in there?"

"That wouldn't be a problem," Copley chipped in. They turned and looked at him with interest.

"It'll be easy to check." He delved into his pocket and pulled out what looked like a mobile phone.

"What good is a mobile phone? Are you thinking of ringing them to tell them we're coming?" Perkins asked.

"It's a camera," Copley said simply.

"And we don't want to take snaps either," Farrel said sharply.

With that, Copley turned up his jacket collar and from beneath it pulled out a length of cable. He plugged one end into a socket at the base of the camera and switched it on. The screen lit up and the three watched together as Copley pointed the other end of the cable in different directions. The pictures on the screen changed as the end of the cable changed its orientation. Farrel and Perkins were intrigued.

"It's made of optic fibre so it can become a lens for the camera," Copley explained. "If you want to, you can see round corners or even see behind you," and he demonstrated. "You can also push it under doors and even through keyholes if need be."

"You haven't been . . . ?" Perkins asked in sham shock and incredulity.

"No, no," Copley assured him with a laugh. "Might be interesting though, mightn't it?"

"You devious little bugger," Farrel said, but with tone of something approaching approval in his voice. "I hope your uncle doesn't find out about your little tricks."

Copley laughed apparently enjoying his apparent newfound notoriety. "Don't worry, he already knows I'm keen on electronic gadgets and he shows quite a lot of interest in it himself, particularly where it could help our work," he said.

"Really?" the other two chorused in surprise.

Copley nodded. "Really," he confirmed.

"I'm not sure I can countenance what I think you two might be cooking up," Farrel said unconvincingly. "Sounds like it could be affecting an illegal entry to me."

"No, no, not at all, guv," Perkins said, as convincingly as he could.

Copley shook his head in his agreement with Perkins. A look of innocence appeared on both faces.

"I'm not sure I . . ." Farrel started, but left the rest of the sentence unspoken.

They decided that there was nothing more they could do that night and so they would meet to make further plans the following day.

"You live closest to here, guv," said Perkins. "Why don't we drop you off on our way back to the office?"

Farrel knew by the tone of his voice that that was not entirely, what Perkins had in mind but he agreed.

At eleven o'clock that evening, he entered his empty flat. He was missing Julie already.

20

Farrel was at his desk by eight the next morning before anyone else arrived. There had been nothing to delay his leaving home after a fitful night's sleep. He sat down and stared at the backlog of work on his desk when he suddenly noticed a large, well packed out brown envelope.

With an almost guilty feeling, he glanced around furtively, as if touching it was something prohibited. Carefully he opened it. It contained a dozen photographs, which he immediately recognised as having been taken inside Unit 5, and a clear, sealed plastic bag containing a few small slivers of wood stained with the same colour that he and Perkins had seen on the end panel of the bench there. A note was enclosed. 'Could not sleep', it said, 'so did a bit more looking around. Have dropped off more samples for forensics to examine'.

Farrel grinned. "Good lads," he said softly. "Now perhaps we can start to make some progress."

*

At eleven that morning, just as Farrel was about to leave his desk for the canteen, his telephone rang.

"The Assistant Chief Constable would like to see you in his office straightaway, Chief Inspector," the Assistant Chief Constable's secretary announced at the other end.

Farrel sighed. *Now what's the problem?* "Certainly, right away," he mumbled, and hung up.

Five minutes later, he stood in front of the ACC's large dark oak desk with the man himself seated somewhat grandly behind it.

"I've had a complaint," ACC Copley announced.

Farrel frowned. "Really, sir?" he said in something approaching mock surprise. "Thank heavens for that. Now I'm sure I'm doing my job properly."

"Don't be flippant, Chief Inspector." Copley was far from pleased.

"Sorry, sir."

"I've received a complaint from a solicitor in Bristol alleging that you are harassing a client of his. He accuses the police in general and you, in particular, of being racist. So . . . ?" He left the question hanging, expecting a response.

Farrel was not surprised. He was usually in control in this type of situation and this was no different. A look of mock horror and hurt appeared on his face.

"Me, sir? Racist? I'm doing my job to the best of my ability and somebody thinks I'm racist. Perish the thought."

"This type of accusation can be bad for us though. You know that, Chief Inspector."

"You're right, sir, of course, but, at the moment, DC Copley, your nephew, is also on this case, and I'm sure *he* will confirm that nothing with racist overtones has occurred."

The ACC hesitated for a moment and cleared his throat. "Of course, of course," he said. "By the way, how is he shaping up now?"

"He's a bloody good copper, sir," Farrel said, "and he's a fast learner to boot. He'll go far."

The ACC gave a small smile of pleasure; it was clear that he was pleased with the report.

"He has a good teacher, Chief Inspector," Copley ceded. "But don't teach him any bad habits."

"Thank you, sir, and I won't," Farrel said as he turned towards the door.

He had his hand on the doorknob when the ACC called. "Be careful with this one. It could become complicated."

Farrel nodded. "Very careful, sir."

"And by the way," the chief went on, "there's an envelope addressed to you on my secretary's desk. I don't know who sent it or where it came from."

"Thank you, sir," Farrel replied somewhat puzzled. Then he left the office and collected the envelope.

Sitting in his car, he opened the envelope. It contained a single small sheet of paper with a number on it. The number meant nothing to him, except that he recognised it as a telephone number; a mobile phone number. He would ring it later, but for now, he tucked it into the breast pocket of his jacket. *It may prove useful, you never know.*

21

Farrel pulled into his road at six o'clock that same evening, and having parked his car, he called into a local shop to pick up enough food for his evening meal.

Life was going to be so different from now on. After the short period that Julie had spent there, he grown accustomed to returning to a beautifully maintained flat, superb food and all the other home comforts that she provided. Now he would have to do all the chores himself and rely on double whiskies to help him get to sleep. He climbed the stairs to his front door, feeling more depressed with each step.

As he reached his door he noticed something strange. The door looked as though it was standing slightly ajar. Had Julie returned? On closer inspection, he saw that it did not fit into the frame properly. On studying it further, he realised that the door had been forced open. There were splinters on the floor and inside the frame was split by the amount of force used. Dropping the bags of groceries, he entered. Tension was building within him. His fists tightly balled ready for any kind of confrontation and God help whoever he found there.

The flat was empty, and it was quite clear that for the second time robbery was not the motive. Each room seemed to have been searched, and except for one or two things that Julie had discarded, nothing else had been moved. *They were looking for Julie!*

His depression now lifted as he realised that if Julie had still been there she could have been abducted or even worse. It also occurred to him that she *had* been seen that evening at the industrial estate. Something serious had happened there, and although she had no idea of what it was, the Slavs obviously thought she had.

He called a friend who came round later and repaired the damage. *Now they know she's not here, they'll leave the place alone.*

22

The next morning, Farrel shared the events with the squad, yet still made no mention of Julie by name, or of the fact that he had moved her to Elizabeth's place. That would have invited trouble.

The observations on the two units continued and Copley reported that the pattern of their use continued much the same.

*

Around midday, Farrel received a phone call from a very worried Jill Franks, asking if he could meet her somewhere where they could talk privately. They agreed to meet at Café Antonio, which, due to its location and prices, was unlikely to attract the type of person that Jill would know, nor the type of people that he would come into contact with.

They met at four o'clock that afternoon. Farrel could see by Jill's face and body language that she was even more concerned than her voice had indicated earlier.

"What's the problem, Jill?" he asked, after ordering a pot of tea and two teacakes. It was important, he felt, to make her feel more relaxed and not to draw attention to themselves as they sat at a table in one of the alcoves.

"I'm scared, Mr Farrel," she replied, and Farrel could see that her hands were shaking. "I still haven't heard from Tommy. It's been nearly two weeks now and he's never done anything like this before."

"Don't worry," Farrel replied, "I'm sure he'll show up soon." However, he did not feel at all sure that what he was telling her was correct. In fact, the longer Tommy stayed away, the more Farrel suspected that the rumour he had heard was likely to be closer to the truth.

"I was going through some of his things a couple of days ago," she said, "when I came across a sort of diary that he's been keeping over the last few years. I know he was never a big shot, or ever likely to be, but he had enough sense to write a few things down so that if anything ever happened he would not be left to take all the blame. He always said he knew enough to take a lot of people down with him."

"Very wise of him," Farrel said and nodded, but thought it was precisely that which would make Tommy even more of a target to be eliminated.

"Anyway," Jill continued, "I read through some of the pages and he's right, he does know a lot of what went on and still does go on. Some of it is about people we both know and people I would not want to get into trouble as they have been good to Tommy, but it seems that other people have come along. People much more dangerous and sinister, and they seem to have taken over most of what goes on here. Even Big Mick is a bit scared of them."

Farrel nodded thoughtfully. "What type of things are going on Jill, and who are these other people?"

"They're foreigners. I don't know where they come from, but from what I can gather they are really bad men and I think Tommy has somehow got himself tied up with them."

"That was not very bright of him," Farrel thought aloud.

"No," Jill agreed, "but that's not helping things right now, is it? I know he wants to get out."

Farrel agreed. It was no good making vacuous statements and perhaps alienating a good source of information, but he recalled what had happened to Harry Coulter, Liz's husband, who had been murdered by one or more gang members some years earlier. "When did you last see Tommy?" he asked.

"Ten days ago I think it was."

"Did he tell you where he might be going?"

"He said he had to go France for two days."

"Was it for Big Mick?"

"I don't think so, that's why I'm so worried."

Farrel decided to change the line of questions. "About this diary of Tommy's?" he asked. "Does it say anything about what he was doing just before he . . . went away?"

"I haven't read a lot of it. After all, it's his and it's private . . . and I really don't want to know too much."

Farrel thought about it and could see her point, but he would dearly love to get his hands on it. "Could you read some of the latest stuff in it and let me know what it says?" he asked.

"No. That would be betraying Tommy."

Worth a try though, Farrel thought. "So, why did you ask to see me, then?" he asked as kindly as he could. "If there's nothing to tell me, we have both wasted our time. We both want to find Tommy but for our own reasons."

"I don't have the diary now," she said. "I've put it in a safety deposit box in the HSBC Bank for safe keeping and I've left a letter with the manager telling him that if anything happens to Tommy or me, Chief Detective Inspector Farrel of the local police should see it."

"Why wait until something happens to you?"

"Tommy's a bit of a fool sometimes but we go together well and I don't want to lose him."

Farrel could not find fault with those sentiments: he knew how he felt about Julie.

"Well, Jill," he said, "I appreciate how you feel and I admire you for it, but I'll still be looking for Tommy. I hope he's okay and not in any trouble. That way we'll both be happy, won't we?"

Jill nodded. "Thanks for listening, Mr Farrel," she said on draining her cup and standing up, "and thanks for the tea and teacake." Then she turned and left.

Farrel watched her as she exited the café, hoping, perhaps against hope, that Tommy would be restored to her soon. Her loyalty to him deserved at least that.

23

At the next morning's briefing, Farrel brought the squad members up-to-date on what he had learned the previous day. Just before the session broke up, he mentioned that Jill had found Tommy Acton's diary, but purposely left out the fact that it currently resided in the bank's safety deposit. As he spoke, he shot a quick glance at the faces of the men there. Could one of them really be a 'mole'? Most showed a mild interest when Farrel relayed that Jill had refused to share the contents with him but they were not surprised. Rowles' face showed interest but nothing more. *Interesting*, Farrel thought but said nothing.

Copley was still monitoring the videos of the suspect units, but there was little movement and certainly no reason for the squad to risk another debacle.

"Are we going to have another go, guv?" Perkins asked after the meeting.

"Not for the present," Farrel confirmed. "Don't want to make ourselves look too foolish, too 'Mr Plod-ish', do we? Remember 'softly, softly, catchy monkey.'"

Perkins nodded.

*

The following day was one that Farrel hoped would never arrive.

"One piece of bad news is always too much," he announced as the squad congregated in the office, "but two is something we just don't need."

Immediately he had the men's undivided attention. No muffled yawns now. They all wanted to know to what extent the enquiries had progressed.

"It looks as if the rumours we heard about Tommy Acton could have some substance," he said grimly. "The tide in the Channel was very low yesterday and a body was picked up from the Goodwin Sands. It wasn't secured to an anchor, as was suggested, so perhaps it's some other poor bugger: fisherman, illegal immigrant or such. On the other hand, we shall have to wait for a positive ID."

"That's going to be awful for Jill Franks," DS Preston said. "She's been worried sick about him."

"It's not that easy, George," Farrel said with a sigh.

Preston, along with the others frowned. What had happened?

"Jill has not been seen since the day before yesterday either; not since after I saw her, in fact."

24

The next few days brought nothing to light and Farrel began to consider that Jill might have suffered the same fate as Tommy. It was still only a gut feeling and he was convinced that it was all tied into Units 5 and 6 and the Eastern Europeans who used them for their business.

Damn it, he would be so pleased to walk in there with his search warrant and find something, just *anything* incriminating, but somehow they were always a step ahead of them. Somebody had to be tipping them off, yet he could not believe for one moment it was anyone he knew.

There was no point in raiding the premises at this stage as the surveillance equipment was working fine and Copley tended it as if it were a loving member of his family. There was no alternative but to get everyone in the squad out on the street asking discreet questions. After all, he did not want any members of the Underworld picking up on his discomfiture, and so he made no mention to anyone that he had the feeling the gang was being kept up-to-date on the police's progress. That information was shared only with Preston, Perkins and, of course, Copley.

Not much was seen of the squad members in and around the office during this period, but from time to time they would all meet up to report on any progress, which, as they all expected, was precious little. Consequently, Farrel decided to change the patterns of work.

Each officer worked staggered hours and was in and around the town and local area during all hours of the day and night. Farrel decided he would work during the evenings and into the early morning. He had carefully noted the features of each of the men he had seen on searching the premises and he wanted to know if any of them could possibly be working or staying locally.

The report back from forensics had confirmed that the stain on the bench in Unit 5 was in fact human blood; group 'O' positive, they said. During their search of the premises, Farrel had noticed how clean the inside was. The bench was so clean that it must have been almost new. That, in turn, meant that the bloodstain must also be new. It further strengthened Farrel's feeling that something rather serious could have happened there the night Julie had heard a loud, sharp noise, but as the sample had been collected in a clandestine manner, neither he, nor Perkins or Copley could mention it, and, in the meantime, it was becoming vitally important that they find Jill Franks.

*

It was the middle of that same evening when Farell found himself at The Rising Sun, a small village pub in Cranton some five miles west of Larchester. He had not been there for a very long time and no one appeared to recognise him.

During a lull in serving at the bar, Farrel propped himself against it, ordered his pint and fell into conversation with the landlord, Jim Carrow. He was a large man: about six foot two and built like a barn door. He could obviously look after himself and defend his premises. Farrel picked up his glass and took a sip.

"It's been a long time since I was last here," he said starting the conversation.

"Really?" Carrow replied. "I wouldn't know about that, I've only been here for a year. Where are you from?"

"Larchester. I used to come out here a lot with my ex at one time, but that was a long time ago and the place was not a patch on what it is now."

Carrow smiled and looked around, as did Farrel. *Good move, Farrel,* he considered. *I think you've made contact.*

"You like it, then?" Carrow asked.

"Yeah, it's very nice. What's your food like? Or am I too late to ask?"

"It's good . . . and you're not too late. What'll it be?"

Farrel decided on a lasagne and continued chatting. "It's quiet here now but I guess it's not like this very often," Farrel said, fishing.

"No, it's getting near closing time and don't forget it's Tuesday. This is usually the quietest night."

Farrel nodded his understanding and sipped his beer. "Cranton's a very small village," he said. "I suppose you get people from all around the area."

The lasagne arrived and he took it to a table next to the bar and close enough that he could continue the conversation. The customers were beginning to leave and shouting their 'goodnights' until Farrel was the last one in the place.

Carrow being the gregarious type was happy to carry on talking. "This place had problems and was about to close down when I came here," he volunteered. "Business started slowly and then the 'big house' just over a mile away was taken over and someone refurbished it and then opened up the derelict farm on its estate as well. That's about a quarter of a mile the other side of the house."

"Really," Farrel said, not sure what he was about to discover, but he was a copper and any information could be useful. He took a mouthful of the lasagne and chewed it slowly. If he could spin this snack out a little more, there was no telling what he might find out.

"Yeah," Carrow said, "it seems the farm is a lot bigger than anyone in the district had ever realised. It surprised even old Harry, my oldest customer; he's in his eighties and has lived here all his life, and he was saying that he never remembered so many people working there, even when they had horses and carts and threshing machines."

"Really?"

"That's right, but even at the beginning Harry was not happy about it 'disturbing the peace', but, as they say, 'every cloud has a silver lining', and I found that a lot of the blokes were coming here to drink and eat."

"Good for business then," Farrel encouraged. "What are the blokes like? Do you get any trouble from them?"

"No trouble at all. They're all foreigners. They don't speak a lot of English and they keep themselves to themselves when they're in here. They seldom come in on their own. Sometimes they do, but not often."

Farrel finished his lasagne and his pint. "That was very good, very good indeed," he said. "I'll be coming back here again."

"Be pleased to see you," the other man replied. "But now it's closing time. Take it easy around these small roads. They can be dangerous in the dark and we've had quite a few fatal accidents in the last year, particularly with young joy riders driving like madmen."

"Really?" Farrel said again sounding surprised and making a note to follow up those fatal accidents—where they had happened and to whom. *Could prove interesting.*

He remembered visiting the area years before and knew what the lanes between the villages were like then. To reacquaint himself with them, he drove back to town by a different route.

This bought him close to the 'big house' that Carrow had mentioned. He could not see much in the darkness but sufficient to see that it had been smartened up. Lights shone from a number of the windows. At the entrance to the drive, two large stone pillars sported shining lamps. The area in front of the main door, which was some one hundred yards away, was well lit and he could see a number of cars—expensive ones—parked outside. As he drove further on, he could just make out through the trees of a small spinney what must be the farm. It was not clear what the buildings were, but in addition to the old farmhouse and barns, he could make out some newer buildings. This was a place that could do with some further investigation. It was a good distance from any town and could well be of interest to Farrel and the squad, but not just yet. He needed more information about it before sharing it with all and sundry, and was certainly not about to let the perceived informer know.

25

The squad were busy with enquiries in an effort to find Jill Franks and at the same time they waited for the results of the post mortem on what had turned out to be Tommy Acton's body. Farrel, in the meantime, was out in the countryside finding out as much as he could about the 'big house' and farm just outside Cranton.

In the daylight, he could see much more of the extent of the farm. From a distance, the long-standing farmhouse looked lived in and its rickety barns used but not well kept. The large new barns that he had seen that first night were much bigger than they had at first appeared. He could see little or no activity of farming going on around the farm itself and he assumed that whatever was being produced was being done within the controlled environment of the large, prefabricated buildings.

It could, of course, be factory farming: eggs, animals, mushrooms even, or, on the other hand, it could just as likely be something much more sinister. Farrel, being a suspicious copper, tended to consider the latter more of a possibility.

However, there was one thing that caused him to exercise his powers of deduction: why were the two units on the industrial estate in Larchester being used if indeed the two locations were linked?

Was something coming in and then out through them? They were certainly not large enough units to handle anything of any size—at least nothing on an industrial scale. It could be another activity completely. Maybe something was being brought in through Larchester and going out a different route. Very interesting thoughts passed through his mind. There was also the possibility that more than one activity was being carried out in this chain of business. He considered it high time that he found out a little more about the farm.

He drove back to the office where he caught up on the latest news before going back to his empty apartment.

*

Early the next morning it was overcast with a hint of rain in the air when Farrel had left the office earlier. He had delegated the day's running of the team to DS Preston, with particular instruction for Copley to monitor the surveillance equipment and record anything that could be of use. He knew that Copley would take this to mean record absolutely anything and everything that occurred. If something later proved to be worthless, then it could be erased. Copley was certainly adept at his job and it irked Farrel a little to think that he was so super-efficient.

He left Larchester, heading west towards Cranton and the 'big house', which he had found out was called Cranton Court. Unsurprisingly the farm was named Court Farm.

His visits to the village over the last few days had tended to be at staggered times as he wanted to build up a picture of what happened in and around the area and when. It was not an onerous task and Farrel used the excuse of enjoying walks in the country as well as visits to local pubs.

The locals were friendly, particularly when Farrel made complimentary remarks about the village and the countryside around, and it was a simple matter to engage many of them in conversation. Of course, they all knew of the 'big house', as they all called it, and as it had been called ever since it was built in the eighteenth century.

Over the years, the vast majority of the local population had for at least part of their lives worked there or at Court Farm, but these days no one knew anything about what went on there. It irked them to think that foreigners had come in and taken over part of their heritage.

The best source of information was Harry, the oldest inhabitant in the village. 'He must be well over ninety,' they said. He had lived there all his life and in the same small two up, two down thatched cottage with its outside toilet. He had been married, but his wife had died many years before, so long ago that most people could not remember when she had died.

Harry kept himself clean and smart and was always a popular customer at The Rising Sun. His thick grey beard was well stained with smoke and nicotine from his old briar pipe, which he seldom took out of his mouth except to down his pint and, Farrel assumed, when he went to bed. Perversely, he even considered in his mind's eye Harry lying in bed still sucking it.

Harry was always good for a tall story or two after a couple of drinks. The other customers would laugh and ply him with more and Harry was always happy to oblige by dipping into his apparent limitless supply of stories. When, however, Farrel spoke with him in the village, or when he saw him out and about in the lanes around the village, he found him a fascinating character. It wasn't long before he considered that he knew just as much about the area as most of the villagers who had lived there for years.

"So when did the foreigner take over at the 'big house'?" Farrel asked Harry when he encountered him whilst out that morning.

Harry took his pipe out of his mouth briefly to send a stream of nicotine-stained saliva into the grass at the side of the lane. Farrel studied him closely and decided that this action translated as a modicum of dislike or distrust of the occupier of Cranton Court.

"Oh, I don't know exactly," he replied in his broad, rustic dialect. "It must be three year ago now. Places were falling down very near both the house and the farm and this foreign bloke turned up out of nowhere and there they were. Been there ever since."

"What do they farm?" Farrel asked.

Harry took the pipe from his mouth, hawked and spat onto the grass again. "Bugger all, as far as I can see," he replied. "They ain't farmers—not of the land at least. That's good farmland there and they don't till it. Whatever they do, it's done in them barns over there. Everything seems hush-hush. We never see them folks from the 'big house' in the village, only when they drive by in their flashy cars."

"What about the people who work on the farm?"

"Funny blokes, they are. They come into the village once in a while and go to The Rising Sun. They all sit together and talk quiet like. They don't mix and they talk foreign. They ain't any trouble though. One night, one of them had had a bit too much to drink and got very loud. The others tried to shut him up but he wouldn't stop. He was shouting his head off about something or other—nobody knew what it was, but it sounded angry and it upset a lot of people in there. He never came back again, not even with those who we thought were his mates."

"Really?" Farrel said. "Do the same people still come though?"

"Oh, yeah, but they're still not friendly. I think they're hiding something, you know. You always know when someone's not being open and honest about things, don't you, 'specially in a little place like Cranton?"

"That's for sure," Farrel said. He above anyone else could understand that.

The conversation finished after Harry asked Farrel if he was likely to be at the pub that evening.

"It's usually midweek or the weekend that they come," Harry said, and Farrel immediately made up his mind that Harry *was very likely* to see him then. They parted company and Farrel returned to his car.

*

He drove around the area for a while and at around eleven thirty found the lane that would take him as close as possible to Court Farm. He pulled into a small lay-by at the side of a spinney.

The small wooded area masked his car. He reached into the glove box and removed a small pair of binoculars that he always kept handy. Then he climbed out of the car and went to the back where he opened the tailgate. He took out a pair of wet-weather over-trousers that he had worn whilst playing golf some years earlier but still kept in the car. Then he slipped his feet into a pair of wellington boots and pulled the trousers over the outside of them. He slipped off his overcoat and put on a waterproof jacket. He always carried his wet-weather gear with him; it was his belief that whenever he had to attend a murder or other crime scene, it was either raining or in a muddy field. He slipped on a slouch hat and tucked his binoculars into a pocket.

Now, he looked the part of a rambler and with that he set off down the lane looking for a gateway into a field from where he could approach the farm and find out a little more about these secretive foreigners. Was it possible he would see Ivan Minski here? *You never know,* he mused.

26

The clouds were low and a light rain was just beginning to fall as Farrel set off along the lane. Some fifty yards from where he had parked, he found a wooden five-bar gate into the field on his right and another into the field on his left. These allowed easy access from one field to the other across the lane for cattle and machinery.

Farrel chose the gate on his left, the one that would lead him closer to the farm. It was possible to see that in years past, this had been a busy route across the farmland linking the large area of the farm to the outlying fields and woodlands, but now it was obvious that no use was being made of it. The grass was long and thistles occupied large patches in the field. As he looked around at the adjoining fields he could see the same patterns. This farm was used neither for raising animals, or crops, he decided, it was so neglected.

The gate to the field was in poor repair. The hinges had not been maintained and this left the side with the large wooden latch deeply embedded in the earth and difficult to open. Farrel decided to climb over at the hinge end to avoid the gate collapsing under his weight. He noticed too that along the top rail of the gate, barbed wire had been fixed and that it appeared to be a recent job. It was not enough to stop people climbing it; just enough to deter them, but, all the same, it was illegal.

He climbed over the gate and decided that rather than walking across the field from one side to the other and leave an obvious trail, he would walk around it, a matter of three or four feet inside the hedgerow. He could not be seen from the other side of the hedge, as again, it had not been cut for a very long time and was overgrown, and, at the same time, from the same side, being dressed in dark green clothing, he did not really stand out.

At intervals where the hedgerow permitted, he looked through the openings to gain a mental picture of the layout of the adjoining fields and where the farm was situated in relation to them.

If his suspicions had any foundation, he may need to visit with a view to searching the farm, and that would need an army of men coming from all directions along well-organised routes. He thought of the immense use young Copley had been and how much more use he could be and decided at this point he would leave the planning of such a raid to Copley, who, he knew, would use his computer to identify every possible path across the fields. *He'd probably locate every cowpat for you as well.* However, as he looked around again, he realised you need cows to have cowpats and there were no cows. *Strange, very strange.* He pressed on. A heavier drizzle was developing and his boots dragged through the thick, wet un-mown grass.

Reaching a vantage point where he could see the outbuildings of the farm, he stopped. He took out his binoculars and did a quick sweep of the area. As he had thought, the old barns appeared not to be in use. The doors stood open or ajar and the half stable-type doors had their top halves fully open, even if the lower parts were closed. There was no activity going on there. A little way ahead, he was able to see the new barns: some thirty feet high and constructed of grey-coloured metal. Such was their appearance that Farrel decided they were newer than even old Harry knew.

There was little activity going on there either, and all the doors and any panels higher up that could possibly be opened were closed. As he watched, from time to time he noticed a worker would leave one of the buildings and immediately close the door after him, leading Farrel to think that the interior of the sheds were artificially lit. He couldn't spot any type of generator so he assumed that it was either kept somewhere that he could not see from his present position or that the power was provided by a local electricity board. He would leave Copley to look into it. *He's a good lad. Pity he has to have an uncle who's one of my bosses.*

The rain began to fall faster although Farrel had not noticed— such was his interest in the things going on around there.

Suddenly a voice behind him startled him.

"What you think you doing here?" a foreign accent, very reminiscent of Ivan Minski, asked.

Farrel turned quickly to find a man dressed like a typical English gamekeeper, complete with a double-barrelled 12-bore shotgun.

"Pardon?" Farrel responded, trying to cover his surprise, and at the same time trying to think of something to say.

"I say, what you think you doing here?" the man repeated, even sterner than the first time.

"I'm bird-watching," Farrel replied indignantly, holding up his binoculars and rather relieved to have thought of something so quickly. "What do you think I'm doing?"

"You not allowed being here."

"Why? It's a free country and I'm visiting the countryside to watch for birds."

"You not allowed being here," the fake gamekeeper insisted. "You leave now."

"Just a minute, sonny Jim," Farrel said again indignantly, and beginning to feel that the other man was not entirely sure about getting into an argument, "I come out here to watch out for rare birds. I'm what we call a 'twitcher'."

The other man frowned and Farrel felt he had gained the higher ground despite the fact that the foreigner was holding a gun.

"I came out here," he explained slowly and deliberately, as if he we explaining something to a very young child or an idiot, so as to let the man believe he was a crazy Englishman, "to look for rare birds. I had just spotted a—" and here he cast about for a species that the man would not know and not knowing himself if this one actually existed, "lesser spotted pied wagtail, and you have just scared it away and it's the first one I have ever seen."

The man frowned again, clearly not knowing what Farrel was talking about and what to say in response, but then he seemed to remember his lines.

"You not allowed to be here," he repeated. "You not go, I call the police."

Farrel chuckled inwardly. *If only you knew, sonny Jim.* But he said nothing in response.

Instead, he became grumpy, which for him was quite easy, and mumbled something about 'it's not a free country any more'. He turned, allowed his shoulders to droop and set off back towards the field gate.

The gamekeeper appeared to be satisfied.

After a short while Farrel turned to see if the other man was following him, but he had disappeared as quickly as he had originally appeared in the first place.

When Farell reached his car he found only the signs of his being there earlier. No one appeared to have checked his vehicle whilst he had been absent from it. He climbed out of his wet-weather gear and stowed it in the boot together with the wellington boots. He slipped into his more comfortable attire and climbed back into the vehicle.

The rain was falling much more heavily now. Farrel grinned. The gamekeeper, whoever he was, was now getting very wet. *Serves him bloody well right, messing up my day. Now for a swift pint at The Rising Sun and back to the office just in time to instruct Copley on what he has to do.*

*

The log fire in The Rising Sun was very comforting after the downpour outside, yet Farrel was the only customer. Jim Carrow was there, of course, and they struck up a conversation as Farrel drank a whisky to warm himself.

"What brings you out here in this weather?" the landlord enquired.

"I like walks in the country. Didn't I tell you?"

"Yeah. But in this weather?"

"Why not?"

"I suppose it takes all sorts."

Farrel smiled as he nodded and thought about it.

As the conversation ended, Farrel walked towards the door but then stopped and half turned back towards the bar, frowning and as if deep in thought. "Tell me," he asked, "is there such a bird as a lesser spotted pied wagtail?"

"I don't have a clue. Mind you, I'm not a real country boy. Why?"

"Well, I said it was a very rare species," Farrel said vaguely. With that, he turned back towards the door and raised his hand in farewell to a puzzled Jim Carrow.

27

Around 2.15 p.m. as he sat comfortably in his car in the car park of The Rising Sun Farrel rang Elizabeth on his mobile phone. It was answered quickly and he heard Liz on the other end.

"Is everything okay?" he asked.

"Yes, everything's fine," she answered, but, somewhere in the tone of her voice, Farrel detected some tension. Perhaps it had not been the best idea to take Julie to her home. It was the safest place he could think of as a matter of urgency, but now, on reflection, he knew that both women would have figured out what his relationship with the other was.

"I'm still out of town, but can I call in on you both when I can, just to make sure everything's in order?" he asked.

"That would be nice," Liz replied lightening up a little. "We'll all have a coffee together."

"See you later," Farrel said and disconnected.

He started the engine, pulled out of the car park and headed in the opposite direction from which he had come earlier in the day.

There was a great deal of diplomatic work to do later and he wasn't exactly the most diplomatic man in the world. He needed time to think everything through.

He had grown very fond of Julie but he was old enough to be her father. Elizabeth, on the other hand, was the same age as him, and he was becoming fonder of her by the day. *You have to sort this out Farrel and damn quick.*

The lane took him along his earlier route to the lay-by where he had parked previously. Beyond, he passed a large gravel pit, which was now full of water and which he considered could be used by fishermen or boating enthusiasts. However, as the secretive Cranton Court landlord was likely to be the new owner, those activities were unlikely to take place.

About half a mile farther along the lane on the right hand side he noticed that it ran parallel to the main railway line, which had various stops at some local villages, and along which ran faster non-stopping inter-city trains. A short way after the road sloped upwards as the railway entered a cutting and the road ran along the top of the embankment. Quite suddenly, there was a sharp ninety-degree bend to the right, taking the road across the bridge over the line. Dirty, worn black and white chevrons barely marked the dangerous bend, and Farrel was forced to brake hard and drag the wheel over sharply to negotiate it. He crossed the bridge and found that there was another dangerous turn, similarly poorly marked, to the left, that took the road again parallel to the railway line but on the opposite side. *Bad bends in the dark,* he considered but then thought no more of it.

*

It was around five in afternoon when he arrived back at the office. All the squad were out on enquiries: some relating to the whereabouts of Jill Franks and others on unrelated matters. Copley was the only one in and quite naturally seated at his workstation.

He rang Elizabeth to tell her he was running late . . . very late.

"Anything new turn up?" Farrel asked.

"No, guv, just running a few things through trying to tie up the loose ends. There are a lot of those at the moment."

Farrel nodded his understanding and turned to study the large white board, which was beginning to show a few more names and addresses but nothing that he did not know already.

"Can you get maps easily on that thing?" he asked nodding at the computer screen.

"Oh yes," Copley replied lightly. "Where do you want to go? Hawaii? Seychelles? Just say."

"How about Cranton," Farrel said, bringing the young man down to earth.

Copley pulled a disappointed face but replied, "Yes, of course," and he turned back to the screen.

"I don't want to see it all right now but what I would like to have is the layout of Cranton Court in Cranton village in relation to the surrounding countryside. I would also like to know the same information for Court Farm, which belongs to the estate."

Copley busily made notes as Farrel spoke.

"That will be easy. Will you need print-offs done for everyone else as well?"

"Not at this stage. I want you to do this without saying anything to anyone else, okay. And I mean anyone."

Copley nodded. He had learned not to question the DCI even if he did not fully understand the reasons behind the instructions.

"I would also like you to get me small-scale maps of the estate there, as up-to-date as possible, that show where the field boundaries are as well as the footpaths, both private and public, and how they relate to the buildings and the lanes around and the roads farther afield. Can you do that?"

"Yes, of course. The local library will have all those things somewhere in its archives or on disc or microfiche."

"Whatever," Farrel said raising his eyebrows and shaking his head, mainly in admiration for Copley's grasp of all things modern and electronic. He never seemed to miss a trick.

"Good, I'll leave you to it then," he said, as he headed towards the office door. Then he hesitated and turned back to Copley.

"How long do you think it will take you to get that info, in addition to all the other stuff you're on?"

"Realistically," and he thought for a few seconds, "three days—at the most, that is."

"Make it two," Farrel shot back and turned towards the door again. As he passed through the doorway, he heard Copley's voice come back in a resigned manner.

"Okay, guv, two days."

Farrel strutted down the corridor and smiled. Copley was definitely an asset and not afraid to work hard. He would go far and Farrel hoped he would be there to see it.

He reached the outside door to the car park, smiled again and nodded his agreement to his own thoughts.

Sitting in his car, he remembered the slip of paper in the envelope with a phone number on it. He punched in the number and waited. It was several seconds before it was answered. The person on the other end had a foreign accent, possibly Slavic but not for definite, it occurred to Farrel.

"My name is Farrel," he stated.

There was a short delay. Then came a shattering statement—something that he had never thought he would ever hear.

"There is a traitor somewhere at your end."

The line was not clear and the voice on the other end was almost a whisper.

"I don't know who or where," the voice whispered as if the owner was afraid of being overheard. It sounded hurried and laced with fear.

"Who are you?" Farrel asked incredulously.

"I cannot say. If anyone finds I am telling you, I am a dead man."

The phone went dead.

Farrel sat for a long time considering this latest development. *We have a mole in our set up.* The thought appalled him, but as he sat thinking about it he realised, *but so have they. The thing is who is it in our side?*

It was clear by now that his worst fears, however outrageous they had seemed originally, had just been confirmed.

He sat, still unable to take it in. It was clear now that he had to rely on very few members of all the local police service. At least Inspector de Large still appeared to have someone in there in his set up. Perhaps both his agents were still operating.

28

Farrel arrived at Elizabeth's apartment around 7.15 p.m. Things were moving faster now in both his professional and personal lives. *What is it people say,* he thought, *life's a bitch, and in the end, you die.* He rang the doorbell and Elizabeth opened the door. She flashed her usual broad smile at him and kissed him.

"Good evening, Superman," she said a little tartly.

Farrel made no reply. He could not think of one at that moment.

They stood just inside the locked door but did not go further into the apartment.

"Hello, Liz," he said quietly so that Julie, somewhere nearby in the apartment, would not overhear. "Is everything okay?"

She nodded. "We've had a good day together. Julie's been telling me all about it so far. You didn't tell me how dangerous it is. The poor girl's in a pretty awful state."

"How bad is she?"

"She's doing very well considering what she may have to face, I'd say."

Farrel breathed a sigh of relief. "Good," he said. "What have you been doing all day?"

"Well, for a start, after she had told me the story from the beginning, I got her to write it all down again."

"And . . . ?

"It's thrown up a few more details. She has remembered a few more things since the time she wrote out her first statement."

"Really?" Farrel was pleasantly surprised.

"Really, and I think that with a bit more digging, she may remember even more now that she's more relaxed and feeling more secure. I think it's the front door that gives her the confidence. Her spelling and grammar are absolute rubbish though."

Farrel smiled and nodded.

"But she's no dumb blonde," she added.

Farrel smiled again and nodded his agreement.

"Anyway, come in and have a cup of coffee or something a little stronger."

Farrel slipped off his coat and hung it on the hallstand and they went into the living room. Julie looked up from her position on the two-seater sofa. She was frowning, and he assumed that it was because he had spoken to Elizabeth quietly for some minutes in the hall and excluded her from the conversation rather than going straight into the room to see her. He smiled at her and gave her a wink.

"So, how's my star witness?" he asked.

The look disappeared immediately. Now he was sure that the frown had been there to make him feel uncomfortable for neglecting her.

"Better now you're here," she said as she stood up and approached him. She put her arms around his neck and kissed him full on the mouth with her lips well parted. She knew Elizabeth was watching from the doorway but she wanted to let both Farrel and Elizabeth know how she felt about things. He felt strangely gratified to think that both these attractive women had designs on him but he knew what had to happen and what the outcome would have to be.

"I have to pop to the shops for a few minutes, so I'll leave you to look after her," Elizabeth said. "But it'll be for only a little while," she added emphatically. "No time for any hanky-panky."

She left the room and a few moments later Farrel heard the heavy security door close. *Now what?*

"Did Liz tell you I had done more to my statement?" Julie asked.

"Yes, she did and that's brilliant. I haven't seen it yet, but she said there's extra information that may well be useful."

"I hope it will be too. Do you want to see it?"

"That's a good idea."

"I have it in the bedroom. Would you like to come in and read it over with me?" she teased.

"I think you had better bring it out here for me to read. You know how weak-willed I am," he replied, ducking the temptation.

She went into the bedroom and came out with a couple of A4 sheets of paper, which she handed to him.

"I'm sorry the spelling's rubbish and the grammar's crap," she said.

"That's not a problem," he replied. "It's the facts I want. Are you sure you haven't *imagined* this is what you saw and heard? It's so easy to do," he said as he scanned the scrawled lines.

"No, sitting here and with Liz just talking quietly to me, I was surprised at how much extra I remembered."

Farrel noticed in the writing that there was much more description of the events and of the people involved.

"You've done well, Julie," he said.

She moved closer to him. "Is that all the thanks I'll be getting then?"

Farrel smiled and put his arm around her shoulder and gave her a hug, but the result was not just the cuddle that he intended to give her. She lifted her face to him, her mouth reached up to his again and they kissed. Her lips were apart and her tongue sought his. He did not resist, although he knew that this was not what he should be doing at this moment and he could see over her shoulder her bedroom door standing ajar, almost as an unspoken invitation; *what a dilemma.*

"You do still care then," she said.

He nodded. "Of course I do."

She sat down on the two-seater sofa and chuckled.

"What's that laugh for?" he asked. She chuckled again. This was getting maddening.

"Liz is nuts about you too, you know," she said. "She hasn't said as much, but after being with her for only a day or so, it's obvious. So what's to do about it?"

Farrel heard the key turn in the lock of the apartment outside door.

"Nothing for the moment," he said. "We've all got to work together at keeping you safe, and that means Liz and me."

The living room door opened and Elizabeth walked into the room.

"So, you have been behaving yourselves," she said.

"Sort of," Julie replied rather sullenly. "You certainly didn't take your time."

Farrel said nothing. Best to keep quiet, he knew.

They spent the evening drinking coffee and the obligatory whisky and talking about the case in general. There were the occasional interchanges between Elizabeth and Julie, which contained friendly, if somewhat veiled barbs, but altogether it passed off in a very amicable fashion.

Farrel left around ten thirty. Elizabeth saw him to the door and they arranged a meeting the next morning to discuss future directions. Julie was safe as long as she stayed locked away behind the door.

29

At ten thirty the next morning, Farrel and Elizabeth met in the Café Antonio where he had previously talked to Jill Franks. It was almost full and with some difficulty they found a table towards the rear of the establishment. Farrel considered that it was really quite fortuitous as they were less likely to be noticed by either any of Elizabeth's acquaintances or indeed any of his adversaries. They ordered coffees and sipped them in silence for a few minutes.

"We have to get this all sorted out," Elizabeth began.

Farrel nodded. "It's beginning to get a bit intense," he said. "I think we shall be making moves on the foreigners very soon."

"I'm talking about Julie," Elizabeth retorted matter-of-factly. "I'm quite happy to have her stay for a short while but things are getting a bit fraught."

"Oh, I'm sorry. What's the problem?"

"She's absolutely crazy about you, for a start, and it's beginning to get on my . . . nerves," she replied.

Farrel said nothing.

"She doesn't think about how it affects me. On about it all the time," she continued. "I wish you could find her somewhere else soon. She's a nice kid and she's had a rough time, so don't get me wrong, I want to help, but she really does overdo it about you."

Farrel thought for a moment and then ordered two more coffees.

"How do you really feel about things, Liz?" he asked, as he reached across the table and covered her left hand with his right.

"I'm nuts about you," she replied brusquely, "and I'm jealous, aren't I. You must know that."

Farrel looked her straight in the eyes and she returned his look. They both knew something had happened between them. It was serious and they had to come to a decision, which they knew would affect not only their lives but Julie's as well.

"Life's been a bit of a roller coaster for me in more ways than one," Farrel said, "and Julie is a lovely girl, despite her past, but if you think it would work out for her and me, you're mistaken. The age difference is too great, and although I think she has stick ability, I really don't think she's someone I could feel would go along with my job and hours. I know what that was like from before. It's a no-brainer."

"So where does that leave me?" Elizabeth asked with an enquiring look on her face and her head tilted to one side.

Farrel lifted her hand, which he had held during their conversation and kissed it. "In pole position, I hope," he replied.

Elizabeth relaxed noticeably and smiled. Farrel was glad to see her instantly happier.

"Pole position, eh," she said and laughed. "Does that mean you're looking for your own personal lap dancer?"

Farrel's jaw dropped, his eyes opened wide in mock shock and then he laughed. "Well now," he replied, "that is an intriguing thought."

They both enjoyed the joke.

"So what do we do about Julie?" Elizabeth asked as they sipped their coffee. "I know we have to keep her safe, particularly with what seems to be going on, but, *please* Ian, can't you find her a more suitable place?"

Farrel knew she was right and that all the time Julie was under Elizabeth's care, both women were vulnerable.

He nodded. "It's going to be difficult to get Julie to agree," he said, "but I think between us and our promise of being with her when she needs us, she will. She's very sensible, after all."

"And it will give us more time to concentrate on our relationship," she said.

Farrel nodded and smiled at the thought.

"By the way," she continued, "I'm fascinated—what's 'the pole' position?"

Farrel's mouth fell open and he gave a short laugh.

"Liz, you are incorrigible."

30

At eight o'clock that evening, the Rising Sun in Cranton was nearly full when Farrel entered. Most of the tables were taken up, so he sat on a bar stool at the opposite end of the bar from the dartboard and from where a rather noisy game was in progress.

"Evening, Jim," he smiled when Carrow ventured along the other side of the bar to greet him. "Good business tonight."

"That's right," Carrow confirmed. "It's like this most Fridays. A bit noisy, but the lads enjoy a game of darts and the other people don't seem to mind the high spirits, if you'll forgive the expression. What'll you have?"

Farrel ordered a pint and a Ploughman's as he settled down to people-watch. He liked to do that. You learn a lot about people that way he always said. Their body language gave away many things about them and it could be amusing as well. From his position, he could spot those who had downed a few and were at the friendly stage, and he noted too those whose tempers could be short, judging by their voices. He was by no means an expert on people's behaviour but his experience had increased his understanding of it.

"Harry not in tonight?" Farrel asked in an off-handed way.

"Not yet," replied Carrow. "He's late, but he'll be here though," he said looking at the large old railway clock on the wall between two racks behind the bar; one holding the various bottles of shorts—a wide selection Farrel noted. The other held a selection of clean glasses. The clock was showing a quarter past eight.

The door opened and Harry came in, complete with his old briar pipe protruding from the corner of his mouth.

"There you are, Harry. You're late tonight," Carrow pointed out as Harry approached. Then he added, "You'll have to put your pipe out whilst you're in here. I keep telling you about it."

Harry swore under his breath as he removed the old pipe from his mouth and stuffed it into his pocket.

"And don't set fire to your coat," Carrow advised.

"If there was another pub in the village, I'd go to it," Harry grumbled.

"If there was another pub in the village," Carrow answered with a grin, "you'd still have to put your pipe out. It's the law."

"Bloody stupid law if you ask me," Harry commented miserably.

"Hello, Harry," Farrel greeted him as he approached his end of the bar, "come and sit here. I can't see any free tables at the moment."

"That's another thing," Harry complained, "some nights a regular can't get a bloody seat."

Farrel smiled. "I know what you mean," he sympathised. "What can I get you?"

Harry's face quickly brightened at the thought of a free drink. He ordered a pint of his favourite ale and then looked more closely at Farrel.

"Ah, you're the bloke I was talking to the other day, ain't you . . . er . . . ." he waited for a name.

Farrel nodded. "That's right. Name's Ian."

They fell easily into conversation until Harry looked across the crowded bar and frowned. "It's them bloody foreigners here again," he complained in his local dialect. "Look, they're taking up all the seats and they don't usually drink much, do they, Jim," he said turning to Carrow.

"They're customers, Harry," Carrow answered wishing to appear neutral. "Maybe not as good as you are, but they're customers all the same."

Farrel looked across at the group sitting around one of the tables. On closer inspection, he recognised the man who had appeared dressed as a gamekeeper on his recent 'bird watching' escapade, and he thought he recognised two of the others from the industrial estate in Larchester, but as they were side on to him he had only a profile view. Harry looked at the group and muttered his disapproval of foreigners in general and foreigners in his 'local' in particular.

"That little bugger over there at the end of the table," he nodded towards the group, "he downs a few. The others don't, but he does. He don't seem to be able to hold it very well either."

Farrel watched the man carefully as he continued his conversation with Harry. The man did seem very familiar, and when he turned his head towards him just a little, Farrel was certain that he was one of the men he had seen in Unit 5 on the industrial estate. What a pity Perkins was not at the pub; he would have confirmed it for sure. Farrel did not recognise the other men there, but this one that Harry had pointed out, was definitely one with whom Farrel decided he needed to 'have a little chat'.

As the evening progressed, Harry reminisced over old times and told Farell many amusing stories of the local people now long gone, yet all the time Farrell's eyes were drawn towards the foreign customers.

During a natural break, Farrel found it necessary to pay a visit to the gents. His path to the toilet brought him much closer to the group. On passing, he made a point of ignoring them and received little attention from the gang in return. As he returned from the toilets to the bar, however, the small man Harry had pointed out looked up at Farrel as he approached. His flushed face showed that he had drunk rather more than was perhaps good for him and he appeared to have a problem with focusing clearly on things around him. Farrel glanced at him and noticed that the other man had clearly recognised him. His expression indicated it, particularly when their eyes met. The Slav was trying desperately not to show it, but Farrel saw a look of fear spread across his face. Farrel continued back to his bar stool and carried on his conversation with Harry and Jim Carrow whilst still closely studying the foreigner, who was showing signs of now being very disturbed. The man's gaze continually returned to look sideways at Farrel.

Had Farrel spooked him? Perhaps—he would soon find that out.

A few minutes later, the man left his comrades, made his way unsteadily towards the door leading to the toilets and went out through it. When another customer used the same door moments later, through the opening Farrel saw the man turn away from the bar towards the direction where Farrel knew there was a door to the outside and to the car park.

Farrel bade a very quick 'see you later' to Harry and Jim Carrow and rapidly followed the same exit route taken by the other man. When he reached the car park through the side door he saw the fugitive turn, look at him, then turn back and run unsteadily towards a car.

"Just a minute," Farrel called after him, "I want a word with you."

This appeared to strike even more fear into the man and his stride quickened as he rushed towards the vehicle. He fumbled with the door lock but managed to open the door and half fall into the driving seat. Again, he fumbled around in his haste to push the key into the ignition. Then the motor burst into life.

"Don't drive in that condition, you fool," Farrel shouted, but the man either did not understand him or, more likely, did not hear him. The gears grated as he found first and the car leapt kangaroo-style forwards until it gained some momentum. Its tyres threw wet stones and sand up from the surface of the car park.

Farrel dashed to his own car, muttering obscenities and something about wanting to have a word with this stupid drunken foreigner. He gunned the motor into life and with much less drama he quickly left the car park and turned in the same direction that the other car had taken.

Farrel smiled. *Now this is just like the old days when I was young—always loved a good car chase—wonder if I still have it in me—and all those old skills.*

A few minutes later as he rounded one of the bends in the lane, he saw the other car's taillights some one hundred yards away approaching another bend. It was travelling far too fast for the width and state of the lane and swerved crazily from one side to the other.

"Pull up, you idiot," Farrel shouted through the windscreen, but it was only in frustration. He knew the other driver could not hear.

The car ahead continued its mad path along the narrow country lane. From time to time, it left the metalled surface and careered onto the narrow, wet grass verges on either side. There were places where drainage ditches ran between the hedgerow and the edge of the road, which, had the driver put the car wheels into it, he would have slowed rapidly and come to a halt—but that was not to be. On two occasions, the car left the road and side swiped a tree, taking off pieces of bark and wood, leaving large areas of bare white tree trunk exposed and metallic grey paintwork in their place. Farrel noted the route the driver was taking was towards Cranton Court.

He's trying to get home, he thought, and knew that if this were the case, it would be an ideal opportunity for him to get a much closer look at the 'big house', or the farm. If anything illegal was going on there, it would become apparent and the drunken driver would be putting himself in a great deal of bother, or even danger with the owners, his employers, assuming they were themselves involved in illegal activities.

As they approached the gates to the 'big house', the car in front made no attempt to slow down, but carried on past, in its apparent rush to escape Farrel, who was, at that moment, hoping and praying that they would not meet another vehicle coming from the opposite direction.

More mud was churned up from the verges of the road in the car's headlong dash. At one point, at a sharp bend, the car scraped along a wall constructed of local stones, built to prevent vehicles leaving the road and falling over a steep slope into a field some ten to fifteen feet below the road. Part of the wall fell away on impact, and the remainder, like the trees earlier, collected a considerable amount of the car's paintwork.

As both cars' headlights lit up the road ahead, Farrel recognised the approaching rise of the road and the starting point of the railway cutting.

"Slow down, you idiot," he shouted uselessly once again.

The other car carried on at speed. Then in the headlights of the cars Farrel saw the dirty, badly maintained chevrons ahead at the bend indicating the sharp right turn over the railway bridge. He braked hard to slow down quickly but not enough to skid and possibly lose control. The other driver appeared oblivious to the chevrons until the very last moment. His brake lights lit up but there was very little effect. His speed and obvious state of inebriation prevented him from reacting properly and made it impossible for him to slow down in time to take the bend. The car continued straight on, mounted the grass verge, demolished the chevrons and the fence behind them and disappeared over the rim of the railway cutting.

Farrel did not see whether it hit anything else, but as he got closer he could see in his headlight beams the airborne car rolling onto its side and then the front end hit the side of the cutting. The car began to cartwheel downwards. End over end it fell, finally coming to rest upside down and partially on the rail track. The car did not explode, but after a moment, which for Farrel felt more like an hour, it burst into flames with a loud 'whoosh'.

He watched the events in horror. It seemed as if it was all happening in slow motion. The fast southbound train that seemed to appear from nowhere was travelling in anything but slow motion. As the car came to rest on the track and burst into flames, the train was less than a hundred yards around a slight bend the other side of the bridge from the burning car. There was no time for it to stop. Farrel held his breath.

"Oh my God," he said aloud, "Oh my God."

The front of the train collided with the burning wreck but thankfully it did not de-rail, instead, it flipped the car over and off the track onto the side of the cutting where the grass was too wet to ignite.

Farrel watched, his heart rate greatly increased. Did he really need to be part of this scene? He decided not. He would hear all about it in the morning. The driver was in all probability dead. A post mortem would confirm that he had excess alcohol in his blood and that would be the cause of the accident. The police would then find out the particulars of the dead driver, as well as details of the owner of the vehicle—and who could tell what can of worms that would prise open?

No, he wanted to stay on the sidelines and out of sight as long as he could. He was sure no one had noticed him as he left the Rising Sun car park and followed the other car, and, anyway, it would be very difficult for anyone to tie him in with the car chase. He felt bad about it, but there it was; he had his job to do and he would do it his way.

A little farther along the lane over the bridge he saw a gateway. He pulled into it and turned around. He wanted to be clear of the area before the emergency services arrived. After all, this was deep in the country and the train had taken something like half a mile to come to a halt.

He drove back the way he had come and returned to Cranton. He parked in the car park of the Rising Sun and after taking a few minutes to gather himself he went back inside. He saw that the foreigners had all left and Harry was now happily sitting at a free table enjoying another pint.

"Hey, Jim," Farrel called to Carrow, "Did I drop some keys whilst I was in here a little while ago?" He needed to create some kind of believable alibi. "I was halfway back to Larchester when I felt in my pocket that they weren't there."

Carrow looked around.

"No. I haven't seen any," he replied. Then he called over to Harry. "Harry, did you notice Ian here drop any keys when he was in earlier?"

Harry shook his head. "Not that I noticed," he replied.

Farrel shook his head feigning worry then slapped at his jacket pockets as if to re-check them. He did the same with those in his coat. Then he smiled and looked up in mock relief. "Sorry," he said, "they've been here all the time. I couldn't feel them and I was sure I must have dropped them in here. Never mind, I won't have to sleep in the car tonight. Good heavens, is that the time?" he asked drawing everyone's attention to the clock. "I must be off soon, but there's still time for a swift half, eh."

*

He arrived back at his flat around eleven o'clock that evening, threw his coat onto a chair, kicked off his shoes and left them one each side of the hall. He hung his jacket on the hallstand and went into the living room.

There was no one there now to correct him and tidy up after him. He missed that. A million thoughts invaded his mind but they were so diverse that he could not seem to get them into any order, or indeed string any of them together, so he did what he always did: poured a very generous double Scotch and sat in his armchair. Hell, there was nobody to say 'no' or 'take it easy on that stuff'. This was the worst part of the day for him, and it had been since Julie had left.

First things first: he had just chased a drunken member of what he felt sure was a foreign criminal gang through the country lanes. The foreigner's car had crashed onto the railway line and burst into flames, and he had left the scene of the accident not knowing whether the driver was dead or alive. That was something he was not at all proud of at this moment. Perhaps the Scotch would ease his conscience. It did not, so he poured another.

The next problem that occurred to him was that three women were also exercising his mind a great deal.

There was Jill Franks, the girlfriend of a dead local criminal. She was missing, and to complicate matters, Farrel knew that if and when she was found, he would have to tell her of her loss.

Then there was Julie, the young woman who had reawakened a part of his life that had lain dormant for something like four years but who was half his age. She was completely besotted with him, and although he did not feel quite the same, there was a strong urge to be with her again.

The other woman, Elizabeth, was, he considered, the one with whom he wanted to share much more of his life. Their relationship was beginning to blossom again and he liked the idea, but he could not go to her and talk through his troubles as he had put her and Julie together in the same apartment. So now, he had to tough it out alone. A third double whisky did not help matters either, so around one o'clock in the morning he poured another.

Sitting in his favourite armchair in an alcoholic haze and with all the characters and problems circulating uncontrollably in his mind, he drifted into sleep.

31

At six the next morning Farrel awoke in his armchair, where he had spent the whole night in an alcohol-induced sleep, with a high-pitched electronic buzzing in his ears. Slowly he opened his eyes; the light hurt them so he closed them again, but the buzzing continued. Moments later, he realised that the sound was coming from his alarm clock. It was loud, damn loud, and it was coming through the open door of the bedroom. It would continue to do so until he did something about it.

He staggered up from the chair cursing, stiffly stumbled into the bedroom and slammed his hand down on the off button until it became silent. Then he sat down again in the chair to gather what thoughts he still had. His head felt as if there were a blacksmith inside it beating enough horseshoes into shape for a troop of the Household Cavalry. The taste in his mouth and on his tongue made him feel as if he had been sucking on some filthy much-used carpet and his stomach was certainly not holding back in its complaining.

I wonder if Jim Carrow's beer was off last night, he considered perhaps unreasonably. In an effort to give himself a feeling of being part of the human race again, he took a shower and shaved—he felt a little better. He needed something to eat, so he did what he had often done before in his bachelor days: he made a bacon sandwich and a pot of very strong, black coffee. Both tasted good, but he had the feeling that his stomach would rebel at some point later in the day. However, he would take care of that when it arose, and anyway he felt much better now. It was amazing the difference the three or four cups of coffee made.

He looked around before he left for the office and tidied up the place as much as he felt it needed—which was not much. He was easily satisfied. As he left the apartment, he made a note on locking the door to get someone to come and tidy up the damaged woodwork and paint it.

He went down to his car, climbed in and switched on the ignition; the clock showed seven-thirty. He was aware that at that moment he still had far too much alcohol in his system to safely drive, but if he was very careful and did not get into any scrapes on his way to the office, he would be early. That would give him some more time to recover and possibly get some paperwork done.

He was sat behind his desk at seven forty-five but had no inclination for any paperwork, so he decided to go to the police canteen for a little more breakfast. Another bacon sandwich and two more cups of very strong, black coffee made him feel much more alive, and he returned to his office at eight-fifteen.

Five minutes after his return his phone rang. He picked up the receiver. "Farrel," he announced in his usual curt manner.

"Mr Farrel, it's Jill Franks," a small and very frightened voice came from the earpiece.

Farrel breathed a silent sigh of relief and offered up a prayer of thanks.

"I just thought I ought to let you know that I am okay. I haven't been out a lot and I'm staying with friends."

"I'm pleased to hear that, Jill," Farrel replied. "Where are you?"

"I'd rather not say," she ventured. "You know how stories get out, and I don't want *anyone* to know, and I do mean *anyone,* until Tommy comes back. By the way, have you heard anything about where he might be?"

"No, not yet," he lied, "but when we hear something, we'll let you know, and you're quite right, don't let anyone know where you are. Ring me when you can, and I'll see what I can find out about Tommy."

"Thank you, Mr Farrel," Jill agreed and hung up.

So, she was still around, scared witless, but still alive, which was more than her late boyfriend. He would have to let her know eventually and he decided to do it the next time she contacted him.

*

The morning briefing was different from most of the others. There were many items to discuss and information to share. Between the time he had spoken to Jill and the time that the briefing had started, he had received details of Tommy Acton's post mortem.

Tommy's lungs were indeed full of seawater, but that was not what had really killed him. It was only a contributory factor. Even if he had been a strong swimmer, he would not have swum far with the massive overdose of heroin that was present in his blood. That in itself, in the opinion of the pathologist, would have killed him in 'next to no time'.

The doctor also ventured that he would have been barely conscious when his body entered the water. During his thrashing about as the cold water revived him for a few moments, it was likely that he ingested a huge amount of it and that was why he had the seawater in his lungs.

The information was disseminated and there was great concern yet not much surprise when the cause of death was announced. The next piece of information that Farrel gave out interested everyone.

"I heard from Jill Franks this morning, just a little while ago, in fact," he announced, "and she tells me she is fine; scared, but fine, and that she is staying with friends. I don't know where and at this stage I don't want to. She is safe. That's the main thing and she will contact me as and when she needs to."

There was a murmur of relief that she had not joined Tommy in the next world. Farrel cast his eye over all the men gathered there but did not notice any of them showing any undue surprise.

"Now, there is one thing you should know," he confided in something of a conspiratorial tone. "Tommy Acton kept a type of diary and in it he wrote down what he was doing and where he was going. I understand from Jill it was, if you like, some sort of safety net. He had expressed the sentiment that if he was ever picked up and sent down, he would take others with him."

The squad appeared stunned for a moment or so.

"Never thought he was the vindictive type," George Preston opined, "but there you are, everyone's different."

"Where's the diary, guv?" DC Dick Johnson asked. "Do we have it?"

Everyone was eager to hear Farrel's reply.

"No, we don't have it, yet," Farrel answered. "I do know where it is but I'm not at liberty to say, and, anyway, it's not going to be easy to get at it, at least not for the time being."

"Jill knows where it is then," Perkins thought aloud.

Farrel nodded and then dismissed the others to their assigned inquiries.

*

Later that afternoon Farrel made a few discreet enquiries. He also received a report from the local traffic department that contained details of the fatal accident near Cranton. The report stated that there was only the driver in the car when it crashed onto the railway line and burst into flames. The driver appeared to have been killed by the impact, but his body was also badly burned. According to what remained of the charred documents that survived, his name was Dimitri somebody. Most of the documents were destroyed in the fire and it was quite by chance that that particular small part had not been burned. It turned out that the East-West Farms Ltd. Company owned the car.

The report also stated that immediately before the train collided with the wreck, the train driver, for some strange reason, had the impression that there was another car in close proximity to the bridge, but when pressed he was unable to substantiate his impression and so it was assumed he was mistaken.

Farrel added this event to the growing amount of information on his beloved white board. He would share it with the squad later and suggest that perhaps yet another member of the criminal fraternity had upset the leadership and pursued the unfortunate man to his death. He knew that his explanation was good enough to satisfy the squad, at least for now, and that there was no reason anyone would need to ask him about his own whereabouts that night.

There was one thing that crossed his mind though and at the first opportunity he spoke to Copley. "This company—East West Farms; can you find out where the head office and the registered office are for me?"

Copley, true to character, came up with the answer within half an hour. "East West Farms, guv," he announced in a manner as if that was the easiest question that he had been asked in a long time, "Head office is at Cranton Court and the registered office is . . . where would you hazard a guess?"

"At that solicitor's office in London?" Farrel ventured.

"Right first time, guv. Joseph Kos and Sons."

"They're all in it together, aren't they?" Farrel concluded. He did not feel surprised.

Copley nodded his agreement.

Farrel made a telephone call to one of his colleagues in the traffic department. He requested that as there was an ongoing enquiry relating to all foreign workers in the vicinity, he would like to accompany the traffic department officer when they visited Cranton Court, or Court Farm regarding the fatality. His request was readily granted and immediately he sought out DC Copley, the 'electronic whiz-kid'

32

The following morning, Farrel arrived at Cranton Court together with an old colleague, Inspector Frank Davies of the Traffic Department. Inspector Davies could have made the visit the previous evening, but Farrel had suggested that if it they made it during daylight hours, it could be more advantageous. After parking the car on the forecourt of the 'big house', Davies rang the doorbell. Farrel quickly checked that the various tiny electronic equipment gadgets secreted on his person were positioned so that they were not obvious and no wires were visible.

Two tiny cameras, one on each cuff to appear as links, should be enough to record anything that Farrel considered he might need. He had requested two just to make sure that they matched, so that people's attention would not be drawn to an odd-looking pair of cufflinks. The ultra-thin wires to the recording centre passed up his sleeves to the small box positioned carefully in his inside jacket pocket. A microphone, which was also connected to the small recording device, was carefully concealed behind the top button of his jacket. That way he could quietly record his observations of the places he was able to visit without others hearing, and, in addition, it could pick up any stray conversations from anyone employed at the 'big house', or the farm.

He did not have permission to carry this equipment, so, strictly speaking, his actions were not legal and therefore any evidence collected would be inadmissible in a court of law. Farrel, however, had his own way of doing things and Copley had readily agreed to provide him with the equipment. *So different from his bloody uncle,* Farrel thought for the umpteenth time.

A man dressed in a dark suit answered the door and seeing a uniformed police inspector, ushered them inside. As he looked around, Farrel could see that this was the business section of whatever was going on.

Doors led off the main oak-panelled hall but they were all closed. Farrel quickly took two or three photographs to capture the layout before they were shown into a large room, a modern office that retained remnants of a bygone era.

The man seated behind the desk did not get up as they entered but he indicated for them to sit on chairs facing him.

"I suppose you are here to talk about that accident," the man behind the desk surmised. His voice was heavily accented and he spoke with similar intonations as Scarface.

"Yes, we are," Davies replied. "I'm very sorry to bring you the news. The man was found to have far too much alcohol in his blood to drive and it appears he lost control of the vehicle at the bend near the railway bridge. I understand that he worked here at Court Farm, so I have to inform you of the facts as we have no one else we can contact to let them know of the tragedy."

The man let out a snort of disgust. "The man was a fool," he snapped, shaking his head vigorously and angrily. "I bring him over here to work so that he can send money to his family, and what does he do? He drinks too much so that he cannot do his work properly. I give him many warnings, but he does not take notice and look where it has got him." Again he made the same sound of disgust.

"I'm sorry to put you to more bother, sir," Davies went on, "but I shall need to interview the men who were with him and those who worked with him to ascertain his state of health and mind during that day."

Farrel noticed the other man stiffen very slightly; for some reason he was not comfortable with that arrangement.

"Is that really necessary?" he asked. "The man is dead. He drove a car when he was drunk, and now he is dead. I will tell his relatives in Ukraine what has happened and I will tell them it was just a sad accident. Surely that is enough."

"I'm afraid not, sir," Davies persisted. "I have to make a full report about the accident. My headquarters office needs to know, and, of course, all the statistics have to be sent to the Home Office in London."

The man stiffened again and bridled. "Really . . . I do not see why all that is necessary. In my country we go by the facts and leave it at that."

"I'm sorry, sir," Davies insisted. "I really must see the men."

The other man was patently very displeased but he picked up a telephone and gave out some terse instructions. Moments later, the same dark-suited man entered the office. He immediately saw that his boss was angry. His demeanour changed from reasonably friendly to extremely formal, and the look on his face indicated something approaching fear of his superior.

"Come with me, gentlemen," he said holding the door open.

They left the office. The top man inside, Farrel knew, was seething.

"Are you happy so far, Ian?" Davies said quietly to Farrel, so that their guide could not hear as they followed him.

"Magic," Farrel answered back quietly. "You're a good lad, Frank."

The man escorted them towards the back of the house where the decor was less opulent. Farrel imagined that it was originally the area where the kitchen staff and servants would perform many of their duties. Now, dotted around, he could see small desks and cabinets with a few computers. The man introduced himself as Kristof and Farrel had the impression that Kristof was a man used to doing exactly as instructed—nothing more and nothing less. He explained that Dimitri had worked at Court Farm and that it was he and his workmates who had been at the Rising Sun that fateful night.

"I need to see the men," Davies said.

Kristof inhaled deeply. This request was something he too was very nervous about and his hesitation and body language interested Farrel. *Looks as if we are getting somewhere after all.*

Kristof made a quick call from a nearby telephone and a few minutes later a man dressed in the clothes of a farm worker appeared at the door that lead to the outside. They were conducted the three hundred yards or so to the farm where they were shown into the main room of the farmhouse. It had originally served as a kitchen and dining area and Farrel could see that its purpose appeared to have changed little. There was a large, solid fuel cooking range, a food preparation area and a very large table, surrounded not by chairs but by the old-style long forms on which, he considered, anything up to fourteen people could sit around at any one time. He hoped the cufflinks were working correctly. They were not offered a seat; such was the less-than-friendly atmosphere.

"The men who were there will come in a short time," their escort informed them.

"Don't worry about that, sir," Davies assured him in a relaxed manner, "just take us to where they work."

Both policemen realised that this was something that was not going to happen.

As the farm worker turned towards the door Davies looked at Farrel. "Interesting things seem to be happening," he said pulling a face. "Is that why you wanted to tag along?"

Farrel nodded.

"Thought so," Davies murmured.

*

The interviews took place over the next hour and a half. Each man confirmed to Davies what had happened, not once giving Farrel a second glance. When they finished, it was apparent that there were still three other men, not only colleagues of Dimitri but close friends, who were not there at the farm that day, or that is what they were told.

"When will they return?" Davies asked. "I must see them as well."

Farrel knew that it was not important to see these extra men about the death, but it was the Inspector's way of doing everything he could to help his old colleague. All the time that Davies had interviewed the witnesses, Farrel had been circulating the room. Ostensibly, he listened intently to the proceedings, but, in truth, he took as many photographs as he could of both inside the room and through the windows to the outside where the large new barns were located. He also recorded as many conversations as possible, both official and anything that the microphone could pick up from extraneous sources. Later he would bring in an interpreter and get a proper word-for-word translation.

As they walked around outside the farmhouse Farell continued to take as many images as possible. On closer inspection of the newly constructed metal barns they appeared huge, and as they passed any open doors, which were sometimes left open for the large farm vehicles to use, Farrel quickly photographed as much of the inside as he could.

The story was that they produced mushrooms and eggs at the farm. *Must listen out for chickens,* Farell made a mental note to himself. That was the reason for the production to be kept under cover. *I wonder what else they are producing* crossed his mind. He was sure that there was more.

The visit ended and the two of them drove out between the two large stone gateposts and onto the lane. They made a quick visit to the site of the crash. For Davies, it was to make sure that all the evidence had been collected, the fence repaired and a fresh set of bright, shiny chevrons erected. Farrel was more interested in what the surface of the lane showed. There were the skid marks that Dimitri's car had left, only about fifteen feet before the corner, ruts left as the car ploughed across the grass verge through the hedge and into the field. Then there were the signs of the car's path down the embankment.

"Look at that," Davies exclaimed. "How the hell did that happen?"

Farrel made a face and shrugged. "He was that drunk, I guess," he replied, looking back down the lane to where the previous evening he had found it necessary to brake hard. He needed to confirm that his car had left no tyre marks and therefore not suggesting the involvement of another car. When he confirmed the lane surface was clear, he relaxed.

On their return journey, Farrel was able to tell Davies something of their enquiries, but he kept the vast majority back. He did not need any more chances of leaks occurring.

33

Farrel sat waiting at his desk the following morning for the results of his photography expedition the day before together with a transcript of the observations he had made.

He was becoming slightly irritated and impatient. Surely, Copley could have done something for him by the morning, but then he remembered that Copley was doing another piece of research for him that would help greatly if, and when, the farm had to be raided.

The young officer was beavering away on his computer, and, from time to time, Farrel was aware that he kept glancing in his direction, obviously aware of Farrel's impatience. Copley knew the DCI was waiting for every piece of information he could garner and he wanted it 'yesterday' at the latest.

"It's okay, Richard," Farrel called across, at last aware of the young man's discomfort. "Do it as quick as you can. No pressure, eh."

Copley smiled. "It's coming along, guv," he answered. "I'm just waiting for the last of the maps. The photos will be ready within the hour. The transcript will take a bit longer; I'm not a typist. Perhaps you could get one of the secretaries to do it. That would speed things up a bit."

"And it would be all over the division in no time flat," Farrel grumbled. "No, Richard, just do it as soon as you can."

Copley nodded and returned to his 'beavering'.

The telephone rang distracting Farrel. He answered in his usual brusque, efficient manner. The person the other end would know that now was not the time to bother him with trivia. He only wanted good information. The information, however, did indeed interest him.

"Hello, Alan. What have you got for me?" he queried. He listened intently, nodding from time to time. "That sounds interesting. Did he recognise you?" He listened again. "All right, as long as he hasn't realised who you are. Get to the counter and find out where he's booked to. If you need to, use your warrant card but otherwise sweet talk the booking clerk."

There was a pause.

"Low-cost flight. Find out exactly where he's going. We need to be on that flight too, so if you think it appropriate, reserve two seats. Let me know as soon as you can and I'll make arrangements this end. I'll wait to hear from you." He hung up.

Copley looked up; interested to know anything that was likely to take place.

"Something could be about to happen—a wild goose chase maybe, but you never know," Farrel explained.

Copley returned to his screen.

Ten minutes later the telephone rang again. Farrel answered it. "You found out then? Good. When and what time?" He listened again. "All right. Get yourself back here as soon as you can. It'll take about three-quarters of an hour to get to the airport."

Then he rang off.

"It looks as if the taller of the two men that were in Unit 5 when we searched it is making a move," he told Copley. "He appears to have booked a flight, a cheap flight," he stressed 'cheap flight', "to Paris, and so Alan and I will be travelling with him—hopefully without his realising it—and tailing him. We'll need to liaise with your Inspector de Large, so I'll leave it up to you to let him know what's happening. Get him to find us when we arrive."

Copley nodded. "Okay, guv. Paris, you say," he said with a half smile.

"It's not a jolly," Farrel quickly reminded him. "I only wish it were."

*

Farrel and Perkins arrived at the airport with plenty of time to spare, so they tried to keep a very low profile, not wanting the Slav to see them. Farrel reflected on the previous evening when his pursuing of this man's colleague had resulted in the fatal crash, but perhaps this man would lead them towards another piece of evidence for them and Europol.

They held back as the queue formed in the departure lounge waiting for their quarry to board. It was getting late and Farrel thought that the Slav would not show up, but then he caught sight of him standing behind them apparently waiting to board.

"He's here, guv," Perkins whispered.

The queue moved slowly forward.

Just as the two policemen approached the departure gate, the man suddenly left the line and walked quickly to a gate two or three away from the one for the flight to Paris. He showed his papers to the member of staff at that gate and passed through.

Farrel suddenly realised that the man must have spotted and recognised Perkins in the travel agent's office where he had booked his flight and must have changed the flight afterwards.

Both detectives swore copiously under their breath, but, there it was, he had fooled them.

Just before he disappeared from sight, they saw him turn slightly in their direction, offer a hint of a smile and salute them with one finger. There was nothing left to do but get back to the office. Farrel had been outsmarted and he did not like it one little bit.

"I'll have you," he muttered, "and God help you when I do."

"He's going to Amsterdam, guv," Perkins said. "I'll let Richard Copley know. I'm sure he'll take it from there. He's in touch with the Frenchman, and I reckon the Frenchman's in touch with the Dutch."

Farrel nodded but said nothing. There was nothing he could do except mutter another string of obscenities. Things remained that way until they reached the office.

"I'm sorry, guv, it was my fault. I didn't think he'd seen me," Perkins apologised.

"Don't worry about it, Alan. We'll just take it from here." But Farrel would not stop worrying about it. He needed a long time to let this settle.

*

By the time they arrived back at the office, Copley had been in touch with Europol and reported that his earlier advice was not correct. De Large had not really been surprised and said that he would contact his counterpart in Amsterdam. It had to be left there. However, Farrel's vile mood improved when Copley presented him with all the processed photographs and a copy of the transcript. The maps they needed would be finished by the following morning. Farrel felt a little better.

The photographs were inspected and judged for their usefulness. Some were discarded, whilst others appeared much more valuable, particularly one, which showed a dark blue van in the shadowy interior of one of the buildings. The registration number was clearly visible although Farrel had not seen it at the time. They noticed that after comparing the photographs taken at the industrial park, it was that same van.

"So, the two places are linked. Now what I would like to know," Farrel mused, "is how does whatever it is that comes from the Continent get to Larchester? Does the white van with all its different numbers go all the way to France, or does a vehicle come from the ferry and swap its cargo somewhere and then return?"

"I'll get onto that, guv," Copley spoke up. "As far as I am aware, they use CCTV to check on vehicles that use the ship. I'll get on to Inspector de Large and the ferry line to see what they can do."

*

Farrel left the office at five o'clock that afternoon. At that particular moment, there was nothing else for it but pay a visit to Elizabeth and Julie. He was not sure of the sort of reception he would get. Perhaps it would be good, perhaps not, but he needed to sit down and talk to someone. It could not possibly be the type of therapy that Julie had given him, but to be with them, he knew, would make him feel better.

The reception he had was very cordial. Both women made him feel very welcome, although he knew that the atmosphere between them was not always sweetness and light, yet they both made a good effort to hide any negative feelings in front of him. They had drinks and a meal and later they watched some television with another glass of wine.

The news came on the television and halfway through the bulletin there was a report of a plane crash. The report said that a plane had crashed whilst trying to land in a squall. It had landed and skidded off the runway, striking a small concrete building as it slewed round. It was a miracle that there had been only one fatality.

Farrel wasn't really paying much attention to the news. His thoughts dwelled on the merits of Elizabeth and Julie and he considered that he was extremely fortunate to have two such attractive women so close to him, yet so far away at the same time.

"Where did that happen?" he asked, suddenly coming out of his reverie.

"Amsterdam, this afternoon," Elizabeth replied.

Farrel suddenly came to full concentration, particularly when the flight number and photograph of the dead passenger appeared on the screen. The newsreader announced that anyone with any knowledge of the man should get in touch with the authorities.

"*It's him,*" Farrel exclaimed without really believing it. "*It's him, damn it.*"

"Who?" the two women chorused.

Farrel related a very brief account of what had happened earlier that afternoon but missed out all the important parts. They seemed to be satisfied. *God, if this keeps happening, we'll be chasing them all to death and never know what they've been up to.*

✳

The next morning it was the talk of the squad room. Inspector de Large had been in touch and had indicated that the French and Dutch police did know of the man and his links with the Eastern European group. Farrel was now in possession of another piece of the puzzle.

34

For some days nothing happened at the units in the Industrial Estate, and nothing appeared to be happening at Court Farm either. Farrel waited, more impatient by the day, for some news. Nothing came through from Europol, so he surmised that his squad were back to doing everything in isolation. So far, Elizabeth was coping with Julie, and occasional visits indicated that they were getting on reasonably well, but he still felt uneasy whenever he went there.

Another piece of the puzzle was added before long. Copley had received advice from the French that the British-registered vehicles never crossed the Channel from Dover. Each time the Continental arm of the business, as they called it now, moved something, it was a French-registered vehicle which crossed to England. The same vehicle returned to Calais on a ferry usually about an hour, or, at most, two hours later.

"Have they never searched the vehicle?" Farrel asked rather incredulously.

"Yes, they have, guv," Copley replied, "and with dogs, but each time they do, it turns out the same as it has been for us. The van is clean. There is a feeling that there must be some concealed spaces somewhere in the vehicle, but after so many abortive searches and the ferry traffic being so heavy, the French are waiting, like us, for something to happen. The police there have had the company's legal team screaming 'hassle'."

Farrel nodded his appreciation of the situation. "I bet they have," he muttered and left it at that.

*

Later that evening, Farrel enjoyed a quiet pint at the Royal Oak on the Barnchester Road whilst thinking through everything that had and had not happened in the last few weeks.

He was completely oblivious to the tall, thin young man about twenty years of age and with such a sallow complexion that he looked decidedly unhealthy, who approached the table where he sat.

"Hello, Mr Farrel," he said, doing his best to make it look as if he were surprised to see the Inspector, but failing miserably. Farrel looked up as the newcomer spoke and a frown spread across his face.

"Good grief," he exclaimed quietly and almost to himself but loud enough for the young man to hear. "Look what the cat's dragged in. Mr Roy Rogers."

The man's name was actually Tony and not Anthony. His parents were both almost illiterate, but, for obvious reasons, he had acquired the nickname of Roy. For a moment Farrel smiled. The old cowboy of those long-ago films was quick on the uptake, good with his horse and fast with a gun, but this Roy Rogers was quick at nothing.

"Well, what does Big Mick's right-hand man want from me? Perhaps I could arrest you for loitering on a pedestrian crossing or something."

The young man stuck the tip of his tongue through his lips at the side of his mouth. A frown settled on his brow and a worried look appeared on his face. He was too slow even to realise that Farrel was joking.

"I ain't done nothing wrong, Mr Farrel, honest," he bleated, believing what he had just said about himself. He slid onto a chair at the next table to Farrel.

"Mr Jeans is very worried," Roy confided.

"About what?" Farrel asked.

"He says he doesn't know where Jill Franks is and he wants to know if you have done anything with her."

"I think you mean he *would like* to know where Jill Franks is, don't you."

Roy screwed up his face again trying to work out if there was any difference in what he and Farrel had both said.

"No, I don't have a clue where she is. I've heard from her, but I don't know where she is."

Roy thought hard. It was obvious he had been told what to say at his 'surprise' encounter with Farrel, but now Farrel's answer had completely thrown him off balance and the usual vacant look once more spread across his sallow, pock-marked face.

Farrel waited a moment for Roy to gather his thoughts, or memory, and then said, "Look, Roy, you tell Big Mick, I'll be here having a quiet pint tomorrow evening at eight. Do you think you can remember that?"

Roy's face registered the difficulty of remembering.

Farrel repeated it slowly as if he were speaking to a hard-of-hearing foreigner who had landed on British soil five minutes ago and who did not speak any English.

"Tell Mick I shall be here at eight tomorrow night. I think he should come himself if he has a problem. Remember, eight tomorrow night. Got it?"

Roy nodded.

"Here at eight, tomorrow night," he repeated as Roy turned to leave. "If he wants to call me, he's welcome to."

Roy nodded. He had a lot to remember.

"Well done, Roy, you'll go places," Farrel called out to him, and then added under his breath. "Wormwood Scrubs, I shouldn't wonder."

Farrel returned to his pint and his thoughts. Something else had been thrown into the melting pot at this point. Big Mick Jeans knew Tommy Acton well and would know Jill to the same degree. He was likely to know all Tommy's friends, and, in addition, where they all lived. So, why send 'thick' Roy to ask where she was? Was he aware of Tommy's fate? It was highly likely that he was, as all the news of criminals spread very quickly through the Underworld.

However, Mick Jeans did not call or turn up the next evening, nor any of the subsequent evenings.

35

At the following morning's briefing Farrel reported on the previous evening's meeting. There was an audible intake of breath around the squad room.

"So," Farrel concluded, "we don't know where Jill Franks is and Mick Jeans' bunch doesn't know either. I think she's safe for the moment but in hiding somewhere, otherwise it means we have a real missing person on our hands."

"Don't we have any idea where she might be?" George Preston asked.

"Not at the moment. So, we'll have to have a look around and visit absolutely anyone who knows Jill or knew her in the past. Putting it simply, we just have to find out where she is."

The meeting broke up. The most important thing to do was to find Jill Franks or where she had been seen last, before anyone else did. If she had already been found and in particular by the foreigners, she could already be dead. If that were the case, he had to get to the package that Jill had deposited in the bank. Until he knew for certain, the bank manager would not be content to release it.

*

The first thing he did was visit Elizabeth's apartment where he broke the news to her and Julie.

"It's not done to frighten you," he warned, "but I have to make sure you know what the position is and to ask you to take even more care."

"But I have to go out from time to time," Elizabeth protested. "I need to do some shopping."

"And I'm going crazy locked up here like a prisoner," Julie added.

"I know it's difficult," Farrel agreed, "but at least we know you are alive. At this stage we can't be sure about Jill. The last time I heard from her she was in hiding, but that was then."

"But we must buy food," Elizabeth insisted. "I can go out and do that. We do have the security door of the flat and the C.C.T.V camera above the lift door looking along the hall outside."

Farrel considered for a few moments.

"All right," he agreed, "but only you go, Liz. Julie, you must stay here inside. We can't risk you being seen out and then followed back here."

The two women agreed. Elizabeth could get out and Julie would have some time alone. Farrel looked at the two before him. *There must be something in Muslims being able to have more than one wife*, he reflected.

*

By late afternoon, Alan Perkins reported that he had located the place where Jill had been staying. It was in a small village some four miles away from Larchester. Jill had gone out the evening before Thick Roy had met Farrel and still hadn't returned. There was nowhere else that her friends—a seventy-year-old couple—could think she could be. She would certainly have let them know if she felt she needed to move to another place. There was nothing left to do but to keep looking. The longer the search went on, the more chance there would be of finding her, or, more likely, her body.

A visit to the bank manager revealed that none of her credit cards had been used and neither had money been drawn out using an A.T.M.

What about the packet that he had for safekeeping? No. It was not possible to let Farrel have it as nothing was certain about Jill. Farrel argued but the bank manager was adamant. No.

*

Two days later, Jill's car, a smart red mini was discovered almost completely submerged in one of the many gravel pits around this part of the county, but Jill was nowhere to be found. There was, however, evidence of people being in the area. The ground had been scuffed up, but being gravel it was impossible to take any useful casts of any of the indentations or arrive at any conclusion as to the size of footwear or tyre tracks.

The gravel pit was a very old one. It was flooded and everyone knew that it was deep with very steep sides. The car had been pushed into it from one of the less steep sides, and it was quite fortuitous that it had been trapped on a ledge just below the surface of the water and had not slid to the bottom, thus never being seen again.

A thorough search of the car yielded Jill's mobile phone, found in the glove compartment. That could prove useful to locate anyone that she had spoken to over the last few days, and to discover where she had been when she had made the calls. However, Jill was still missing and things did not look at all encouraging to the squad.

The search was widened and after another three days Jill's body was found. A dog-walker discovered it when his dog ran off to sniff out something on the steep, bush-covered side of another gravel pit. This quarry was some three miles away from where her car had been found.

Forensics was called in and the police surgeon estimated that she had been dead for some days. Death had been caused by strangulation using a rough cord. It was clear that Jill had struggled with her assailant as her shoes and legs were covered in scratches and remnants of gravel and sand. Comparisons would have to be made in an attempt to find exactly where she had been killed.

The bank was closed and so Farrel decided to get the papers Jill had left there the moment it opened. A photograph of Jill's body would no doubt convince the manager.

Farrel needed as much information as he could get his hands on right now. So much had happened in a short space of time, and it appeared that anyone who was likely to know anything about the newly arrived criminals was being eliminated one by one. The worrying thing for Farrel was that Julie was very likely to be on that list. After all, someone had been in her apartment and when they realised she was no longer there, they had intensified their search for her, even breaking into Farrel's own place.

It was time to look more closely into the private lives of Jill Franks and Tommy Acton.

Tommy usually kept on the move. Each time he had been arrested, the form which had to be completed showed N.F.A.—no fixed address. That was only for official purposes. Farrel and his squad knew that he could be found at any one of five addresses. It was just that he had never settled, preferring to pay friends or relatives rent whilst he was living with them.

The occupants of the five addresses would always vouch for Tommy's whereabouts, say what a dependable young man he was, and, if he needed an alibi, they wouldn't fail to provide him with one. There was obviously a good chain of communication between them all because none of the five ever contradicted any of the others. This was what infuriated Farrel. Tommy's friends and family were all well known to the police, not only locally but also in the surrounding counties. The fact that to Farrel they were all rogues did nothing to help in apprehending him. Proof was always needed to gain a conviction, but over the years, ever since his early teenage, no one had quite been able to break down that code.

Farrel despatched various members of the squad on enquiries to each of the five groups, and although he considered it a probable waste of time, it was one of those lines of enquiry that had to be done. He, however, together with DC Copley visited the family of Jill Franks. She was, after all, a piece, albeit just a small piece, in the jigsaw. She was a pleasant enough young woman but did not really have the criminal tendencies that Tommy or his friends had, nor the required amount of intelligence not to tell the truth. It may not be the full truth, but at least there was a much greater element of it than there would be from his other associates.

It was Farrel's task to inform the parents of Jill's death. He was always very formal during this sort of occasion, but Copley was surprised at the amount of sympathy and concern that Farrel displayed towards Jill's parents, particularly the mother.

The tearful outcome was that they knew Tommy, who seemed to them to be a pleasant and caring young man, but they did not approve of his apparent criminal activities even though Jill had tried to convince them that he had had a tough upbringing and was misunderstood for the most part. They had heard that his body had been found, but they knew nothing about the way he had died. They also knew that for some time Jill had been worried about him because he had been associating with some new people who had arrived from the Continent. Jill had told them that Tommy saw this as a way to better himself and make more money. At first, she had been happy with his progress in the group. The amount of his disposable income was impressive, but, as time passed, she became fearful of his deeper involvement with the gang.

"Did he say anything to Jill about anyone from the gang being missing?" Farrel asked.

"I think he must have said something," Mrs Franks replied through her tears, "because that's when she showed signs of worry and then she became very scared. That's why she went to live with her aunt and uncle, my brother-in-law and sister, in Till Cross, about five miles away from Cranton."

There was nothing more that the Franks family could add that was helpful. Farrel gave them his business card and assured them the police would do everything to bring the killers to justice. If they needed any help or remembered any piece of information, all they needed to do was to ring the telephone number on the business card. Then they left.

They climbed into the car and began the drive back.

"Bloody ironic, isn't it," Farrel sighed.

"What do you mean, guv?" Copley queried.

"She went to Till Cross to get away from the gang, little realising that in a small village she would stand out even more. Then there's the fact that she was actually moving closer to their centre of operations. Moth to a flame, like."

Copley nodded and made a face. "I see what you mean," he said. "I guess we now have to go and see the aunt and uncle."

Farrel nodded. "Bitch of a job, isn't it."

Again, Copley nodded in agreement as if to say, *a real bitch of a job.*

*

The visit to Jill's aunt and uncle proved to be of little use. She had moved to their home only two weeks before and for the first few days had preferred to stay inside the house. After that she had ventured out in her car to pay a visit people she knew. It was quite clear to Farrel that these little jaunts out had drawn the gang closer to her. They would know the registration number of the car. It was all too easy.

The last time that the relatives had seen her was three nights before, which turned out to be the probable night of her death. Someone had telephoned the house and the aunt had answered. It was for Jill and shortly afterwards she left in her car saying that she would return by ten thirty, but she had not. They thought she had met someone and was staying with them.

"You know what these youngsters are like these days," the aunt tutted disapprovingly.

Farrel agreed but had a distinct feeling it was likely that she had met someone who had made sure she did not return by ten thirty.

"Was it a man or woman on the phone?" Farrel enquired.

"Oh, it was a man's voice," the aunt replied. "Come to think of it, it wasn't a local accent, more of a foreign sound to it."

That was the end of the conversation and there was precious little more to go on. At least those foreigners seemed to be involved somewhere.

They left the house.

"Well, that's just a little more we know," Farrel said. "Let's get back to the office to see what else has been unearthed."

36

Late that afternoon the detectives all met in the office. It was an opportunity for everyone to report on any progress, or lack thereof, before they left for the evening. As information became available, the white board was beginning to fill with details and photographs. Farrel went through what he and Copley had learned and this was followed by reports from the other members.

No one had found much of any interest. The families had all confirmed that they knew Tommy and Jill and that Tommy had stayed with them from time to time. As far as they were concerned, he was just a misunderstood youngster who had fallen foul of the law.

However, George Preston and Dick Johnson had called on a family who had given a slightly different account of things. Yes, they knew Tommy had been in trouble but nothing too serious until now. Just lately, he had seen less of his old friends, including Mick Jeans, and had been associating with some newcomers. He had become somewhat cocky at first, giving the impression that he was now in a bigger league. His new companions had international status; not just on the local level like Mick. Tommy had been away from home on occasions, sometimes for two or three days, and when he returned, they noticed that he always had a considerable amount of money to spend.

He had told the friends he was staying with at the time that he had been to the docks to pick up a consignment, but he was not forthcoming about what the consignment was, or even whether he knew. On two occasions, he had been to France with another group member and seemed to enjoy what he was doing.

Some two weeks before he had disappeared, he began to show signs of stress and possibly fear. He said very little to his hosts and indicated that he was considering leaving the gang, although he was not sure how to do it. His hosts got the impression Tommy was in deep, too deep, and to leave the organisation was not an option.

The last time they saw him, Tommy seemed very unhappy and also very unnerved. He had been instructed to go with a vehicle to France to pick up what he said was an important load, and perhaps after this he and Jill would be able to 'get lost', as he had put it.

Who the men he was working with were, he could not say. They all spoke with foreign accents and in a foreign language when they spoke together. This, and their attitude, had increased Tommy's mistrust and fear.

The details were logged as appropriate on the sheet. DC Perkins' visit had come up with, as he put it, a big fat zero and Peter Rowles reported the same.

"So," Farrel concluded, "we know we are up against some big boys and we have a pretty good idea that they could be very dangerous, so we still have to keep looking and digging."

37

The bank manager was a little less than helpful when Farrel sat opposite him across the large, highly polished oak desk the next morning.

At least now I know what my investments are used for, he mused as he looked around at the expensive furniture and equipment.

The phone rang and the manager answered it. He listened for a moment.

"I'm busy at the moment, Karen," he said into the phone. "Ask him to ring back in say, fifteen minutes." There followed another pause. The manager's face revealed he was annoyed. He looked uncomfortably at Farrel. "Oh, put him through then," he grumbled. There was another pause.

"Oh, hello, Mr Jeans," he greeted the caller brightly, but Farrel felt sure that he felt highly embarrassed.

Hello, Mr Jeans, Farrel thought incredulously. *Son-of-a-bitch, that's why he's trying to put me off, but he's not going to bloody well do that.*

"I'm very busy at the moment, can I call you back?" Another pause.

"I have Detective Chief Inspector Farrel with me at the moment," he announced, as if warning the caller that he could not possibly carry on the conversation, "so if I may, I'll ring you back shortly."

There was yet another short pause and the manager replaced the phone without the usual 'goodbye'. He looked askance at Farrel. "Mr Jeans is one of our customers, you understand," he stated rather uselessly.

After some twenty minutes, Farrel cradled the valuable package in his hand.

"Did Mr Jeans mention anything about this?" Farrel asked.

The manager huffed and puffed a little but finally said that it had not been mentioned.

Not yet, but I'll bet a pound to a pinch of 'whatsit' it soon will.

As he left the bank, Farrel slipped the package into his briefcase, closed it and patted it almost lovingly. He climbed into his car and threw the case onto the passenger seat next to him. "Perhaps this is where we get some luck going our way, Ian, old boy," he said aloud to the empty vehicle.

Before he had chance to start the engine, his mobile phone rang.

"It's Liz."

She sounded very worried.

"What's the problem?"

"Julie's not here."

"What!"

"I had to go out this morning, so I locked everything up as you said and left Julie safely inside. Anyway, when I got back five minutes ago, she wasn't there. She's gone."

"Gone?"

"I think you should come here as quickly as you can. I won't move anything. See what you think."

"Give me twenty minutes," Farrel replied. Now he was worried.

For some reason, before he gunned the engine into life, he pulled the package from his case, pushed it into the glove compartment and locked it.

"Damn," he complained loudly, "we get once piece of luck, but then this."

*

It took him only fifteen minutes to complete the journey. When he arrived at the apartment block, he took particular notice of everything that appeared strange or out of the ordinary. The lift received the same quick scrutiny, as did the hallway leading to Elizabeth's door.

He rang the doorbell. Moments later, the door swung open and Farrel noted the worry etched on Elizabeth's face. He stepped quickly inside but didn't venture any further into the apartment. He gave her a quick kiss and hug in an attempt to reassure her that he was now in charge.

"Now, tell me everything from the beginning: what time you went out, where you went, and what time you came back, and apart from Julie not being here, what else you found."

As he listened he surveyed the space around him.

"Everything is just as I found it," she said, waving her arm around at the interior of the apartment. "When I called to Julie that I was back, there was no reply. Then I saw that her coat was missing, yet she had left her purse with all her credit cards on her dressing table. There are some things lying around on the floor in her room. Not big things, mind you, but items that were usually put away tidily. As you know Julie is a very tidy person."

Farrel summed up the situation before he made his way further into the apartment.

"What do you think, Liz?" he asked, looking into her eyes and waiting for an answer he did not want to hear.

"I think she's been taken."

"But how? Who knows she's here?"

"Well somebody does, it appears. You and I are the only ones who know that she's here, and I certainly haven't told anyone."

Farrel thought back to conversation that had taken place in the detectives' office, and what information he had disseminated. He could not remember giving out such delicate stuff, but then he remembered the anonymous person on the other end of that phone call. 'You have a traitor', it had said.

"I kept my cards close to my chest," he insisted, still at a loss to understand just how Julie could have been snatched away.

"Someone has tied you in with her. They searched her flat, and yours, remember," Elizabeth pondered quietly, "and they somehow tied you in with me and tried their luck here."

"But how did they get in? Oh, I know it's possible to enter through the street door if the person waited for someone else to exit or come in, but how did they get into the apartment?"

"The C.C.T.V. is always working," Elizabeth said encouragingly.

"We'll need to get in touch with the security company," Farrel confirmed. "That, at least, will be a start, but I suppose it'll take time to locate the relevant part of the disc. I'll get it. Young Richard Copley will be eager to sink his teeth into something like this."

Without more ado, and with feelings of fury and worry, he visited the security company office that dealt with Elizabeth's apartment block. He was relieved to find that the chief man was a retired colleague from his earlier police service.

When Farrel explained some very brief details, the hard disc containing the period during which Julie had disappeared, was removed from the relevant machine and made available to him.

"It's the latest piece of equipment we have, and it's pretty clear," his friend assured him. "Well, as clear as anything is these days."

Farrel left with the disc and with the good wishes of the security man.

*

On his return to the office, Farrel found that most of the squad had finished for the day. They had done as much as they could by this stage and as it was half past six in the evening, they had gone their separate ways. It irked Farrel to some degree, but he had to consider that some of the men had families to go home to, whereas he hadn't. His only respite had been with Elizabeth and Julie, but now Julie was missing and somehow he could not bring himself to make the trip to Elizabeth's apartment, certainly not in these circumstances.

Copley, however, was still at his workstation, pondering every possible angle that presented itself to him.

He'll make a damn good copper, Farrel assured himself for the umpteenth time when he saw Copley still working.

"Just in case you're getting bored, Richard, here's something else for you to get your teeth into," Farrel said, as he placed the disc next to Copley's keyboard.

"What's that?" asked Copley. "Something interesting?"

"Julie's gone. I think she's been abducted and this is the disc from Elizabeth's apartment: the one covering the hall between the lift and the apartment door. Have a look at it and let me know what you think."

"Right, guv. When do you want it? Yesterday?"

"Cheeky bugger," Farrel grumbled, but not unkindly. "But it is important though, Richard. It may alert us to something important. Julie's a potentially vital witness."

Copley nodded. "Yes I know, guv. Leave it with me. I've nothing much to do, so I'll have a look before I go home. I'll let you know if anything crops up tomorrow morning."

"Good man!" Farrel had noticed how quickly Copley had melded into the squad and how he instinctively knew what was important. "Good man," he repeated rather absent-mindedly.

He turned to leave and as he did so he laid a hand on Copley's shoulder. He was worried, it showed, and Copley noticed it.

Farrel drove back to his apartment deep in thought. He wanted to see Elizabeth and talk things over with her to reassure her that he was going to do everything he possibly could to find Julie. He knew that she and Julie had seen themselves as competition for his affections, but now it was clear to him that Julie was currently ultra-important.

*

He arrived back at his apartment around seven in the evening. His first task was to pour himself his usual whisky. Tonight he poured not a generous double, but something much larger. He kicked his shoes off, leaving them near the hallstand where he had slung his coat and then he sat down in his favourite chair in the living room where he started to sip the warming drink. Still he could not really think through what was happening to him. This whole thing was now so personal. Perhaps he should hand it over to another officer.

He had this murder enquiry on his hands, but there too in the background was the thought of this lovely young woman who had, he was sure, been abducted. She had become very special to him. Was it as a lover, or perhaps because she was so much younger, more like a daughter. He had often thought of what he would do to any man who had abused or done anything to a daughter he might have had. He knew he wanted to take care of her. The poor young thing had experienced a hell of a life up until now, but his conversations with Elizabeth just lately had indicated that Julie was anxious to leave her past behind and strive for something much better for the future. That had pleased Farrel and he felt whatever Julie wanted he would help as much as he could.

There was also Elizabeth. He knew she was, in his terms, 'a hell of a woman' and it was perhaps this thought running through his mind that had made him want to go to her this evening. He also felt it was not the thing to do. He would ring her a little later, somewhere between his microwaved lasagne and his last whisky. He decided not to leave it too late and not too close to his last drink.

The lasagne was reasonably tasty he decided, but nothing like the meals that Julie had prepared—God, he missed her. His dessert was lemon-flavoured yoghurt—good grief, how he had slipped down the ladder.

He finished his meal and poured himself another whisky, roughly the same size as the first. He was becoming maudlin.

"Better ring Liz before I reach a ridiculous state," he ordered himself.

He picked up the phone. It rang out and was answered very quickly.

"Hello, Liz, have you heard anything?" he asked.

"No. I was hoping that your call might be from Julie."

"If you hear anything, you *will* be sure to let me know, won't you?"

"Of course I will. We really must find her. She's changed so much. I never thought it possible, but I'm actually really fond of her now."

"If I hear anything, you'll be the first to know," Farrel promised.

"Are you coming over tonight?" Elizabeth asked.

"No, not tonight," Farrel replied softly, "I've got a lot to get through."

"How's the bottle of Scotch?"

"Not much left."

"Keep it that way."

"Sure, don't worry about me."

"But I do. Take care. Miss you," she whispered into the phone, and repeated, "miss you."

"Miss you too, goodnight."

"Goodnight," Elizabeth echoed into his ear, and he heard the sound of a kiss blown into the mouthpiece the other end.

He hung up and tossed back the whisky. He could handle a murder enquiry and he thought he might be able to handle two women he was keen on, but put the two together, and it became something of a Gordian knot.

Before he poured his third whisky, he decided he should do the washing up, so he deposited all the utensils and plates into the kitchen sink. Then he decided they could wait until morning, and he poured another whisky.

Around midnight he decided to go to bed. He had all the details of the case firmly in his mind, even with the whisky now in his blood stream trying to muddle the facts. He had always been able to sort the facts into the right order when it came to police work. It was those personal parts of his life that never seemed to slot into place.

He went to bed with the fourth whisky nightcap. It did the trick and he fell into a surprisingly dreamless sleep.

38

Farrel awoke with a splitting headache at six o'clock the next morning after six good hours of sleep. Plenty of black coffee, his usual antidote to a binge the previous evening, seemed to work well, and after a shower and a breakfast of two bacon sandwiches, he returned to feeling human again.

There was nothing to hang around the apartment for so by seven thirty he was at his desk. One of the desk sergeants from the front office reception knocked on the office door and entered.

"Morning, guv'nor," he greeted Farrel brightly. "Lovely day."

"Hello, Alf," Farrel replied slowly. "I suppose it could get better."

The headache was beginning to recede.

"Ah, I see." Alf gave him a knowing look. "I don't usually get to see dead men walking around, at least not this early in the morning."

He paused and Farrel smiled weakly back at him.

"We received a phone call earlier this morning from an Inspector de Large," Alf went on. "He sounded foreign to me. He didn't say much but he wanted to speak to you."

"How much earlier?" Farrel queried rather aghast that someone other than shift workers were at work that early.

"Around six thirty."

"Good grief, they must start early in France. The accent was French, Alf."

"Oh, I see. Don't forget they are an hour ahead of us."

"Yeah, well they would be, wouldn't they? It's still a bit early for me at the moment."

"Anyway, he left a message for you to ring him when you can. I got the impression it could be urgent." He dropped a sheet from a message pad onto Farrel's desk with a telephone number. It had the French international dialling code on it.

"I've no doubt about that, Alf. I hope he has some better info than we have so far."

"Nobody's heard any more about the young woman as far as I know," Alf sympathised, "but as soon as the uniform boys find anything, they'll inform you too."

"I'm sure of that, Alf, thanks."

The sergeant left the office and Farrel to his thoughts. He would leave the phone call for Copley to make; after all, he had all the dealings so far with the French Inspector.

For half an hour Farrel considered all the places he should send the men to search plus all the people that should be interviewed. It was unlikely that Julie was being held at the industrial estate, assuming, of course, that she was still alive. It was that frightening thought that gave him so many problems. This gang was ruthless and it was certain that they would cover their tracks as quickly and completely as possible. On the other hand, they must have invested a huge amount of time and money to reach the stage they were now at.

The farm and the 'big house' at Cranton remained the best bet, but there was no concrete evidence on which to go on to apply for a search warrant. Snooping was the only answer, but he knew that DC Copley's uncle, the Assistant Chief Constable, would certainly not approve. The Chief Constable himself would not give the green light to anything clandestine, although if end result proved useful, he would find a way of justifying the activity. He had done that in the past. That is why Farrel respected the man.

The more he considered this approach, the more it seemed to be the only way. He thought back to the evening when Richard Copley had produced his electronic equipment for making observations on an 'unofficial' basis. The young man had subsequently revelled in the notoriety he had seemed to gain, and Farrel considered on reflection that 'dodgy' methods would reach neither the Assistant Chief Constable's ears, nor desk, through his nephew. Farrel knew he could trust the young man implicitly, even if his uncle was less of an ally.

The detectives were all at their desks by eight fifteen and after a résumé of where they were at, each man left the office, except Copley, whom Farrel had asked to remain behind.

"Remember Inspector de Large?" It was a rhetorical question.

"Yes, guv, of course," Copley replied, frowning.

"He rang the front desk this morning and left a message for us to contact him." He pushed the paper across his desk for Copley to read. Copley nodded and noticed the 'us'. He looked quizzically at Farrel.

"I thought I'd leave it to you to do the honours. After all, you have spoken to him before and seem to be buddies, and, as I understand it, your French appears to be excellent."

Copley smiled. "Well, not quite buddies," he grinned, "but I'll be happy to talk to him for you."

"Good man," Farrel said. He had now started to refer to Copley as 'man' and no longer son, and Copley responded well to the trust being accorded to him.

Copley made the call. It was only very brief but before it ended, Copley had referred to Farrel.

"He wants to meet you face to face," Copley announced. "He's not happy about using post or emails, so he says he'll travel over to England by ferry to meet you to talk. He's suggested somewhere discreet. He has a file to give you. It seems it's a duplicate of everything he has."

"When does he want to meet?" Farrel was pleased.

Copley returned to the phone then turned towards Farrel. "As soon as possible."

"Tomorrow? After all we have two bodies that we know of and a missing person."

Copley nodded and returned his attention to the phone, making a few notes as he continued the conversation.

"Tomorrow is fine, he says," Copley reported. "He'll come over on the ferry that arrives in Dover around ten in the morning. It seems that our friends, for the want of a better word, never use the really early ferries, or at least haven't done so far."

"Excellent," Farrel nodded, feeling more at ease with this step forward. "Tell him we'll meet him at the closest motorway rest area to Dover." He paused. "I'll leave that up to you to organise."

*

By the evening, all the local places had been checked out. Jill's room had been searched but nothing of any help had been found. Tommy's various places of abode had been looked over too, but again there was nothing to go on. Careful observations had been carried out on the buildings on the industrial estate, but no one had visited it all day, and judging from what nearby businesses had reported, it had not been used for two or three days.

"I don't care what happens, that place is going to undergo a minute search," Farrel thundered. "There must be something there. Isn't there a law of physics to confirm it?" He looked at Copley with a look of query on his face and a smile. The other men also glanced at the young man. Copley shrugged and smiled.

"Can't help you there, guv," he replied. The others all laughed and Farrel and Copley joined in. Copley knew he was being ribbed and he was quite happy to take it.

"By tomorrow morning, George," Farrel stated, "you and the rest of the boys are going to give that place such a going over. I want anything and everything that looks as if it could be evidence collected. I don't care about the consequences. I want anything that could yield DNA through bloodstains or the like. Now Dick and Alan, I want you to go and baby-sit those two places right now. Guard them as if they contain the Crown Jewels. I don't want anyone getting wind of anything until after tomorrow afternoon."

He remembered the warning about the 'traitor'.

"Where will you be, guv?" DS Preston asked. "Will you be with us or here when it's all happening?"

"I have another meeting arranged," Farrel said, "and Richard here is coming with me, aren't you?" he added as he looked across at Copley.

"Am I, guv?" Copley looked surprised, "Oh, yes, of course I am."

That left everyone wondering why Farrel would want to take the Assistant Chief Constable's nephew with him. Farrel imagined that some of them probably thought he was trying to sweeten a meeting with the ACC. *If that's what they think*, thought Farrel, *so much the better*.

39

Half past seven the next morning found Farrel and Copley heading towards the Channel port: a journey of about two and a half hours. As they left Larchester, Farrel decided it was a good time to tell Copley why he had chosen him to accompany him.

"You were the one that came up with the idea of contacting Europol," he said, "and so, therefore, I think it best that you continue this line of enquiry. And, of course, you speak French, just in case our Inspector de Large has problems with English!"

"I speak enough to get me around, guv," Copley explained. "I had a gap year in Paris."

Should have known, thought Farrel.

During the two-and-a-half-hour journey, they talked about tactics, and Farrel became more and more impressed by Copley's grasp of what was needed. His squad was a very loyal group, but there were times that Farrel thought that it should not be necessary to explain things in so much detail, yet here was a young man seemingly streets ahead of the general level of policeman. *He'll definitely go far*, he thought, *a bloody sight further than his stupid uncle.*

Between the time the squad had been dismissed the previous evening and now, Copley had located a restaurant just outside Dover where he thought it appropriate that they could liaise with the French police inspector and he had emailed a vague message that would only have any meaning to the Frenchman.

"From what I have learned," Copley said, "it's a small restaurant and it's located somewhat off the beaten track. Few ferry travellers will use it and it seems a good place to meet up. If anyone is tailing de Large, it is unlikely they will follow him there."

"Good thinking," Farrel commended, "although I'm not really sure what info he has to share with us."

"Whatever it is, guv, he doesn't want to risk someone hacking into his computer system or ours. Delivering it by hand is his preferred method."

"A careful sort then," Farrel opined. "He sounds like my type of guy."

They found the restaurant quite easily and parked their nondescript police vehicle in the side car park. When they entered, they chose a table to one end with an uninterrupted view of the whole of the car park outside. They ordered coffee and croissants and settled down to wait.

Copley consulted his watch. "The ferry should have docked about fifteen minutes ago, guv," he noted, "so, give him half an hour or so to clear the docks and a twenty-minute drive, and, assuming that his satnav is up-to-date, he should be with us in about thirty-five to forty minutes."

"Good," Farrel replied, "I think I could manage another coffee and croissant."

True to Copley's calculations, in forty minutes, a small, black Citroen with French registration plates pulled into the car park. Two men climbed out, and whilst one stayed behind, perhaps to check they had not been followed, the other man, around six feet tall and possibly fifty years of age, walked towards the restaurant. He was slim and had the air of a man of authority.

Farrel stood, and leaving Copley seated, he crossed towards the newcomer.

"Inspector de Large?" he ventured quietly.

"Ah, Detective Chief Inspector Farrel, I presume," the Frenchman replied, also quietly holding out his hand and smiling broadly.

"I have a table over there," Farrel nodded towards Copley as they shook hands.

De Large followed Farrel to their table where Farrel introduced the two.

"I am pleased to meet you, monsieur," de Large said as they shook hands. "I think it is with you I have been having contact, yes?"

Copley nodded. "Yes," he replied. "I'm very pleased to meet you, sir."

The second Frenchman arrived.

"This is Pierre, my assistant," de Large said, introducing him. There were handshakes all round and then they called for more coffee.

"We need to return to Dover as soon as possible," de Large told them. "We must be on the very next ferry back to France. There is much to do."

Farrel nodded. "I understand," he said.

Inspector de Large took a large black briefcase from Pierre, unlocked it and removed a brown package. He slid it across the table to Farrel.

"This is all the information we have on the case that we are working on together," he confided. "Any more and we will send it to you, even if we have to meet like this. These people are very, how do you say, very astute, and I am not sure that our Internet communications are completely secure from them."

He looked at his watch and stood up as he finished off his coffee. The other man did the same.

"We really must go now, Chief Inspector. We must catch the ferry, you know. If we have been followed at least some of the way, we must try to keep them guessing, yes?"

Farrel smiled. "Of course, Inspector. It has been good to meet you. Let's hope the next time will be in much more relaxed circumstances."

The four of them all shook hands and de Large and Pierre left.

"They'll get the same ferry back okay," Copley confirmed, looking at his watch.

Farrel peered into the open end of the large envelope. He carefully slid the sheaf up out of the envelope, just so that he could read the title, which was type written on the top in capital letters: HYDRA.

"Hydra," he puzzled, recalling the name from his school days but not quite bringing its meaning to the fore, "what the hell is that?"

Copley thought for a few moments. "Hydra," he said, "is a microscopic creature, or something from Greek mythology. If it's the latter, it's talking about a multi-headed serpent. When one head was cut off, two more grew, but there was only one head that was mortal, and to kill the Hydra it was necessary to find that head and cut it off. That's all I can think of."

Farrel stared at him. "If it's what I think it is, then we have at least one mountain to climb with this case, possibly more."

Copley took a closer look at the typescript. "It looks as if it's all in French, guv," he said.

"Can you translate it?"

"Yes, I think so. There's a lot by the looks of it, but I'll get the gist as soon as I can, and then the rest as and when it's possible."

"Gist of it by when?" Farrel asked raising his eyebrows with the question.

Copley looked at his watch and drained his coffee.

"We should be back in the office around half past one. Say a basic idea by tomorrow morning when we get together again. There's also the disc from Mrs Coulter's apartment."

"Right," Farrel agreed, "but I want to digest it all before I say anything to anyone. I'm not happy about what's going on in Larchester."

Copley frowned but said nothing. If Farrel wanted to keep it close to his chest, then he had a very good reason for it.

40

Farrel was at his desk early the next day at six thirty. He had not slept well the previous evening; even three whiskies had not helped him relax. There were far too many things running through his mind to allow space for sleep.

Inspector de Large's visit, for one thing, had raised so many issues, particularly the mention of some multi-headed monster running a crime syndicate. However, the thing that exercised his mind and worried him most was the whereabouts and the condition of Julie.

It was strange, he thought, in those small hours when he could not get to sleep, how Julie had somehow invaded his life. He knew her background yet the relationship had become very intimate, so much so that the physical aspect of the relationship aside, he felt he was responsible for her well-being. After all, she had no family and life was a struggle.

He put the thought of her past to one side and mused upon the fact that, after all, he would not really mind having her as a daughter now. Of course, he would have to discount the fact that they had been lovers.

The more he thought along these lines, the more he realised that perhaps this was the real reason he felt so close to her. Then there was Elizabeth. She too had a past, and had connections with the Underworld since their very close relationship in their earlier years. His feelings for her were more intense now than ever before, and he felt that the future did perhaps hold something for them both.

Sleep had come eventually and he dreamed of holding both women in his arms and at the same time trying to fight off a multi-headed monster. The monster had taken a grip on Julie and dragged her away from him. He awoke in a sweat and thereafter found it difficult to get back to sleep. He could live with Elizabeth, he thought, but he would need Julie around to make the circle complete.

He was, in truth, glad when his alarm clock dragged him back from his troubled sleep at six o'clock the next morning. He got up straightaway, showered, and quickly ate a breakfast of orange juice together with toast and marmalade, and, of course, the usual strong black coffee. He did not have time to waste doing chores in his lonely apartment. *Let's get into work and find out what Copley found out, however little it may be.*

It was seven ten when he arrived at his desk. The office was deserted. He looked at his watch. *Where the hell are they all?* He was anxious to get the wheels rolling, what with Julie missing too.

Copley was the first to arrive.

"You look as if you've been up all night," Farrel observed.

Copley certainly gave the appearance of a man who had had very little sleep. His eyes were red rimmed with dark patches underneath. He smiled weakly.

"Not quite all night, guv," he mumbled as he sat down wearily at his desk in front of his computer.

Farrel felt impatient but fully realised that the young man had been working and not out on the town since he had seen him last.

"Did you find anything interesting in the file?"

"You could say that."

"Tell me."

"Well, according to the French police, they have been in contact with many other countries before we had even heard anything about this situation. This Hydra organisation is a problem, a really big problem. Even now no one knows for sure just how big, but it appears to be global." He paused.

"This doesn't sound good at all," Farrel remarked quietly. "Go on."

"As far as I can tell, every developed country in the world is having a problem with them to some extent."

"Now us," Farrel interjected.

Copley nodded. "Now us."

"It even has the CIA and the FBI very concerned, to say nothing of Interpol, Europol, the South African BOSS and even MOSSAD in Israel."

"What else have you been able to glean from the file?" Farrel asked. "Any good news?"

"Not a lot so far, but it seems they have their fingers in many pies. The French police haven't lost their two agents. They are still working deep under cover and it's these two men who have provided a lot of the important info. According to these agents, Hydra is moving drugs around, into Europe as well the US. They are using channels from places in the Far East and Afghanistan through Iran, Iraq, Turkey and Eastern Europe. Then from South America into the States via the usual routes, through Mexico etcetera, and to Europe through South Africa, West Africa and Morocco, to Spain and France. It's big, very big, to say the least."

"You can say that again," Farrel remarked. "So, we are looking at a worldwide group smuggling drugs, not as we thought, just from Eastern Europe?"

"Right," confirmed Copley, "but, unfortunately, that's not the end of it."

Farrel looked at him with one of his quizzical looks.

"No, it seems they are into a lot more. They're into people smuggling as well. Not just the little bits of illegal immigrants from the Third World all wanting a better life in the West; that's very lucrative for them, of course, but they are also moving the less desirables about as well. These are the important ones. If they have any trouble with the little men, they can lose them, ditch them or just get rid of them, but these other people are often what would have been called in the old days 'agent provocateurs'. These days, of course, we tend to call them terrorists. Some come through Afghanistan, Iran, and Iraq, like the drugs, others perhaps from the Indian sub-continent. And others, particularly as far as the US is concerned, from South America."

"Sounds more like a covert world war," Farrel thought aloud.

Copley nodded his agreement. "Absolutely," he confirmed grimly, "and it doesn't end there."

"I thought you were going to say that," Farrel grumbled.

"No, as I said, smuggling drugs and people has given them proven routes and it doesn't take a lot of imagination to realise that they're into gun running as well."

Farrel rubbed his chin and shook his head almost in disbelief.

"Tell me more," he sighed, "I'm all ears."

"They're running guns into the UK. It appears that there is more than one dissident group in Ireland that wants to either arm or re-arm, and, to round things off, it seems that they'll do anything for any terrorist group that pays enough."

Farrel sat quietly, reflecting on the report,

"Is there *any* good news at all?" he asked finally, letting out a long, slow breath.

"Not that I have found out so far, guv. What do they say? Everything comes in threes?"

He paused and then said, "Give me a bit more time and I should be able to report with more info as time goes on."

"Do we know if they own any politicians or policemen who might be involved as well?"

"No one knows for sure, but the organisation is so large and powerful that it's highly like that a fair few are in their pocket."

Farrel's mind went back to the phone call: *there is a traitor.* Where or who, no one knew; police or civilian, high position or low, it was still a mystery. He had to keep so much of this to himself until he knew whom he could trust.

"Well done," Farrel commented eventually, then again he repeated, "Well done? What the hell am I talking about 'well done'? There's nothing 'well' about anything I've heard this morning, but, then again," he said looking at Copley, "you know what I mean."

Copley grinned and nodded. He knew exactly what Farrel meant.

"By the way, guv," Copley said, "I have the disc from Mrs Coulter's apartment block hallway, but I've only had a quick look at some of it."

"And . . . ?" Farrel looked up quickly.

"Nothing yet, but there's a great deal on it, of course, and . . ."

"Yes. Of course," Farrel agreed. "When did you do that?"

"Last night."

"But you did that report too . . ."

"Amazing what strong black coffee can do, isn't it?"

"Sure as hell is," remarked Farrel, "but be careful the coffee doesn't kill you."

Farrel looked at the young man and they both laughed at the thought of what coffee might do. It was Farrel's way of showing his concern for Copley and saying 'don't go over the top'. Copley for his part appreciated Farrel's concern for him. He was now beginning to realise fully why the other members of the squad were so loyal.

There were sounds of people arriving in the corridor outside.

"Keep this to yourself. We're not in a position to divulge any of it yet," Farrel counselled as the door opened and George Preston entered.

Copley nodded briefly and started work on his keyboard.

41

"We used the search warrant yesterday, guv, whilst you were away," George Preston reported, as soon as he arrived at the office.

"Any good?" Farrel enquired.

Many things must have been left behind but were they of any use? The gang appeared to have deserted the two units and moved on to a place they considered a lot safer for them, so it was unlikely they would knowingly abandon any evidence, but one could always hope.

"We did a fingertip search of the whole place. It looked squeaky clean but we picked up a lot of stuff anyway. It's all at forensics now," the detective sergeant continued.

"So, how long is it going to take before we can see the first results?" Farrel asked.

"Shouldn't be too long," Preston replied. "Three or four hours and we should start to get the first set of details."

"Okay," Farrel nodded. "I'm off out. I have some enquiries of my own to make. I'll be on my mobile, so let me know the moment anything comes through."

"Right, guv," Preston replied as Farrel left the office. "Okay then, you all know what you have to do," Farrel heard him say to the rest of the detectives as he walked down the corridor.

*

Farrel looked at his watch. It was five thirty. *Time for a drink at The Rising Sun and a chat with old Harry, if he's there.*

He drove to Cranton and parked the car in the pub's car park. Inside, he found no one except Jim Carrow behind the bar polishing the glasses. Farrel ordered a small lager and sat on his usual barstool at the end of the bar so he had a view of the whole area. He didn't want to miss a thing.

"Is Harry likely to be in tonight?" he asked.

"Harry's always here around half six, usually without fail, but, sometimes, like the other night, he doesn't come in until after eight," Carrow replied. "He has a couple and then he's off home quite early. Says he likes an early night so that he can rise early in the morning. Says an hour in the morning is worth two at night. I know what he means but I pull his leg. I always ask him if it was always like that when he was a lot younger and married. He chuckles and taps the side of his nose with his index finger. His eyes sparkle, 'That's for you to wonder sonny,' he always says. He's a real character."

Farrel smiled and nodded.

"A real character," he agreed. "There aren't many of them around these days."

"You can say that again," Carrow concurred. "And he's as honest as the day is long too. Ask him anything about Cranton and he starts off at the year dot and tells you all the history."

"What about recent history?"

"That too—knows it all. He doesn't like much of what's happening here though with the influx of the foreign workers.

He doesn't like them and he doesn't trust them. He'll tell you over a pint."

"Why?"

"He doesn't say. I think he knows something but doesn't let on."

"Really?"

Carrow nodded.

Farrel finished his first beer and ordered another. At precisely six thirty Harry strolled through the door. He nodded to Farrel and greeted Carrow.

"How are you keeping, Harry?" Farrel asked.

"Pretty good for an old 'un," was the bright reply.

Farrel wanted to talk to Harry even more now as Carrow had intimated that he knew everything about everything that went on in Cranton.

"Let me pay for this one," Farrel suggested. Harry's eyes lit up and he smiled.

"Thank you very much," he said. "I'll have my usual—a pint of the best, if you don't mind."

"My pleasure," Farrel replied and laid a crisp ten-pound note on the bar.

Carrow moved away after he had pulled Harry's pint and busied himself at the other end of the bar and in the snug.

"So what's going on in Cranton these days?" Farrel asked.

Harry looked down at the bar where Farrel had left the change from his pint—maybe another one was in the offing.

"Well, not a lot in the village," he drawled in his local dialect, "but I don't reckon them foreigners is up to any good."

Farrel raised an eyebrow in an unspoken query, encouraging Harry to continue.

"I know they keep themselves to themselves mostly," Harry went on, "but they come in here from time to time, and I know that they look at us as if we're country bumpkins, but we ain't."

"I know that," Farrel assured him.

"Anyway, when I've been out walking around the area, I've seen things that I don't like."

"You know the area around here well, I imagine," Farrel supposed. "Lived here a long time. Done a bit of poaching—in your younger days, of course," he added quickly, but with a knowing smile, once a poacher, always a poacher out here in the country.

"I know you're a copper," Harry confided, "but you ain't the sort of copper what's interested in a bit of poaching."

Farrel's face broke into a wide grin. "Spot on, Harry! No, I'm not interested in someone taking a bit of wildlife—or even semi-wildlife, if you know what I mean."

Harry nodded and smiled. "You're interested in them foreigners too, ain't you?" he intimated in a conspiratorial fashion as he tapped the side of his nose with his index finger.

"You could say that," Farrel admitted. "Things have been happening around here and somehow, in my sneaky little copper's mind, I can't see it being a coincidence."

"There's a lot of action that goes on at night—during the hours of darkness, I think you blokes call it. A lot of movement of vehicles coming through the village—light vans and such, so they don't make a lot of noise and they go up to the 'big house'. Well, maybe they go to the farm as well, I can't be sure. There's also something dodgy about them big new barns."

"What do you mean?"

"Don't rightly know, but I've got a funny feeling about 'em."

"Do you hear strange noises coming from that area when you're taking a walk?"

"From time to time—bangs usually—not often though. I put it down to somebody dropping something big and heavy onto something very hard."

Or a shot, Farrel thought. The same type of story had come from Julie about events in the industrial estate in Larchester. *Oh my God, Julie could be there.*

"How often do you think these activities take place?"

"Twice, sometimes three times a week. I took a walk along the road the other day and passed the 'big house' with its big wide gateway. Everything seemed all right then. After a while, I saw where something had hit a wall at the side of the lane and then further along where something had hit some trees. I guess that could have been what that stupid drunken bloke did before he went off the road at the railway bridge over the cutting."

Farrel nodded. "You're most probably right about that," he agreed. He knew damn well Harry was right.

"Funny thing that," Harry went on, "quiet road with nothing much about and he drives like a madman. Still, I reckon that's one less to worry about."

Farrel nodded again.

The door to the bar opened and three of the foreign workers entered. They looked around and when they saw Farrel and Harry talking at one end of the bar, they made their way to a table at the far end where they sat down. One of them approached the bar and ordered their drinks after which he took them on a tray over to the table.

Farrel and Harry paused their conversation for a moment or two as they watched the men settle down, then they resumed it, but in lower tones. Farrel was facing the three men and immediately recognised two of them as having been at the unit in the industrial estate.

The men were talking quietly and then one by one they turned to take in Farrel and Harry talking at the bar. In Farrel's mind, they did not look happy; their eyes darted from one to the other, then to their drinks and back to the two at the bar. *Shifty individuals with something, if not a great deal, to hide,* he considered. *Need to have a much closer look at the 'big house' and the farm as soon as possible.*

Farrel looked at his wristwatch. "Time's getting on Harry," he pointed out. "I must be on my way."

With that, he placed his glass back on the bar, slid off the bar stool and began to make his way to the door. Then he dug into the inside pocket of his jacket and produced one of his business cards. "By the way, Harry, pop this into your pocket. If you see anything going on that you feel shouldn't be happening up there," he tossed his head to indicate the direction of the 'big house', "give me a call."

Harry took the card and read it. Then he nodded and made a face when he saw Farrel's rank.

"So, I was right then. You ain't just a copper who's interested in poaching. You're after bigger game, ain't you?"

Farrel smiled, nodded and touched the side of his nose indicating for Harry to keep it under his hat.

"You can rely on me," Harry confirmed.

Farrel turned back to the door.

"What about your change?" Harry called to him.

"Oh, buy yourself another, Harry. Thanks for the chat."

Harry smiled, picked up the change and ordered another pint of the best. "Thank you too," he called.

*

Farrel drove back to the office. Some of the forensic reports from the two units were in with more to come. It was always frustrating to wait for the results, although he knew that some would take a long time to complete. Most reported oil—motor oil, bits of detritus from what would have been a working environment, but then there one which indicated the presence of blood—human blood—not in a great quantity but sufficient to suggest that the injury was the result of something more that a cut finger. It confirmed the clandestinely taken and inadmissible evidence.

There was no news of Julie and Farrel was becoming more convinced that she had been abducted. It was highly likely, in his opinion, that she was being held at the 'big house', or the farm. There was little more he could do. Copley was not in the office but he had left a note asking to see Farrel early next morning before the rest of the squad arrived. *What has he discovered now?* He was intrigued but knew that it would have to wait until morning.

When he arrived at his apartment, he tucked in to the burger and fries he'd bought on his way from the office and poured himself a whisky. Feeling guilty about that, he made himself a coffee: black, no sugar. Then he rang Elizabeth to bring her up-to-date as much as he could without mentioning too much of his work. It was very little, but he was glad to hear her voice and have her to confide in, and it was obvious she derived some comfort by talking with him too.

"How's the whisky bottle?" she asked, as she always did when they were about to end the conversation.

"It's still okay," he replied. "I'm drinking coffee at the moment."

"Where's the whisky glass?"

"About three inches to the right of the coffee cup!"

"Be careful, Ian," she advised, her tone very concerned. "I worry about you."

"I'm okay," he assured her. "Good night and sleep well."

"I'd sleep much better if you were here," she said. "Good night."

"I'd sleep a lot better if I was with her too," he announced to the coffee cup and the whisky glass after placing the phone into its cradle.

42

Farrel woke early the next morning. He had not slept a great deal for thinking of Copley's note. What had he found?

Seven fifteen and he was seated at his desk and at seven twenty Copley appeared. He looked as if he was worried about something—something he was going to have to bring to Farrel's attention.

"Morning," Farrel greeted him wearily.

"Morning, guv."

"Found something?" Farrel enquired.

"Well . . . I think so . . . but I'm not sure. I hope I'm wrong, but . . ." He said no more and sat down at his workstation to power up his computer. He appeared to be running something through his mind before saying anything that could make him appear foolish again.

"Guv . . . would you take a look at this, please?" he asked hesitantly.

"What have you got?"

"I hope I'm wrong but I don't think I am."

Farrel left his desk and went to stand behind Copley so that he could see the screen more clearly and what Copley was scrutinising so intently.

"What have you got then?"

"I've been through the security company's disc from Mrs Coulter's floor."

Farrel realised that Copley had an inkling of what there was between him and Elizabeth, but, always the diplomat; he still referred to her as Mrs Coulter.

"And . . . ?" Farrel encouraged him.

"I found the time when it appears the witness was abducted."

Farrel drew in a deep breath, pulled up a nearby chair and sat beside Copley. He leaned forward so that he could clearly view what was on the screen.

"Look at this," Copley pointed at the screen. "It's from this point onwards."

A figure with its back to the camera over the door of the lift suddenly appeared and walked to the door of Elizabeth's apartment. It was a man dressed in a short dark raincoat, dark trousers and a hat pulled well down on his head. He pressed the doorbell and after a short while, in which Farrel considered Julie had looked through the security viewer, the figure moved close to the side of the door where the door handle was. He appeared to be speaking to Julie through the door, which was still firmly shot at that point. Then the door opened a little, as far as the safety chain would allow, and a short conversation ensued. The door closed and then opened wide enough for the figure to enter.

"Well, we know one thing for sure, Julie knew the man," Farrel surmised.

"My thoughts precisely," Copley agreed. "But now watch."

Some five minutes later the door opened again. Julie had put on a coat and the man had her by the arm. He held her with his left hand. Julie seemed to struggle, but it appeared that the man's grip on her left upper arm was so firm it was causing her a lot of pain. In his other hand he carried something covered partially by his raincoat sleeve.

It could be a small gun or a knife, Farrel thought.

He edged closer to the screen and peered hard to try and see the man's face. The problem was his collar was turned up, his hat pulled down well over his features, and he was now wearing sunglasses, so his face was entirely masked. Farrel had the impression that all the time he was talking to Julie. His body language gave out extremely aggressive signals. The pair then turned away from the lift towards the stairwell and disappeared from view.

Farrel slumped back in the chair and ran everything he had just seen through his mind.

"Play that again," he said.

Copley did so, and after that, a third time.

"There's something very strange about this." Farrel was now thinking aloud again. "I am convinced Julie knew who it was by sight, or why else would she think it safe to open the door?"

Copley looked at him carefully and Farrel knew that the young DC had similar thoughts. But how similar or how different from his own?

Copley gathered his courage. "A customer?" he asked uncomfortably.

"I don't think so," Farrel replied shaking his head, now having to consider that in the recent past Julie had a customer or two, but certainly not in Elizabeth's apartment. "She hadn't been doing it for more than a couple of weeks."

"Well, she certainly knew and trusted whoever it was," Copley observed at something of a loss of what to say.

"So, what's your guess, or, should I say, your possible guess?"

Copley made a face. This was going to be a tough thing to say. He was obviously considering a way of saying something that had the probability of sounding ridiculous and sending Farrel through the roof.

Farrel saved him any embarrassment he might have been feeling. "You think it could be one of our men—a copper?"

Copley breathed again and just nodded. There was a look of disbelief in his eyes.

"I was thinking the same," Farrel said. "The whole way through that video recording, I had a strange feeling in the back of my mind that something seemed familiar."

"Shall I continue then, seeing as how we seem to be on the same wavelength?"

"If there's more, let's see it as soon as possible and, hopefully, before the rest arrive."

Copley loaded another disc and set it to 'run'. "This is from the camera on the wall of the station here overlooking the police car park. If it's a copper, it may show up here."

They watched as the activity took place. Cars, both police and public, came and went. Then Copley paused the play.

"Watch this next piece," he suggested.

They watched as members of the detective squad arrived and departed. Then they saw a figure walk away from the building to one of the cars and climb into it before driving away.

"Want to see it again?" Copley asked.

Farrel wanted to see it again that was for sure, although he was not quite sure of what he was looking for. "What are you getting at?" he asked.

"Watch how the man walks."

They watched the replay several times. Then Copley brought up the two video recordings side by side on a split screen. Both men watched very closely.

"It's the same man!" Farrel stated incredulously. "I'm sure of it!"

Copley nodded. "That's what I thought too," he concurred.

"Who is it? That's the next question."

Copley zoomed in onto a still of the car.

"That's Peter Rowles' car!" Farrel exclaimed in disbelief. He slumped back into his chair as he took in the enormity of what he was convinced he had just seen.

"He normally parks his car next to the wall of the building. It's not visible on the video usually," Copley reported. "It seems to me, he feels he has almost reserved that space there."

"But not on that day! When was that video taken?"

"Yesterday morning."

Farrel sat quietly. Thoughts were rushing through his mind.

"He was on his way to get Julie," he muttered in a voice scarcely above a whisper.

Copley looked at Farrel but said nothing.

"I want to see DC Rowles the moment he sets his foot in the office. He has some explaining to do," Farrel asserted. "All I can hope is that we have made a mistake."

Copley nodded, but again said nothing.

"But we don't think we have made a mistake, do we Richard?"

Copley shook his head forlornly and said nothing.

43

One by one, the members of the squad arrived around eight fifteen, but there was no sign of Rowles. Farrel had never liked men to be absent from their post, or even late, without a good reason. If they were ill or had been on a long duty the day before, that was permissible, but he had always expected a phone call to explain the situation.

Time passed, and still Rowles was conspicuous by his absence. Finally, Farrel decided on the direct approach. He picked up the phone and rang Rowles' home number. His wife answered and when Farrel enquired of the detective's whereabouts, his wife said that he had not been home the previous night. She explained to Farrel that he had phoned her around eleven and told her that he was on an all-night observation. So far, he had not returned, and, in truth, she was beginning to get worried. Farrel hung up.

"We appear to have lost Rowles," he advised Copley, the only other man in the office. "So, it looks as if we were right in our assumption."

"It's a bad do then," Copley said.

Farrel nodded in grim agreement.

*

Farrel was in the canteen on the ground floor when the station-desk sergeant came in with a large 'jiffy bag' addressed to Farrel.

"What's this then?" Farrel asked, looking up over the rim of his coffee cup.

"It's from the photographic department," the sergeant replied. "Somebody just left it in reception. They said you had been busy with a natty little camera."

Farrel took the packet and tore it open along the top. He had almost forgotten the session he had had accompanying the Traffic Department to the 'big house' and the farm in Cranton. Things had not appeared to be too helpful during the visit, but he had snapped away on the understanding that taking a huge number of photographs could bring something up when you have time to sit and study them all more carefully.

He finished his coffee and returned to his office where he sat down behind his desk and opened the envelope. Inside there was a whole sheaf of photographs, and, one by one, he studied them. When he had finished he created two piles in front of him. One pile was made up of the pictures that he considered of no real use; the other, he thought, consisted of photos that appeared to have more potential.

DC Copley returned from his break and sat down as always in front of his screen. Farrel picked up both sets of photographs, took them over to Copley and laid them on the desk in front of him. He showed him the pile that he thought yielded the least interest to him first.

"What do you think of these, Richard?"

Copley flicked through them quickly and silently, as if trying to decide which appeared to be those of particular note. Then he went through them much more slowly. Farrel said nothing as he did so. When Copley finished, he blocked the photos neatly and carefully laid them on the desk. He took a breath, made a face and shook his head.

"On the face of it, guv, I can't see anything, but if we spot something else, it may give us a clue."

Farrel then indicated the second pile.

"What about these?"

Copley went through the same routine and as he did he shifted in his chair and sat forward more eagerly. Something had caught his attention and he was much more interested in this collection.

"Well? See anything?" Farrel wanted to know.

"There's something about the photos of the barns," Copley replied. "They don't look right."

Farrel nodded. "That's what I thought," he agreed, "but I just can't put my finger on it."

They both sat for the next half an hour studying the photos of the large barns. Then, at last, Copley sat back and put his hands flat on the desk in front of him. He had found a photograph which best showed the inside of one of those barns.

"Look at this, guv," he said. "You can see most of the details of the inside of this barn. You caught the light just right." He was paying the DCI a backhanded compliment.

"What do you see?" Farrel wanted to know.

"Well, on the far inside of the building there are two combine harvesters parked just inside the door and along the side wall."

Farrel made no reply but nodded. He had seen them before. He knew there was something about the picture that did not look right, but he could not quite put his finger on it.

"Look at how closely together they are parked—almost nose to tail—from the front to the back. Now, imagine those harvesters parked outside along this nearside wall. What can you see?"

"That's it!" exclaimed Farrel. "It was there in front of my eyes, and I couldn't see it. Well done."

"There's room for at least another harvester along that inside wall, maybe two, so that interior end wall is, to all intents, a dummy wall and there is a rather large area of barn behind it. Wouldn't it be nice to know what's inside and if the other barn is designed the same way?" Copley put the proposition.

They returned to the photographs and in one of those that Farrel had originally discarded the second barn showed a similar set up.

"I think we need to get a search warrant and have another, more careful, look at Court Farm now we have this new information, and, this time, we'll make sure we give the 'big house' a thorough going over too."

Copley made copies of the appropriate photos and carefully annotated those that indicated the main points of interest.

*

Farrel was halfway through his lunch when his mobile phone sounded. He answered it. The caller was someone who Farrel had heard of but not had any dealings with: the police officer who covered the rural beat outside Larchester, which took in Cranton.

"Sorry to bother you, sir," said the officer. "Have you had any dealings with 'old' Harry who lives in Cranton?"

"Yes, what's the problem?" Farrel answered with a sense of foreboding.

"He's in hospital, sir, hurt bad. Apparently, it was a hit and run. I found your card in his pocket."

"How bad is he?"

"Bad—they say critical. I didn't know the best thing to do when I found your card, so I called you."

"You did the right thing. Where is he right now? I'll go and see him."

The man the other end gave him the name of a hospital fifteen miles away.

Farrel finished his lunch quickly and made his way as fast as he could to the hospital. He flashed his ID as he entered the ward and told them he was a friend of Harry's.

A nurse showed him into the intensive treatment unit. Tubes had been inserted into Harry's body in a variety of places. The thing that concerned Farrel was that Harry looked deathly pale. He had seen dead bodies before, of course, and people very close to death before, and he felt sure that Harry had but a very short time left.

"Can I talk to him?" he asked the sister-in-charge. "It's *very* important."

"Yes," she replied, "but quietly and not for long. The poor old man doesn't have much longer."

Farrel nodded his agreement. Then he went to the cot where the old man lay. He took Harry's hand gently in his.

"Can you hear me, my friend?" he asked. The grip was weak, but Farrel could still feel some life there. Harry's eyes fluttered open a little. He saw Farrel and recognised him. Then he smiled, but it was a weak one.

"The bastards got me," he whispered. "A big, black, four-wheel drive. Seen it before, I have."

"From the 'big house' and the farm?"

"Yes. They drove straight at me—couldn't get out of the way." He closed his eyes and the weak smile faded from his face.

Farrel felt the grip on his fingers release. He watched. Harry had stopped breathing and his lips had taken on the blue tinge. He had gone. Farrel slowly and gently placed the dead man's hand onto his chest.

"I'll get the bastards, Harry. I'll get the bastards. Trust me," he vowed. Then he turned and walked towards the nurse's station. The nurse looked at him enquiringly, and Farrel shook his head slowly as he walked to the door, out into the corridor and thence into the car park. Now it was three murders.

44

Farrel arrived back at his desk at the time everyone else was beginning to leave the office after a long day's work. He sat down in the silence that descended. What a mess! He had been the officer-in-charge leading many investigations before, but this was something different from all the previous cases. Was he really just a small-town copper who was getting out of his depth?

He ran over all the details in his mind until he had them in what he considered a good order. No, damn it! He was *not* getting out of his depth. He was not about to invite some big-town organisation in to do his job. He would see this through to the end.

The phone rang and brought him to the surface again. He recognised the voice. It was Peter Rowles.

"Where the hell are you and why haven't you been in today?" Farrel demanded angrily.

The voice on the other end sounded rather muffled and extremely nervous, not at all like Rowels. Farrel could hear him breathing unevenly.

"Is there a problem, Peter?" Farrel asked quickly, changing to a more considerate tone when he realised what state the other man was in.

"I need to talk to you, guv," the voice was shaky.

"There is a problem, yes?"

"A big problem."

"Tell me about it."

"I can't do that, not on the phone anyway. I need to talk to you alone in private."

"When? Right now?"

"No—how about tomorrow?"

"All right. You say where and when."

"Do you know the pub, The George, near the canal lock at Bradbury?"

"Yes."

"I'll be there at ten thirty tomorrow morning. Please don't be late."

"Don't talk to *me* about being late, but, alright, I'll be there at ten thirty."

With that the phone went dead. Farrel wanted to ask where Rowles was, but the chance had gone, and it was likely he would not have said anyway.

He's scared about something. Is he scared of me or someone else? Chances are it's someone else. That mob, I'll bet my pension on it.

Things were getting deeper and darker, and he still had no real idea of where Julie was. He needed to talk to Elizabeth. At 6.45 p.m. he picked up the phone and dialled her number. She answered it on the second ring.

"I thought it might be you," she said when Farrel spoke.

"Have you heard anything yet?"

"Nothing, but can I come over and talk?"

"It's as bad as that, is it?"

"It's been a hell of a day and I need a friend."

"Come on over. I'll have a drink waiting for you and I'll rustle up something to eat. Then you can tell me some more of your troubles." Then she added quickly, "And don't be long. I'm in the middle of cooking, and there's enough for two."

Farrel knew they needed each other and he was grateful for her care. Four years was a hell of a time to go without gentle female companionship. He hung up.

"Thanks, Liz," he said aloud to an empty office.

Farell took time clearing his desk. He closed his office door as he left and looked down at Copley's desk to see if there was anything interesting on it.

The desk was clear. He was always so neat and tidy, hardworking, bright and a good copper. He would make a good chief officer; they never seemed to have a bloody thing on their desks either.

Five minutes later, he left the building and drove the ten minutes or so to Elizabeth's apartment. It was 7.15 p.m. and it was getting dark. He parked the car under a streetlight in the road. He used the lift and when he rang the doorbell, Elizabeth opened it almost immediately. She held the door open and he stepped inside. The smell of food cooking danced around his nostrils. He had not had real home-cooked food since Julie was at his apartment and the aroma awakened his taste buds immediately. *No fast food tonight!*

"Come and sit down," Elizabeth invited. "You look a sight."

"And you look great," he replied.

She took a ready-poured glass of Scotch from the drinks cabinet and handed it to him.

"Now, get that down your neck before you do anything else."

Farrel took a sip. As he expected, it was not a run-of-the-mill whisky. This was quality, real quality and mellow.

He smiled. "That hits the spot," he commented, and it was not long before he had drained the glass. Elizabeth offered him a refill but he declined—he did not want to allow his brain to become unclear at this early stage of the evening.

"Dinner's ready," she announced a few moments later.

They ate a meal, the likes of which he had only eaten once or twice in the past few years. The wine, an excellent Rioja, made the food even more enjoyable, and they finished with coffee.

Farrel offered to help with the washing up but was told there are machines to do that sort of chore these days.

"Look, why don't you go and take a shower and then when you're done you can tell me all your troubles."

A shower was something that Farrel knew would help him relax and he accepted.

"Use the shower off the master bedroom—you *know* where that is—and you'll find something comfortable to put on afterwards," she instructed.

Farrel did as she suggested. He took a long, hot shower and, at last, felt the tension beginning to ease. As he towelled himself dry, he noticed that on a shelf Elizabeth had provided a man's electric shaver and some aftershave, as well as a bottle of cologne. She was not expecting him to have to leave in the same state as he had the previous time. He smiled—this looked to be a promising therapy session.

He returned to the bedroom to find a dressing gown and a pair of boxer shorts lying on the bed. His clothes, apart from his suit which he had worn when he arrived and which was now hanging on a hook, were nowhere to be seen. He shrugged and slipped on the shorts and pulled on the dressing gown.

Returning to the living room, he saw that Elizabeth had also slipped into something more relaxing too—a light blue dressing gown of some sort of silky material and by the looks of it—he had a very keen eye when it came to observation—there was precious little beneath it. She was sitting on one of the two-seater sofas and there was another glass, generously supplied with what Farrel knew was Scotch.

"Come and sit here and tell me all about your day," she invited.

Farrel sat beside her, close beside her. He could feel her warmth and he could smell her perfume. *I wouldn't be surprised if that perfume is called 'the ultimate allure'*, he thought, inhaling it deeply through his nose.

He brought her up-to-date with as much as he thought she should know. She listened carefully, her eyes seldom moving from his. Finally, he stopped talking, not because he had run out of news or things to say, but because he could no longer concentrate on what he was supposed to be saying. It was in her eyes, which were looking into his and which prevented any further talk of mundane subjects.

He had noticed that from time to time, she had 'innocently' adjusted her position on the sofa and that in turn had caused her dressing gown to ride up at the hem and to open just a little but enough at the neck and front.

"Go on then," she was waiting and expecting to hear more.

"I can't," he admitted in exasperation. "You know I can't and you know damn well why I can't. It's impossible for me to concentrate."

She giggled. "Okay," she relented. "Now comes the therapy," and she moved closer still. They leaned towards each other. The first kiss was gentle, the second less gentle, the third passionate and from there on the world ceased to exist for both of them; especially Farrel.

"Feel better?" she asked later when Farrel had returned to the wicked, worrying world.

"Yes, a little, I think."

More therapy followed. Farrel lost all sense of time until Elizabeth looked towards the mantle above the fireplace.

"Good grief," she exclaimed. "Is that the time?"

Farrel's eyes focused on the clock—10.30 p.m.

"I think it's time for bed, don't you?" she ventured.

"Definitely time for bed," Farrel gladly agreed.

Elizabeth turned out the light as they left the living room. The bedroom was low-lit, but Farrel could clearly see what was happening to Elizabeth's dressing gown and also the flimsy thing she had on underneath. There was no point in denying why they were here and so early at that. When they both shed the small amount they were wearing, they slid between the sheets. Farrel reached for Elizabeth and she came to him across the bed. This was not the time to talk of problems at work, about what they were missing on the television, or what the weather was likely to be the next day. This was the time for deep, deep therapy when utmost concentration would be needed for those other important things in life.

45

Farrel awoke. The digital clock on the bedside table showed 6.10 a.m. He was surprisingly wide-awake considering that they had not gone to sleep until somewhere around 1.00 a.m. Something had relaxed him and helped him to sleep relatively peacefully, and it was not the whisky.

He swung his legs out of bed, padded into the bathroom and closed the door before turning on the light. He did not want to wake Elizabeth at this time of the morning. Then he showered and shaved. When he returned to the bedroom, Elizabeth was not where he had left her sleeping: judging by the smell of food coming from the kitchen, she was preparing breakfast. It smelled good.

He dressed in the new set of clothes she had provided. They felt fresh and crisp, and he was surprised they fit so well. When he mentioned it a few minutes later, she replied that she was a woman and knew all these things quite naturally.

Farrel saw that she was dressed in the same silky-type dressing gown as the night before, but before leaving the bedroom, he had noticed her nightdress draped carelessly across the bed. What would he have given not to have to go to work today?

Breakfast over, he prepared to leave. He slipped into his jacket, pondering what the day might bring. As Elizabeth kissed him goodbye, the gown fell open a little, just enough to encourage another passionate kiss.

"Now, Liz," he said, "take special care today. Those men know this place, so keep it securely locked at all times and don't leave unless you really have to."

"You take care too," she ordered. "Try not to be late tonight; then we can have a really early night."

With that, she kissed him and opened the door. He noted, with pleasure, that he was expected back that night. It made him feel a lot happier than he thought he ought to be feeling at this particular moment, particularly with the job he had to do today on his mind.

He tried to organise his plans for the day and put to the back of his mind the previous night. It was difficult.

He arrived at the office before anyone else, but, as usual, Copley arrived less than ten minutes later. They greeted each other.

"A couple of things, guv," Copley said as he switched on his beloved computer and inserted a memory stick into one of the drives.

"What are they?" Farrel wanted to know.

"Have a look at this."

Farrel left the desk in his office and took a seat next to Copley so he could view the screen clearly. Copley had put the two videos he had the day before onto the screen again. They watched the images side-by-side of whom they thought was the same man walking away from the cameras. Then Copley brought the two together so that one was superimposed upon the other.

"Well, what do you think?" he asked.

"Looks like we were right, doesn't it?"

Copley nodded. "Not much doubt now," he concluded. "They're identical."

"That figures right enough," Farrel said. "Peter rang me yesterday in a state. He wants to see me today."

The rest of the squad arrived, the day's briefing took place and they all dispersed to their duties. Farrel looked at his watch. It must be about time to leave for Bradbury. It was some twelve miles away and at this time of the morning traffic could be difficult to manage in and near the town. In the countryside, it would be light so he could leave himself thirty minutes and still get there in time. Rowles had said half past ten, and Farrel did not want to be late. He knew that if Rowles was as scared as he had appeared to be yesterday on the phone, he would not want to be late either.

*

He arrived at The George at ten twenty and made his way into the pub. There was no one there, although the notice outside indicated that it was open for coffee, snacks and English breakfast from ten.

A man appeared from a doorway behind the bar and asked Farrel what he would like. Farrel told him that he was expecting to meet a friend there for a coffee and perhaps some food at ten thirty. The barman told him that he hadn't seen anyone in the pub yet.

Farrel left the bar and waited for Rowles to arrive outside in the car park. The day was overcast, and it began to drizzle slightly—not a day to sit out beside the nearest lock for a drink.

Ten thirty arrived—no Rowles—ten forty, ten fifty and then eleven o'clock. There was still no sign of him. Farrel was becoming impatient and very agitated. What had delayed him? Had Rowles arrived when Farrel was inside the pub and because he couldn't see him leave for fear of someone following him? There was always the chance that something had spooked him somewhere between his home and Bradbury. He dialled Rowles' mobile; no reply.

Farrel rang the police station in Larchester. Copley was there and he looked up Rowles' home phone number. Farrel rang it. Rowles' wife answered. No, he was still not there. He had left very early that morning in a worried state, she said.

"I'm very worried too," she confided. "Something's going on. I don't like it. He never spoke to me about it though, or what was going on."

Farrel told her that although Rowles had not arrived at their agreed meeting point, he was sure he would come—probably caught up in traffic somewhere. Somehow, though, as more time passed, he felt less convinced. He disconnected the call and decided to take a walk to see if Rowles had kept a low profile and was waiting somewhere less obvious.

He walked to the higher lock and looked around. Nothing appeared out of the ordinary; not even a canal boat was in sight. He turned and retraced his steps. As he passed the pub he glanced in quickly. The barman shook his head as if understanding Farrel's look of enquiry.

He walked towards the lower lock but saw nothing extraordinary there either. He walked a little farther. Then he saw Rowles. He knew it was him. He could not see his face, but he knew it was him floating face-down in the water of the canal below the lower gate of the lock. His feet were drifting downwards towards the bottom of the canal whilst his arms were extended sideways at right angles to his body.

Immediately, Farrel called for an ambulance and anyone who was in the police station in Larchester that could give assistance. Then he found a boathook, caught it into Rowles' saturated clothing and pulled the body to the bank. He turned it over just to confirm his fears. It was Rowles all right, and, at this point, Farrel could see a neat hole in the left side of his head, close to the jaw hinge and just behind the earlobe. It was small .22 bullet, Farrel surmised, although he was no ballistics expert. He was, however, certain that it had been carried out by a professional hit man, most probably using a hollow-nosed bullet; one of the weapons, he knew, assassins like to use. He secured the body by using a length of rope he spied close to one of the large, heavy wooden beams that operated the lock gate. And then he waited.

Copley arrived first. Farrel told him the details and between them they pulled Rowles' body from the water. A hard job for the two men as his clothes were wet through, the steep bank was slippery and the water level some three feet lower than the top of the grass-covered bank.

The ambulance arrived at the same time as DS Preston and DC Perkins. The paramedics took one look at the body and gave Farrel an enquiring look as they approached. Farrel shook his head.

"Sorry guys," he told them, "he's dead. You'd better take him straight to the mortuary and I'll arrange for a post mortem later."

The medics loaded Rowles' body into the ambulance and drove away.

Farrel turned to the three officers. "I came here on Rowles' request," he explained. "He rang me yesterday and wanted to talk. He was scared, and I had the feeling he wanted to get something off his chest."

He turned to Copley. "Explain it, Richard."

Copley explained how he had used the two security videos, one from Elizabeth's apartment hallway and the other from the police car park, and then how he had superimposed one onto the other. Preston and Perkins listened without interrupting and remained silent for some time after Copley had finished.

"I hate to say it," Preston said, "but that seems to be the reason they knew what we were going to do and when."

"Never expected him to do a thing like that though," Perkins remarked in utter disbelief.

"Well, we can't do anything more here, so we had better make all the enquiries we can. I'll leave that to you to organise, George. I have to go and tell his wife. I'll go and pick up one of the female constables on duty at the station," Farrel said.

With his hands in his pockets and his shoulders hunched over he turned and walked away. It was a bad day.

46

It was around 1.15 p.m. when Farrel arrived at Rowles' home. He asked one of the female constables to accompany him and had explained the situation on the way. He did not tell her everything. There was no need to at this time he considered. Everyone outside the crime squad would be told that Rowles had gone to meet a contact and had been murdered in the line of duty. It could have been the truth, but Farrel knew in his heart that it was not. Why make too many waves until the whole truth be known?

He explained that he would need to look through the house thoroughly to find anything relating to Rowles and his killer—that at least was true. Perhaps the dead man had left something behind that would be of use.

Together they walked to the front door and the policewoman rang the bell. There was no reply. She rang again— same result.

"Let's go round to the back," Farrel suggested. "Perhaps she's in the garden."

They made their way round the side of the house to the back door. Mrs Rowles was not in the garden. The back door was standing slightly ajar. Farrel knocked on it. Again, there was no reply. He knocked again and nudged the door open a little more.

"Mrs Rowles," he called, "are you there?"

There was no response. He pushed the door wide open and entered. If she saw him, it might give her a fright but at least she would recognise him and see the female officer's uniform. He called her name again as he walked through the kitchen. There was a door in the wall opposite the back door and Farrel assumed it lead to the hallway and the front door. That too was ajar and calling once again he pushed the door fully open. Then he saw Mrs Rowles. She was lying at the foot of the stairs. It was obvious to him from the first sight that she was dead.

"Oh my God," the policewoman gasped.

Farrel spread his arms out to stop the officer from stepping forward.

"Stay where you are, my dear," he counselled. "We don't want to contaminate the scene any more than we have to, do we?"

He took out his mobile phone and for the second time that morning called for an ambulance.

Forensics had been despatched to the scene of her husband's murder, now they would need to divide their resources. He looked around carefully, disturbing as little as possible that could prove useful to forensics.

The body lay on its back; her left arm lying down the side of it. The other was outstretched away from the shoulder bent at a right angle at the elbow and pointing towards her head. The head itself was facing towards the staircase, away from the two officers.

Farrel stepped carefully to the side of the body, put his four fingers under the jaw and turned her head towards him. There was an identical wound in the identical place, or at least as close to identical as Farrel considered it could be, to that of her husband's. Then he carefully and slowly let her head return to its original position.

"Same way Rowles was killed," he told the white-faced young woman as he turned to look at her. "It looks as if it was the type of bullet that killed him. I wouldn't mind betting it's the same gun and the same man, or woman, of course, that did it." He stood up and as he looked around the hallway he said, "Stay here with the body. I'm going to have a look around to see if Rowles kept any private notes on what he had been doing."

The policewoman went back into the kitchen to wait for the arrival of forensics, the ambulance and anyone else from the squad who had been dispatched to the scene of the crime.

Farrel carefully stepped around the body and onto the staircase. He went upstairs and selected the first door he came to. Entering what appeared to be the main bedroom, he was met with a sight that he had seen so many times before. The room had been ransacked. The bed was uncovered and messy and had been overturned. The drawers had all been pulled open wide and left that way—*searched from bottom to top*—a *professional job*. The wardrobe doors stood open and everything that had been inside now lay scattered on the floor. Farrel took a quick look around and then passed to the next room, and then the third. Everything was upside down. Even the bathroom had received the same attention.

DC Johnson arrived a few minutes after Farrel had returned to the ground floor.

"Dick, I want you to go through this place with a fine tooth comb. I'll send George, Richard and Alan over as soon as they get through at the locks. I want everything checked, double-checked and triple-checked. Any piece of paper that you think may be interesting and anything in writing too that you come across."

His mobile phone rang. "We've found Rowles' car, guv," announced George Preston. "Doesn't appear to be anything much around it, but forensics is taking over and they'll bring the car in as soon as they can."

"I'd like to have a meeting in the office as soon as everyone can make it," Farrel told him, "but don't take any short cuts with what you're doing. We already had two murders when we started the day, to say nothing of a missing person and a suspect traffic accident. Now we have a dead copper and the dead copper's dead wife in addition.

47

The squad all met in the office at six o'clock that same evening. It was a sombre atmosphere. Farrel stood next to the white board to which he had added two more victims' names and photographs. He invited those present to sit. "This won't be the usual quick briefing," he declared. Then he went on to explain in full detail everything that had taken place. The first being the suspicious nature of the activities at the industrial estate, and then onto how Julie had been caught up in the affair, how he had kept her almost under lock and key in his apartment and then at Elizabeth's. He brought everyone up-to-date regarding the visit to Cranton Court and Court Farm after one of the men had been killed in a car crash. However, he did not mention the events that had lead up to the crash. Some of the information the men already knew, of course, but not all of them knew all the details. Each one knew that on occasions Farrel worked on the need-to-know basis, but now it was time for everyone to know all the facts. From now on this had to be a team effort. He told them about old Harry being knocked down by a hit-and-run driver, and that Harry had given Farrel a good indication where the car had come from before he died.

He went on to say how he had received some information that there was a mole either in the squad, or in the Force close to it. He did not know who had provided this bit of information. He was not interested at this time in its origin as long as it was good, and now it appeared to have proved correct. There was a murmur of deep concern from those present.

"By an excellent piece of work from Richard here," he continued, looking towards Copley, "and intuition too, it became clear that the late DC Rowles was that mole, particularly when he failed to turn up for his shift. He rang in and said he wanted to meet me. He was scared, I could tell, and so that's why I was at the locks this morning. We went to his home to see if his wife could give us any leads, but, as you know, she was dead by that time too.

"We are waiting for forensics to report, but I'll wager it was a bullet from the same gun that killed both of them. I'm pretty sure it was a professional hit."

"Do we know any more about Julie Jackson, guv?" DS Preston wanted to know.

"No, but the chances are they think she saw something, even though she hadn't, and that's why they abducted her."

"You think she's being held at Cranton Court or the farm?" the DS asked the rhetorical question.

"Where else?"

The men sat in silence, staring at the white board deep in thought, and then at Farrel's face.

"When do we go then, guv?" Alan Perkins asked. "We can't leave it long. If we leave it too long, the girl will be dead by the time we find her and the whole bunch of them will have flown."

There was a noise of agreement from the room.

"Absolutely," Farrel agreed, "I'm going to see the Chief Constable as soon as I can arrange it to put him in the picture and get a search warrant for Cranton Court and the farm. Now,

I don't want a word of this to get out. Be sure of that. I know there are no men in the Force more honest and loyal than your good selves, but this Hydra group is international and will have its contacts everywhere; small fry or even big shots.

Farrel finished at that point and then Copley spoke up. He looked around at the group a little sheepishly; he remembered the last time he had said something when they were all assembled.

"There's a little bit more info that I may have turned up," he said, "and I think this could possibly help more towards getting the search warrant."

He produced an enlarged photograph of each of the farm barns. They were blow-ups of photos taken by Farrel whilst he was there.

"Take a look at these, particularly this one," he suggested, thrusting one forward so that each man could get a closer look. "You will see that there are two combine harvesters inside."

"Yes, so?" someone asked.

"If you look closely, you'll see that they just fit into the barn along one side." Copley looked around at each man as he spoke. "They must be somewhere around twenty feet long with a few feet either end for manoeuvring them around. That makes the barn somewhere around sixty feet long."

There was silence still in the room.

"I've been along to the Town Hall Planning Department in the last couple of days and checked out the plans for these buildings. They were built only a couple of years ago, and the plans showed that they are a hundred feet long. So even with my very poor estimate, I reckon there is another thirty feet, at least, beyond that back wall. So, imagine what may be going on there . . ."

Copley then sat back and waited. He was gratified to see nods and hear sounds of approval coming from his colleagues.

"So, we go as soon as I can get things moving," Farrel announced. "We'll go in mob-handed and have a good number of the firearms unit with us."

The meeting broke up at eight thirty and Farrel returned to his office as the other men departed with a meeting scheduled for half past seven the next morning.

There was nothing more that could be done. He sat at his desk, picked up his phone and dialled Elizabeth's number. Twenty minutes later she opened her door to him.

"My God, you look awful," she gasped.

"Feel it," Farrel replied. "Do you feel like listening?"

"Of course; come and sit down."

As he sat down, she placed a very large Scotch into his hand.

"Now, where do you want to start this time?"

"Right here," he said and put his arms around her and held her close. He needed some sort of comfort. Some kind of sympathetic, warm and understanding human contact, preferably female contact, that he felt keenly at this moment had been sadly lacking over the previous four years.

48

At seven thirty the following morning, the detectives were busy at their desks, sifting through every piece of evidence they had gathered so far. They checked and double-checked their work and each other's on the understanding that a fresh pair of eyes was likely to pick up something new.

Farrel was on the phone in his office behind the closed door. At nine o'clock he spoke to the Chief Constable's secretary. He explained, as best he could without giving away too much, the urgency his meeting with the Chief merited. At last, he was told that the Chief Constable had a thirty-minute slot free before his meeting with the local police authority. Thirty minutes would be fine Farrel had assured her, and, in fact, thirty minutes would be ample. The less he talked about the peripheral problems, the better.

Farrel left his office and forty minutes later he was standing outside the Chief Constable's office. Thirty minutes after that he emerged with everything he needed to continue his case.

The Chief was very interested in the way the case was being handled thus far. At the same time, he was appalled at the suggestion that Rowles had been involved with the criminal element. Yes, there was irrefutable evidence that it was true.

"Young DC Copley did a superb job with regard to that, sir," Farrel reported.

"Better let the Assistant Chief Constable know that," the Chief suggested with a smile. "What with the young man being a relation of his and one of his favourites for a rapid promotion."

"I'd rather you didn't say anything, at least for the moment," Farrel said. "I'd like to keep this op as quiet possible, if you don't mind."

At that moment he could never be sure there were no more 'moles' in the Force, this criminal organisation being global and all. Just who could they not buy?

The Chief Constable agreed. He had known Farrel for many years and knew that if he asked for something, there was a very good reason for it. Farrel had only to pick up the phone and everything would be made available to him.

*

By six o'clock that evening, he had everything he considered he would need when he made the visit to Cranton Court and Court Farm, including a search warrant.

The final conference in the squad room was one in which tension was building. Each man knew his place in the plan and his place on the ground at the time of the raid. They would be armed and backed up by a large contingent of the firearms unit. Those men would be dressed as normal for a raid: black uniforms and carrying a variety of firearms, as appeared appropriate. The detectives too would wear dark clothing. They would draw their weapons from the armoury before they left the police station that evening.

That done, Farrel returned to his desk and ran through the plan several times: he had to make sure he had it right. Did it need changing at the last moment? No. Did it need tweaking? No. There were always things that happened in a raid that had not been planned for and Farrel could not remember anything quite this big in all his years in the Service. Things must not be allowed to go wrong; it was as simple as that.

Eventually he phoned Elizabeth to say he was on his way before he went to the armoury to draw his handgun, a Glock 17 holding seventeen rounds. A gun he had never fired in anger but one that he had used on numerous occasions on the shooting range in the basement of the station. He liked the gun. It fitted him nicely and he had, to his own great surprise, become a damn good shot. Would he be as good in a possible real fire fight as he had been on the range? At least there the targets had never fired back at him. He sincerely hoped his ability would not desert him, but he hoped even more that it would not come to it.

*

He was very quiet when at last he arrived at Elizabeth's apartment. She was very concerned for him as usual and had planned a pleasant evening to help him relax. She knew that something big was about to take place and when he took off his jacket to reveal the pistol in its shoulder holster nestled under his left arm, her mouth fell open and a look of horror spread across her face.

"My God, Ian," she gasped, "what *is* going on? I knew it was a big case for you, but I didn't realise it was as dangerous as this."

"Don't worry yourself about it, Liz. It's just a precaution, a show of force, if you like. The only thing it's going to do is wear a sore spot on my ribs."

He looked around and sniffed.

"What's that gorgeous smell?" he asked brightly, and to change the subject. "And what's for afters?"

She smiled and then laughed.

"What would you like it to be?" she asked, loosening his tie, reaching up and clasping her arms around his neck.

"Now, that is what, in the trade, we call a leading question, ma'am," he replied.

49

Farrel left Elizabeth's apartment at five o'clock the next morning. He felt apprehensive about the coming day but comforted by the 'therapy', as he called it, that Elizabeth had provided. The full breakfast with plenty of black coffee she had made for him fortified him no end.

As he left she clung to him.

"For God's sake be careful," she pleaded. "I've lost you once and I don't want to lose you again."

"Don't worry about me," he assured her, "I'm indestructible."

With that he kissed her and left, arriving at the police-station parade room twenty minutes later.

At five thirty the rest of the 'assault team' had assembled and were finally assigned their duties. They were to work in pairs and approach Cranton Court and the farm from a variety of directions, thus cutting off any lines of escape the villains might take.

It would take longer for those officers coming across country to get to their positions, so timings were critical. When each pair arrived at their designated spot, they would report in using the briefest of messages on their dedicated radios, and then Farrel, DS Preston and DC Perkins would go in as fast as they could with a back up of firearms officers.

DCs Johnson and Copley would act as further back ups, with Copley having the job of coordinating anything that needed any adjustment. Farrel had explained that Copley had his full confidence, even though he was the junior officer, and that his organisational skills were more than sufficient to deal with any hiccough that might occur. No one argued; they had realised over the past few days that what Farrel said was right.

Group by group, they left the station and made their way to Cranton. It would be just as dawn was coming up, so that each group would be sure that if there were a fire fight, they would not be firing at their own colleagues. They had heard of friendly-fire deaths far too often in the not too distant past.

Farrel and those other groups with final positions close to the 'big house' and closest to him left last.

*

The day was grey overcast and a soft drizzle started to fall as they parked their vehicles around four hundred yards from the 'big house' and began their final deployment. Farrel and the other two detectives parked their car in the lane close to the main gate but out of sight of the house. They made their way quietly along the side of the drive on the grass, so as not to make any noise.

Everything was very quiet and the three men looked at each other. It was quiet, too quiet maybe. They approached the door. It was closed and far too solidly constructed to be broken in. Perkins noticed a window slightly ajar a few feet to the side of the columns of the porch, but said nothing. Most times, it would have gone unnoticed, but Perkins was that type of copper—he did not miss a thing—which is why he had been chosen to accompany Farrel and Preston.

It appeared to be an office window, he reported, and Farrel cast his mind back to his first visit. That would be about right—most of the ground floor he had seen had been given over to office space.

By the time Farrel had rung the bell twice Perkins had disappeared. Perhaps he was looking for an easier access point, but unknown to Farrel and Preston, he had prised the window open and disappeared inside. There was no reply to Farrel's knocking. Farell turned and looked at Preston.

"I reckon they've gone, George," he opined quietly and in disappointment. Then, a sound from inside: a key was being turned in the lock. The door opened and Perkins' smiling face appeared.

"What the—" Farrel started.

"Open window, guv," Perkins cut in, nodding in the direction of the insecure window. "Thought they might have left it open for us."

"That's naughty," Farrel tutted quietly and unconvincingly.

"I didn't break anything," Perkins assured him; his face covered in a look of innocence. "It does seem very quiet in here though."

Farrel reported to those in their various positions that all was quiet and that a search of the house was about to start. Those, apart from the shooters behind him, were to maintain their positions until they had further instructions.

It took fifteen minutes to cover every room on the ground floor of the large house, but it soon became evident that whoever had been there had left in a hurry. Papers lay strewn around—a cursory glance indicated that they were likely to be of a business nature, but in any case they would be inspected at length later on.

In an outer office, to the rear of the one in which Farrel had spoken to the foreign man who appeared to be in charge those few days ago, one of the armed officers found a sheaf of papers which seemed to have fallen behind a filing cabinet. A quick inspection suggested to Farrel that it could well be a more interesting collection compared to those they had found so far. As he studied it, it was clear that something of a global nature was, or certainly had been, taking place there.

The documents may have been in code, but that did not worry Farrel at this point. What he noticed was that they were in foreign languages. He recognised English, of course, but there were papers with Chinese or Japanese characters, Arabic, Asian and Cyrillic as well.

"Hydra most likely," he surmised turning to Preston.

Preston nodded. "Big then, really big, guv."

"The big boys have gone, George, that's for sure. I guess it was Rowles' killing that finally did it. They're most probably long gone by now. I wonder if we have another informant among us."

They would later discover that a small number of cars, which when checked out came from the company running the farm, had been seen heading north towards Oxford.

They would, in all probability, have a light aircraft waiting on a small, disused World War Two airfield; but one which was not as 'disused' as everyone thought.

The raid on the 'big house' had been kept low key mainly because of the number of officers available to cover the two places at the same time. It had been a quiet affair. Now, those who had been positioned around the house moved to other pre-decided locations around the farm and the barns.

"Gone but not forgotten," Farrel confirmed as they moved towards the farm. "Now, let's hit the farm and hit it fast and hard. I don't want any gunplay unless it's unavoidable. There may be no one there, but I can't imagine these bastards taking everyone with them. Their 'soldiers' are dispensable. They won't know much. They're most probably illegals who don't speak any English, who don't know what they're doing here and know even less than that about their bosses. Let's just hope they've left someone behind who might prove useful. That man at the industrial estate, for example. I'd like to meet him again face to face."

His mind strayed to thoughts of Julie. *I just hope she's here, and alive.*

The assault force converged on the farm. It was still not light in the heavy, grey overcast clouds and drizzle, which was now falling faster.

50

Each small group of police officers, as well as their firearms, were equipped with a battering ram to use on any doors that were not opened immediately. This was an international organisation and information, good information, suggested it could well be desperate enough to use guns to protect its property and criminal activities.

"Don't open fire unless you have to," he had ordered. "If you do, then make sure you take the target down!"

The instructions were that Farrel would give the order to break the farmhouse door down, and, at that moment, DS Preston would give the order—"Go! Go! Go!" to every group via his radio.

Two uniformed officers accompanying Farrel, Preston and Perkins carried the battering ram, and on Farrel's command broke the door down with one blow just below the lock. Preston had given the order at the same moment, and a second or two later the sound of other doors being broken down by other groups reached Farrel's ears.

With repeated loud shouts of 'Police', the officers rushed every part of the buildings they could. People, who had just woken up and still bleary-eyed, looked in surprise and fear at the heavily armed police. Those sleeping were very soon roughly awakened, dragged from their beds, ordered to stand against a wall and not to move.

Police, who broke into the farm barns some distance away, experienced the same thing.

Later they discovered concealed places that contained a variety of firearms and other weaponry: handguns to heavy weapons, grenade launchers and explosives. In other places, they found large packages containing a frightening array and quantity of drugs.

In one barn, they discovered twenty very scared people—illegal immigrants who were being used as slave labour on the farm, as well being drafted by the mob to other places affiliated to it.

Frightened young women were in another group. They were terrified and had either been used in the vice trade in cities where they had been taken and then brought back to be re-assigned, or had recently arrived and would soon be put to work on the streets.

Farrel's suspicions had been correct all the time. So far, the police raid had been an unqualified success, but Julie had not yet been accounted for and Farrel felt that she was very close nearby and he needed to press on deeper into the farmhouse.

There seemed to be so many doors. Each had to be opened and the rooms beyond them searched and cleared. Those rooms, he knew, could well yield more and more evidence, but, first and foremost, he needed to find Julie. She had been his responsibility from day one, and he felt that responsibility weighing very heavily upon his shoulders even more now.

Most doors he tried were unlocked and the rooms behind them were devoid of people, but Farrel considered they could contain plenty of useful material for the investigation.

Pressing on, he passed through a door into a small, brick-lined passageway. There were doors on either side. Everything had suddenly gone very quiet—eerily so, he thought.

He tried the first door on his left. It was unlocked and the room was empty. It was the same result with the first door on his right and the second door on his left, but it was a different thing altogether with the second door on his right.

He pushed the handle down. The door was locked.

Then he heard the sound of what he thought could be a struggle. He heard a muffled sound of a voice followed by a crash as if something had fallen over. There was a short scream. It was a woman's scream. Then he heard the sound of a shot. The scream ended abruptly. It was Julie. It had to be Julie. He had never heard her scream, but the timbre of the voice sounded as if it must be her.

He felt as if the contents of his stomach were turning to water. *Not Julie*, he prayed silently. *Please God, not Julie.*

He withdrew a little from the door, took the Glock from under his arm, switched off the safety catch and hooked the index finger of his right hand around the trigger. Then he slammed his foot against the door next to its handle. It flew open as the keep and the doorframe splintered.

The first thing he saw was a woman lying in the far corner of the room to his right, propped up against a wall. A large bloodstain was spreading across the front of the white shirt she was wearing. She was lying very still.

All Farrel's fears were confirmed. It was Julie!

Then in a matter of fractions of a second it happened. The sight of Julie lying there changed everything.

Farrel had heard of soldiers and warriors in battles who had turned into berserkers. He had never given it too much credence, but, at that moment, Farrel, completely unaware of it, became a berserker.

Julie was hurt. Perhaps she was dead and a primeval sense consumed him to the exclusion of all else.

He saw from the corner of his eye a figure across the room from Julie standing behind and half-hidden by a desk.

Filing cabinets near the desk were half empty and untidy, and in his hand the man held a gun, which was pointing directly at Farrel.

For some strange reason, Farrel had no idea why he saw it all in an instant. Perhaps it was his highly analytical mind, but it was a vivid 'snapshot' that would forever stay locked in his memory for the rest of his life.

"You bast—" Farrel began to shout, and he raised his weapon to fire at the man. The room suddenly filled with the noise of gunfire and the smell of cordite. It was a battleground confined within the four walls. He pulled the trigger a millisecond or so, it seemed, after the other man had fired, and immediately he felt an excruciating pain in his right shoulder, then another, slightly lower, then he felt a third smash into his ribs on his right side and a fourth into his right thigh.

Somehow he kept firing. He did not know how. The pain was incredible, but he still fired off more shots, how many, who knew, he certainly did not, until he had no more strength to pull the trigger. He had to keep firing. He had to kill the man because he had shot Julie, his Julie.

Suddenly, everything turned black in front of him. He blinked. Yes, it was getting darker. He suddenly felt very weak. He stepped back towards the wall at the side of the door to steady himself, but his legs gave way under his weight. He tried to push upwards and straighten them to stay on his feet, but it was no good. The wall he was leaning against was not able to hold him up. It felt slippery and he slid down towards the floor, unable to stop himself. All he was aware of then was that the room was suddenly silent, but there was still that acrid smell of cordite streaming into his nostrils.

His fight to stay upright was lost and he slid down the wall to finish up in a crumpled heap. *Julie* was his last thought as he lost consciousness completely.

51

DS Preston and DC Perkins were not far behind Farrel when he kicked the door in. They had heard the scream and single shot and they had witnessed Farrel rush into the room. The next few moments seemed to pass in a blur. They heard Farrel shout which was followed by a very brief but sustained time of firing. It could have been six or even twelve shots fired. It was difficult to tell. All they knew was that it sounded like a gun battle with a number of people all firing at the same time. When they entered the room a scene of mayhem greeted them.

They saw Farrel slumped against the foot of the wall. Blood was smeared on the surface above him. He was still. His pistol still gripped in his hand. They saw a woman, whom they recognised as Julie, lying in a corner over to their right, a large bloodstain almost covering her hitherto white shirt. She was motionless. Then they saw across the room to their left another inert body draped face down across a desk. They looked at each other in alarm as they took in the scene.

"My God!" Preston exclaimed.

"Bloody hell! Perkins breathed.

Preston knelt down beside Farrel and felt for a pulse. Then he turned and yelled over his shoulder to anyone outside the room.

"The guv'nor's down. He's hurt. It's really bad. Get an ambulance and be damn quick about it."

Moments later, there was a scuffle from somewhere in the passage just outside the door of the room.

"It's the paramedics," a voice from somewhere behind him called out.

Perkins ran across to Julie.

"She's hurt bad," he announced, "but she's still alive."

The paramedics rushed in and quickly took over the situation.

Copley stepped into the room and surveyed it in horror.

"How the hell did they get here so quickly?" Preston wanted to know, looking in surprise at the paramedics.

"I had a feeling that something like this could happen, Sarge, so I called the ambulance before we hit the farm," Copley explained. Then he asked as he looked down at Farrel, "How bad is it?"

"Bad! Very bad indeed, but he's still alive. How much, I don't know, but if he lives, it will be due, in a great part, to your intuition. Well done, Richard."

At that point, the DS could have hugged the young man. Farrel could be a son-of-a-bitch, everyone knew that of course, but he was also well liked and respected by his men.

The man the other side of the room was sprawled out across the desk. He did not move. He didn't pose a threat, so Preston, Perkins and Copley ignored him until they were sure that Farrel and Julie had been attended to by the medics. When they eventually returned their attention to him, they recognised him as being the one they had seen in photographs taken at the units in the industrial estate; the man with the scar. There was not a great deal of blood on his clothing. He had died very quickly.

Perkins pulled the man's jacket open. "Bloody hell!" he marvelled. "The guv'nor never did do things by halves, did he?"

"*Does* things by halves," Preston corrected him flatly.

Perkins ignored the remark.

"Look at this," he said, "he's been taken apart. Looks like he's got one through his heart, a couple in his lungs, one through his throat and one in his head. It's like I said, the guv'nor never does things by halves. He always said fire low, the gun pulls upwards."

"Call the meat wagon and get this body taken away, then we'll get onto taking this place apart, piece by little piece."

The firearms team left and the forensic department arrived. This was going to be a long job. These criminals were meticulous in keeping their business a secret and ongoing. It was not going to be easy to break everything down into simple, easily understood evidence.

"Well, at least we seem to have given them a bloody nose," remarked Preston. "We appear to have closed this little venture down. I wonder where the next will spring up. What was it Copley said—Hydra was a multi-headed thing. Cut off one head and another grows."

52

Farrel was usually in control of things as far as he himself was concerned, but those damned bullets had swung the balance the other way. He tried to move in the darkness but found it impossible. The pains were horrendous. He had never experienced anything like this before, yet all around him was silent.

The pains seemed to diminish slightly and he felt that he was able to move a little. He thought he opened his eyes and found that he was in a small, dark, smooth-walled tunnel. He struggled to his feet by holding on to the walls for balance and then he moved forward. He could see something ahead. Was it a light? He could not really tell, he could see only a blur . . . He tried walking towards it and found that as he struggled forward, his pain lessened. The light gradually became brighter and more distinct, and the pain faded slightly at the same time.

"Come on, Farrel," he said to himself, "get yourself moving. You've got to get yourself out of this mess."

It was then that he heard a voice from behind him. The voice was faint but one that he seemed to recognise. A woman's voice; it was Julie's voice, a long way back behind him in the tunnel calling to him.

"Ian! Ian! For God's sake, Ian, hang on! Don't go! I need you! I love you!"

Although it was a long way back, it seemed to echo through the whole length of the tunnel.

He paused.

"Julie?" he asked the walls almost in disbelief. "Julie? I thought Julie was dead." Then he heard the voice again.

It was Julie. *Julie's not dead!*

He stood for a few moments, at last comprehending, and then turned back towards the sound of the voice—it was then, the light, which he had seen ahead of him in the tunnel, dimmed and disappeared and the pains returned, and by God how they returned.

Gradually, he became aware of a great deal of activity going on around him. He was moving.

No *he* was not moving; the place where he lay was moving. He tried to open his eyes, but when he did, there were strong lights in the ceiling above him. He tried to speak, but found something in his mouth prevented him by holding his tongue down. He tried to move but it was impossible. He could feel what he thought were straps across his body keeping him secure and preventing any sideways movement, and his head was held in a brace of some kind.

He could hear a siren sounding; he thought outside and not too far away. He realised he must be in an ambulance that was travelling very fast judging by its occasional violent manoeuvres.

Someone must be very sick, he decided. He tried to look sideways to see who it might be, but even the slightest movement was impossible. One thing he did feel, which was comforting, was a small, cold hand holding his. It was not a man's hand—not a medic—a woman's hand, and from time to time it gave a little squeeze.

Farrel was transported back to the times when he was with Julie at first, and then Elizabeth later. It usually meant that something was in the offing—something very pleasant. *Not just now my dear*, he thought before he passed out again.

*

The next time he gained consciousness he was in a place that was not moving. He assumed that it must be a hospital. The pains were much less and the fact that he could still feel pain suggested to him that it was perhaps as well he had not made it to the end of that tunnel. Perhaps it had been him in the ambulance who was sick. He was aware that there were many people all milling around him and that he was surrounded by lots of bright lights shining down on him. The object that had been in his mouth had been removed, leaving a soreness behind.

There was someone calling his name, but not just in a normal voice. It was very loud.

"Ian," it called. "Ian, can you hear me?"

Farrel did not answer.

"Ian," it called again. "Ian, can you hear me?" and the voice came close to his mouth.

The owner of it listened and then his head moved away. Those present saw a smile spread across his face and then its owner was chuckling.

"Did he say anything?" a voice in the background asked. It was a voice that Farrel knew well: DS Preston.

"What did he say?"

The other man stopped laughing long enough to answer.

"Yes," he said, "he said something all right. He said 'stop bloody shouting in my ear. He sounded a bit narked about it too."

"That's him," Preston said sounding amused and very relieved. "That's the guv'nor. He'll make it okay."

Farrel felt a prick in his arm and he passed out once more.

53

F arrel had no idea how long he had been unconscious, nor what time of day it was, or even what day it was. All he knew was that the lights were less bright than they had been when he was last awake, if 'awake' was the correct term.

He felt warm and comfortable and the pains, which he remembered from before, were not so acute. In truth, he felt numbness throughout the whole of his body. Without moving his head, he rolled his eyes from side to side in an attempt to take in what was around him. All he could see above him was a piece of equipment to which a variety of transparent bags were attached. Moments later, the memory of what had taken place inside the room at the farm returned.

How the hell did it end up? He wracked his brain, which was just beginning to function to some extent, and tried to remember more of the details, but they eluded him.

"Good morning, Mr Farrel," a man clad in a white coat greeted him pleasantly as he looked down at him. "It's good to have you back with us again."

Farrel frowned and searched his memory.

"Do I know you?"

"I'm Doctor Peters. We've been looking after you for some time now."

"How long?"

"Well, you were wounded very badly. We removed the bullets that were still inside you. Some had passed right through, and then we had to put you into a medically-induced coma to give your body chance to recover more quickly from the trauma."

"How long have I been out, Doc?"

"Twelve days."

"Twelve days! What's happened in all that time?"

"Well, we've—," the doctor began.

"No, no . . . I don't mean that. I'm still here, so you've done a good job, and thanks. What I mean is, what about my men and my case?"

"I'll leave it to your colleagues to bring you up-to-date on that. They call in to check on you most days."

That's good; I like that, Farrel thought.

"What about Julie?" he asked rather fearfully. He remembered the last time he had seen her, her shirt had been covered in blood.

"Did she make it?"

"She made it alright," the doctor replied. "We kept her in for three days and then she was allowed to go home. I think it was a friend of yours who took her to look after her. A Mrs Coulter she said her name was."

Farrel closed his eyes and offered up a prayer of thanks.

"They have been in to see you every day you've been 'asleep' and they have sat here for a long time on each occasion. Two special friends you have there, Inspector," the doctor commented, giving Farrel a knowing smile.

Farrel smiled.

"Very special, doc," he confirmed.

*

As the next few days passed, Preston and other members of the squad called and filled Farrel in on all the details so that he was fully aware of what had taken place. Although he was incapacitated, he was still the officer in charge as far as they were concerned. He was grateful for their concern and amused when Perkins, in his own inimitable style, gave him his account of the 'showdown'. He described it like a wild-west shoot out and went into great detail about the injuries sustained by the dead gunman and the 'fact' that it took four men to put him in the 'meat wagon', he was so heavily weighted down with lead.

"It's lucky that Julie is such a pretty girl," Preston said. "It seems that she was being held, perhaps as a hostage, but certainly with a view to 'selling her on', and that's why she didn't suffer the fate of Rowles, his wife and all the others."

Farell swore through gritted teeth, but now he was so relieved that Julie was safe.

Elizabeth and Julie visited often. Julie's arm was immobilised due to the gunshot injury she had received, but that didn't stop her from coming to see Farell each time Elizabeth visited.

Farrel appeared suitably embarrassed as they both bestowed kisses on him and fussed over him in the presence of the doctors and nurses.

Elizabeth explained that Julie was staying with her, and when Farrel was fit enough to leave hospital, he would go and stay there too. *Mixed blessings*, he thought, but it had its compensations. He looked forward to that day. He had been told that he would be able to return to work in several weeks' time, and that for the time being DS Preston would take on Farrel's responsibilities.

"An excellent man for the job," Farrel stated.

*

During the third week of his stay in hospital, he was beginning to move around far more freely, undergo physiotherapy, and visit the hospital's rehabilitation centre. It was at this point an event took place that was to change his life entirely—Assistant Chief Constable Copley paid a visit.

54

Farrel had a good workout in the gym. He pushed himself a great deal and felt the strength returning to his muscles. He was able to walk but needed the support of a stick. The effort, however, had brought on tiredness, and so when the Assistant Chief Constable entered, he happened to be relaxing in the large armchair at the side of his hospital bed.

Farrel was dozing but roused and looked up expecting the visitor to be either Elizabeth or Julie, or both. His spirits fell when he saw who it actually was.

"Oh, good morning, sir," he said, pretending to make a slight effort to rise to greet his senior officer, despite having no intention of doing so for ACC Copley.

"No, don't get up, Chief Inspector," Copley said hastily. "How are you feeling?"

In truth, Farrel felt exhausted from his exertions and now deflated by the arrival of the ACC, so he used it in an effort to keep the visit short.

"Pretty good, sir," he replied. "They say I'll be out of here in a couple of weeks, and the specialist says that there's no reason why I shouldn't be back to work four to six weeks after that. All the wounds are healing nicely and the body is repairing itself after the operations. And, after all, I have a score to settle with Hydra."

ACC Copley shifted in his seat and his expression changed.

"Yes, well," he began but then hesitated, "I don't think that will be possible, I'm afraid."

But Farrel saw on the other man's face that he was not really afraid of what he was about to say; rather he was 'politically' afraid, Farrel thought, and relishing what he was about to say, and the message it contained. Farrel was not a gullible man and saw through it immediately.

"Oh?" he queried, somewhat aggressively, suspecting that he was not going to like what the ACC said he was afraid of saying.

"Well, since you sustained such horrific injuries and have had to rest for so long, it has been decided to change your duties."

"Go on." Farrel's voice changed from its usual reasonably polite tone when dealing with a senior officer to one of outright suspicion.

Copley recognised it.

"You will, of course, retain your rank, but, due to the changed health implications you will be moved to admin and replace Chief Inspector Allen when he retires in six weeks' time."

"What?" Farrel almost exploded. "Who the hell decided that?"

"I did, actually. It will be better for you to take a less active job. If you were in the field again, your state of health could well jeopardise any case you may be working on, and also the wellbeing of your men."

"Don't you think that's up to me to decide what I am capable of at the time?"

"I'm sorry, Chief Inspector, but it's already been decided. As you know, I'm responsible for Human Resources, and that's how it has to be. There is also the fact that you shot and killed a man using what may well be construed as an excessive amount of force. The Independent Police Complaints Committee was very concerned about that when I had to advise them of the event. I found it quite embarrassing."

"I deemed it necessary at the time."

"But you killed a man. A criminal, yes, but a member of the public as well."

"A member of the public?" Farrel retorted incredulously. "He was an international terrorist for God's sake, and at the time he was pointing a loaded gun at me."

Copley did not respond.

"Can I appeal the decision?"

"No, I'm afraid not."

He's afraid of a lot of things, Farrel thought, *I wonder why.*

"I'm not happy with your decision, *sir*," Farrel was showing his petulant and rebellious side. He thought that he saw the tiniest smirk appear on Copley's lips. "I don't want to work in a back office pushing a pen and paper about. My place is outside feeling the collars of all the slimy lawbreakers."

At that time, he had a strange feeling that Copley was not feeling very comfortable. "If I can't fight crime, I suppose I'll have to resign."

Copley was back on track again.

"That's your prerogative," he replied, "but of course you won't be able to draw your considerable pension until you reach retirement age."

Farrel knew that was the case and he knew that he would need an income to see him through any intervening time until then. It was clear ACC Copley, who had never seen eye-to-eye with Farrel, had won this particular battle, and he appeared satisfied as he stood up and prepared to leave.

"Well, I must be off, Chief Inspector," Copley said in a polite but off-handed fashion. "I'm glad to see you in much better health. Come and see me when you are fit enough to work."

He stood up, turned and left Farrel sitting in his chair seething.

I'll see you in hell first, Farrel thought. Then he picked up the daily paper he had bought on his way back from rehab. *Typical*, he thought, it was Friday 13th.

*

The visitors he had after the ACC's visit were all appalled at the news of Farrel's impending change; none more so than DC Richard Copley, the man who had impressed Farrel so much in the short time that they had worked together and who had become a close and trusted colleague of his.

Farrel could not help but feel sympathy for the young man. He was so different from his uncle, and when he left Farrel, Copley was clearly disturbed by the situation his uncle had created.

*

The days and weeks passed and Farrel was discharged from hospital. The wounds had healed remarkably well. Apart from him having to use a walking stick to ease the pain in his leg where he had received the least serious gunshot wound, he was in good fettle. The specialist wanted to know where Farrel was going to live. He still needed a certain amount of care. A very attractive Elizabeth, accompanied by an equally attractive Julie, assured the doctor that he would be well looked after.

"I'll be doing everything for him, Doctor," Elizabeth stated.

The doctor looked at her and then at Farrel and smiled. "Everything?" he queried.

"Everything!" she confirmed.

The doctor smiled as he looked at Farrel. "You're a very lucky man, Chief Inspector."

Farrel, embarrassed, returned the doctor's smile with a weak one of his own.

"She means it, Doc," he confirmed and raised his eyebrows. "She'll take good care of me."

*

Elizabeth's flat, Farrel realised, had just the two bedrooms, one for Elizabeth and the other for him. However, that was not to be. He had forgotten that Julie had moved in and Elizabeth had decreed that he should share her bedroom, and, of course, her bed. He did not object, but he feared that a full return to recovery may well be delayed, but what the hell. Julie appeared to be quite happy with the situation too.

The case, Farrel had learned gradually during his sojourn in hospital, had finally been resolved. The main perpetrators had already fled, that Farrel knew. Those who had remained, and who knew little of the operation, had been arrested and very promptly been deported. To all intents and purposes the whole set-up had been closed down.

Maybe it has and maybe it hasn't, Farrel thought privately. He certainly was not convinced, and the longer he thought about it, the more certain he was that Hydra was still in operation and not far very away for that matter.

During the course of the following days, Elizabeth explained that after long discussions with Julie about her future, Julie was adamant that she wanted to undertake further education so that she could have a career. After all, she was still very young.

"And she was crap at her old job!" Elizabeth stated. "And not very successful either. She did mention that there was only ever one guy who was good to her, in more ways than one," and she looked at Farrel with that knowing look.

Farrel made no reply and tried to put on an innocent 'oh really' look.

"I think that she likes to look upon you as the father she never had. So it looks as if we could be a little family."

Farrel approved. Maybe the future was looking up, after all.

55

A week later, a letter addressed to Farrel appeared in Elizabeth's mailbox. It had a typewritten address but the letter inside was handwritten. It was a personal note to Farrel from the Chief Constable himself, and invited, if Chief Constables ever invited junior officers, him to meet him at a pub some twenty miles away in the next county for an 'important and private' meeting.

Farrel was on time, as always. The Chief Constable arrived five minutes or so later in his own private car. Farrel knew that normally he would use his official car driven by a police driver. Something was different. Was this meeting for a good reason or something that the Chief Constable wanted to keep away from the public gaze?

With a pint in front of them both on a table in a quiet corner of the lounge bar, their meeting began.

"How are things, Ian?"

That was a good start. The big boss calling him by his first name, but there again, they had known and respected each other for many years.

"I'm getting there," Farrel announced.

The CC nodded and appeared pleased. "I have some news which I think you may be pleased about."

Better and better.

"I heard all the details of your meeting with the Assistant Chief Constable," he continued. "Not from him, I might add. And I heard that you are not happy with the intended outcome."

Intended outcome. I wonder what he's leading up to.

Farrel nodded slowly.

"I'm not happy about it either," the Chief went on. "I've looked into it and taken it up with the Chairman of the Police Authority, strictly on a personal and private level, you understand, and he is not happy about it either. He had been button-holed by someone else. He wants officers like you in circulation and doing what you're good at."

Farrel was listening carefully.

"Mr Copley has a point about your injuries though, and the rules back him up . . ."

Farrel was about to interject but the Chief held his hand up to stop him.

"So," he continued, "under the circumstances, it has been decided, strictly between the Chairman and myself, that instead of you being moved to admin, you should, if you wish, be allowed to retire from the police service on a full pension. You would then be free to follow another line of business, BUT," he stressed before Farrel could interject, "under the circumstances, we would expect you to be available, after all your previous experience, to be called upon as a consultant if, and when, required."

Then he sat back to allow Farrel to digest what he had just said.

"Of course. What else can I say?" Farrel was at a loss to say anything else. He did not even need to take time in making such a decision. He was a copper through and through. "I was considering a security-type service and this sounds like an ideal resolution, but tell me—why have things changed so much in the last few days?"

The Chief Constable looked out of the window and appeared to consider what to say next. Farrel knew that it was not just a whim of the Chief Constable, nor the Chairman of the Police Authority that had caused this change of events. The CC nodded and looked back at Farrel. "Let me just say 'keep the idea of security in your mind'," he advised. "If you are content to wait a while, I'll see to it that all the paperwork is completed. It will be done quietly and I'll get it to you as soon as I can."

"Thank you, sir," Farrel said. "I think there's more to this than I know at the moment, but it really seems things are looking up," and he smiled broadly at the other man.

"By the way, sir, I don't suppose you are at liberty to say who it was that put in the good word for me?"

"Let's just say it was someone who wishes you well. Someone who considered it to be an injustice and wanted to do something about righting a wrong."

Farrel frowned and looked enquiringly at the Chief Constable.

"Let's just say it was someone with connections to the," and here he paused, "to the 'funny handshake brigade' as you might refer to it, shall we."

Farrel smiled. Now he knew who it was. The only man who had those types of connections: Richard Copley—the loyal man who would make a 'bloody good copper'.

"I imagine you'll need a licence to practice as a 'private investigator'," the Chief supposed as he got up to leave.

The way he said 'private investigator' indicated to Farrel that there really was far more to the meeting than he realised, but it would be a new challenge for him and he felt all his old confidence beginning to flood back.

Farrel smiled. "Yes, I suppose I will," he replied happily.

"You may well be contacted soon, unofficially, of course, by certain people with connections in security circles," the Chief Constable said rather conspiratorially, as he rose and prepared to leave. But then turned back. "Oh, by the way, we've put you forward for the George Cross," he announced, almost as an afterthought. "I'd almost forgotten about that. Congratulations!"

With that, the Chief Constable left him alone with his pint and his thoughts.

Farrel sat there for a long time mulling over what the Chief Constable had said. He liked the idea. He liked the idea very much—very much indeed

George Cross—almost forgotten; Farrel smiled again. He liked the Chief. *Almost forgotten,* he thought again—*you lying old bugger. You waited to see which way the wind was blowing and whether I would take up your offer.*

Now perhaps he would have the opportunity to look more closely in the future at Assistant Chief Constable Copley. Why would he want Farrel off the street—off detection duties?

But you will be a civilian and not subject to police discipline, you must not victimise him, he reminded himself. *Of course not,* he agreed with himself and allowed himself a wicked smile as he slammed the ferule of his walking stick into the soft carpet on the floor.

And, just to make sure that he was not having a euphoric dream, he checked the newspaper for the date. It was Tuesday 23rd and definitely not Friday 13th.

56

"You look just like the cat that got the cream—a lot of it too," Elizabeth said after she had greeted him back like a long lost lover that afternoon.

Farrel just smiled. "Could be."

She looked at the clock on the mantelpiece. "Dinner won't be for another two hours and Julie's out on the college interview and won't be back until just before dinner. You've been a busy boy today and you're obviously in need of a lie down." She took him by the hand and led him from the lounge. "And I'm going to make sure you do lie down. Come on." She paused for a moment. "Oh, I almost forgot . . ."

Somebody else 'almost forgot something'—this is becoming a habit.

"Someone called to see you whilst you were out, a very smartly dressed man in a dark suit. He had an American accent—at least, I think it was American. I told him you were out. He didn't seem too surprised and he said he'd be in touch with you pretty soon. Does that mean anything?"

"Probably," Farrel replied, "but not just now. Now, I must have my lie down." Still holding her hand, he stepped ahead of her and led her gently across the hallway to the half-open master bedroom door. "I'll tell you all about it when we are all eating."

*

Julie arrived home just in time for dinner. She was delighted and buzzing with the news that she had been accepted on a secretarial and administration course. Now she could have a proper job. She did not say that she had an inkling that something had been going on during her absence.

"What about income?" Farrel wanted to know.

Julie paused. That was something she had not thought about in her excitement.

"Don't worry. That's already sorted," Farrel reassured her. "During your course, you can work for me in the evenings and at weekends as practice and I'll pay you for your work. I'm going to need a secretary and I reckon that between the two of you, you could handle the work. Anyway, I have a very strong feeling that I am going to need someone I can really trust."

The two women looked at him; waiting for what they both felt was going to be news of enormous interest.

He explained his meeting with the Chief Constable and the change that was going to affect his future. They were particularly delighted to hear the news of the George Cross.

Although he would be treated formally as a private detective, the work was likely to go beyond that and that was why he would need Elizabeth and Julie close by. "Work like a big happy family," he said. The women agreed wholeheartedly. *God, I'm a lucky man*, he thought contentedly.

"Could that have something to do with that American man who called earlier?" Elizabeth frowned.

"Quite possibly."

"Is it likely to be dangerous?" Julie asked.

"No." Farrel shook his head and outwardly dismissed the thought for Julie's benefit. Inside himself, he knew it could be highly dangerous, but that was in the future. "I just imagine it's the international police organisations wanting to know what I already know about Hydra, and, at the moment, that's precious little."

Then he suddenly remembered the diary that he had put in the glove box of his car all those weeks ago. The one Tommy Atkins had kept. It should still be there. Would it be of any use? What would the dark-suited American say, 'dollars to donuts' it would be. The more he thought about it, the more it looked as if Farrel had not seen the last of Hydra after all, and perhaps he would be reacquainted with its activities much sooner than he had originally anticipated.

"No," he emphasised to the two women. "It won't be dangerous."

However, just to be on the safe side, he made a mental note to make sure he had a legally held handgun, his Glock 17. He would get in plenty of range practice, just to be on the safe side. Those men, those crooks, those terrorists did not 'play around', and Farrel knew that he would need to be well prepared in order to stay alive the next time he came face to face with them. He was glad that someone else was interested in them; someone who was highly professional and someone upon whom he felt sure he would to able to rely for support because, for sure, there would be another head to lop off the Hydra.

57

Time for Farrel seemed to pass so slowly and however hard he tried he could not get Hydra off his mind. It occupied his thoughts day and night. He dreamed constantly of the last few moments of his contact with them; of the excruciating pain he had felt as the bullets tore into him. He remembered Ivan (Scarface) Minski and the look of hatred on his face as he fired at Farrel. He remembered too the 'tunnel of death', as he now thought of it, and how Julie's voice in the distance behind him had brought him back; back into the world of the living. Dear Julie!

There was a reason he had survived. There had to be!

The more he thought about it, the more he was convinced it was his mission in life to lop off as many heads of Hydra as he could. It was becoming an obsession. Where, he wondered had, or would, another head appear.

The diary of Tommy Acton was beginning to prove extremely interesting. Farrel had somehow 'forgotten' to mention he had it, and he had not handed it in to the authorities. *Why should I? I can't trust anyone, and it may fall into the wrong hands.* He was sure that the late DC Rowles was not the only police officer the syndicate had in its pocket. He had strange suspicions about some past colleagues, but, as he had no proof, he had to dismiss them. They still nagged him, however. For instance, why should Assistant Chief Constable Copley be so determined to get him off the Force?

The diary could prove so useful in the future to a private detective with such inside knowledge. He could even hold Big Mick Jeanes in the palm of his hand. *Now that would really be something.* The first few pages had given Farrel enough information on Big Mick and his associates to do just that.

Set a thief to catch a thief. He smiled as he thought of the old saying. He was also good at 'leaning on people' when necessary. He was surprised too of how diverse Mick's activities were. *What Mick would not give to lay his hands on this little lot,* Farrel had thought on numerous occasions as he read through those pages. *I must keep them very safe.*

Page 68 showed the time that Tommy's allegiance to Big Mick had changed and Page 73 contained the information Farrel now deemed 'dynamite': 'there are coppers who are on the payroll—not only beat men, but one in the CID and a senior cop too. Don't know who he is. Don't suppose I ever will, but he's big'.

Copley, Farrel thought, *ACC bloody Copley.* It was incredible, but it might fit. *I'll be watching him, and very closely too.*

58

Farrel sat alone in Café Antonio in Larchester drinking a coffee and eating a croissant. It was eleven o'clock on a bright morning. He enjoyed the coffee and food there and it was always possible to find a table in a quiet corner where he could watch the world go by, or read his newspaper, or plan for the future: like opening his private investigations business near the town centre. He appeared to anyone sitting close by to be relaxing, but that was not so. Thoughts of Hydra still filled his mind.

From his seat close to the large café window he could see people passing by outside. For some unknown reason, his attention rested upon one particular individual—a man, just an ordinary man. He seemed to be a non-descript type, but as Farrel watched him, he saw something in the man's demeanour that interested him. He was self-assured and focused his attention on the things around him. Farrel turned back to his coffee and took a sip.

Moments later, the same man stood beside his table. He looked down at Farrel.

"Do you mind if I sit here?" he enquired. There was something of a transatlantic accent in his voice.

Farrel looked up then looked around at the other unoccupied tables.

"May I?" the man asked again. "Mr Farrel . . . or can I call you . . . Ian?"

Farrel studied the man's clean-cut face. *Was he friend or foe? Better find out!*

"I suppose so," he replied in a disgruntled tone.

The man slid into the chair opposite Farrel and held out his hand in greeting.

Farrel ignored it.

"My name's Wall, Max Wall."

"Very funny," Farrel grunted, clearly not amused as he remembered the old comedian.

"Well that's what I'm going by here in the UK," the man replied by way of explanation.

"And in which part of the world do you call yourself Bob Hope?" Farrel wanted to know. His voice was sarcastic.

"Ah, sometimes that too," the man smiled. "That's usually in South America."

"So what can I do for you, Mr Wall?"

"Call me Max, it's friendlier."

"Oh, we're friends then?"

"You bet your ass. If we weren't, you could well be dead right now." He tugged slightly at the left lapel of his jacket. Farrel could see the end of the butt of an automatic pistol nestling in a shoulder holster.

"Okay, so we're friends, but how can I tell?"

"You know about Hydra." It was a statement.

"Do I now. That still doesn't convince me that you're my friend."

"You shot Ivan Minski, the guy with the scar."

"That could make you my enemy."

"I shot Vladimir Minski, his brother."

Farrel paused with the croissant half in and half out of his mouth. He removed it. "So come on," he said, "level with me."

Wall inserted his hand into the breast pocket of his jacket, took out a laminated card the size of a credit card and passed it across to Farrel.

Farrel had seen something like this before—Government Issue ID card, complete with Wall's name and photograph.

Farrel studied it, looked back across the table and returned it without comment.

"We're a relatively new set up," Wall explained. "The Americans call it Homeland Security and you're part of it in this part of the world, but I get the impression that you're not fully aware of that."

Farrel shook his head, as if to clear it.

"Since when?" he wanted to know.

"Since you 'retired from the police service'. Didn't your Chief Constable say anything to you?"

Farrel thought back to the conversation with his late employer.

"I guess he did in a roundabout sort of way," he replied, "but don't expect me to change my name to Charlie Chaplin."

Wall smiled. "Don't worry about that. You'll be based here in this region of the UK. There are other people within the organisation that work in other countries."

Farrel grimaced. The quiet cup of coffee and croissant in this little town had suddenly taken on what could be a momentous change in direction as far as his future was concerned.

"Am I just a PI or a full blown agent?" he asked sarcastically.

"PI is your cover, if you like. Do that job day to day, but be ready to switch when you are needed. I will contact you either in the flesh or on this."

He passed a small package across the table.

"A mobile phone?" Farrel queried. "I already have one."

"Not like that one. It's dedicated to our network. No one can hack into it. Keep it switched on and charged at all times."

Farrel took the phone, nodded and slipped it into his pocket.

"Aye, aye, sir," he said a little flippantly, allowing himself a slight smile as he dropped his gaze from the man opposite.

"I'll always announce myself by saying: 'This is Wall, Max Wall. The real Max Wall.' Anything different in the slightest and you'll know it's not me."

Farrel nodded in agreement. There was no need to reply. He understood the instruction well enough.

He allowed himself an inward smile. *I used to play this sort of game when I was a ten-yea-old kid.*

"You'll need this too," Wall stated as he reached into a small tote bag he had been carrying and now kept on his lap under the table. He took out a package wrapped in brown paper. *Oh, yes!* Farrel thought. Something had tickled his wicked sense of humour, but he said nothing.

It was well taped up and Farrel estimated it to be around nine to ten inches long, five inches wide and two thick.

Wall passed it to him below the tabletop level. Farrel took it and knew what it was immediately.

"Like you," Wall explained, "taken out of police service, checked over and in perfect condition . . . better condition than you, at this moment, I would think." And he smiled.

Farrel grunted and hefted it in his hand. He knew it was a Glock, most probably a model 17 like his police sidearm.

"It's the one you had before you retired," Wall told him. "Old buddies, eh?"

Farrel snorted but again made no reply.

"Keep it with you at all times," Wall instructed. "You have clearance to carry it and you may well have to use it. Don't be afraid to."

Farrel nodded. He knew how to use it to good effect.

Wall looked at his watch.

"Must go now," he said. "Duty calls and all that crap. I'll be in touch before long."

He finished the last piece of croissant and drained the remnants of his coffee then stood up to leave.

"By the way," he mentioned, more as an afterthought before he left, "we're still looking for the other informant in the police. *We* have our suspicions and I'm sure you do as well. Maybe they will coincide." Then he turned on his heel and walked from the café leaving Farrel to digest his croissant and everything else that had just taken place.

59

Farrel was 'champing at the bit' all over the weekend. He still had another week before he opened his office officially but he wanted to make an early start.

Elizabeth and Julie continued to insist he take it easy to ensure a complete recovery, but Farrel was Farrel. He had his teeth into something and he did not want to let go.

*

At five o'clock that Monday afternoon he drove to Cranton Court and Court Farm.

There might well be still something out there of use, something that previous searches had missed. It was his intuition that motivated him and that intuition had so often in the past provided something more to go on.

The police had searched Cranton Court thoroughly but had not left it totally secured when they left. Farrel soon found an insecure window and gained entry. The place had been abandoned since the raid, and after half an hour or so he had found nothing. Next, he made his way to the farmhouse. It was late afternoon, but there were still two hours or so of daylight left.

Once again, he found a way in. His search was Farrel-like thorough. Something caught his eye in the large open fireplace in the farmhouse kitchen. The evening sun was low and streaming through the curtain-less window. As it struck the inner part of the brickwork fireplace, Farrel saw, quite by chance, an uneven surface. Closer inspection revealed what he thought might be a loose brick.

He searched around and found an old kitchen knife in a cupboard drawer. He pushed the blade into the joint in the brickwork and moved it from side to side. The brick moved slightly at first, and then a bit more until he was able to grip the end of it. With some difficulty, he managed to pull the brick out. Behind it, he saw there was a small void, and inside, he made out a small bundle of papers rolled up. He used the knife to reach in and lever it from its hiding place.

"What the hell do you think you're doing here?" an angry voice suddenly demanded from the now lengthening shadows behind him.

Surprised and shocked, Farrel swung round to find he was looking into the barrel of an automatic pistol about seven feet away. *It's funny how something as small as nine millimetres can look as if it's a foot across.*

He raised his eyes to see a man shrouded in a heavy black coat with a hood that covered most of his head.

Farrel could see the face . . . Michael Copley OBE Assistant Chief Constable. The face was contorted with what Farrel thought was a mixture of hate and fear.

"Farrel!" Copley snarled. "I should have known."

"*Mr* Copley," Farrel sneered in reply. His old assured self had quickly taken over from the initial surprise. Then he added, "But I think I really knew all along, didn't I? Thought you had me off the case and not snooping around anymore, but here I am as they say; like the old bad penny."

"But not for long," Copley declared. "Why couldn't you leave well alone? You're out of your depth, by definition. You will never close Hydra down. It's too large."

Farrel shrugged his shoulders. "Maybe and maybe not," he argued.

"But *you* won't. You won't live that long."

Farrel saw the index finger tighten on the trigger and he instinctively dived to his right, but not quickly enough.

Copley fired.

The bullet struck Farrel low in the left shoulder. Had he remained standing, he knew it would have been in the heart and Copley would have been right.

The force of the bullet fired at such close range was enough to knock Farrel backwards and he found himself in a sitting position on the floor with his back against the bricks of the fireplace. The pain was excruciating. He remembered the previous time.

Not again he thought desperately as Copley moved closer still.

Farrel looked up at him from his position of disadvantage.

"You're not quick enough, Farrel," Copley taunted. "You know what the Good Book says, 'In this world there are the quick and the dead', and you're not quick enough, so you're dead."

Farrel saw the grim smile on the other man's face, his teeth clenched tightly together. His finger tightened once more on the trigger. Farrel saw it turn whiter with the pressure.

He heard the shot and he smelt the cordite, yet he felt no pain.

What he saw was Copley's head suddenly jerk towards its left side and blood spray from the uncovered side of it. The

Assistant Chief Constable collapsed face down onto the floor at Farrel's feet and did not move.

Uncomprehending, Farrel looked towards where he thought the sound must have come.

Standing, framed in the doorway to his left, he saw DC Richard Copley holding a smoking gun.

"Are you OK, Mr Farrel," the young man sounded very worried almost to the point of panic.

"Guess I'll live," Farrel managed to say through the pain and gritted teeth.

"Some guy called Wall told me you could be in big trouble and he suggested I tail you. He gave me this gun."

"Good job he did," Farrel coughed, "and a good job you took his advice."

The young man crossed to the body lying face down on the floor, kicked the pistol away from its dead hand and turned it over.

When he saw who it was, he stood up quickly and fell backwards in shock.

Farrel saw his face turn white, and for a moment he thought Copley would vomit, but he managed to control himself.

"Oh, my God!" he gasped in horror. "Uncle Michael!"

Aghast and in complete disbelief, he stood absolutely still for a few seconds, which to Farrel, with a bullet in his shoulder, felt like hours, and then he dropped the gun on the floor.

"Oh, my God!" he repeated in shock. "Then it was him who was giving Hydra all the information as well as Rowles. How could he do that?"

Farrel was, by now, thinking that as both the men's name was Copley, Wall needed to know which one could not be trusted, and which one was loyal.

"I'm afraid so," muttered Farrel through his pain. "Now, Richard, could you please spare the time to call someone before I bleed to death and you have two corpses on your hands?"

Still in a daze, Copley used his mobile phone to call for an ambulance and then the CID office. The young man would have some explaining to do. Farrel knew that very well.

Copley turned his attention back to Farrel and at the same time tried to ignore his uncle's dead body as best he could.

"Wall said there could be big trouble," he repeated as if for something to say. "I've had a hell of a shock, you know that, but, by God, I'm glad I was able to help you."

"Me too," Farrel agreed. "What do they say, take a life to save a life?" He groaned. The pain was bad and getting worse. "And there'll be a lot more trouble to follow, you can be sure of that."

"What do you mean more trouble?" the young DC wanted to know. There can't be more trouble than this, can there?"

"Oh, yes there can!" Farrel was unequivocal.

"How?"

Farrel closed his eyes tightly against the pain and touched his left shoulder with his right hand as if it could ease it slightly. Blood still oozed from the wound.

"Liz and Julie are *really* going to give me shit this time," he prophesied bitterly before passing out.

Printed in Great Britain
by Amazon.co.uk, Ltd.,
Marston Gate.